HARM
REDUCTION

HARM REDUCTION

A NOVEL

TODD L. GRANDE

UNHOOKED BOOKS
Independent Publishers since 2011
an imprint of High Conflict Institute Press
Scottsdale, Arizona

Text copyright © 2021 by Todd L. Grande
All rights reserved.

Published by Unhooked Books, Scottsdale

www.unhookedmedia.com

ISBN (paperback): 978-1950057313
ISBN (ebook): 978-1950057320

Library of Congress Control Number: 2021932235

Cover design by Julian León, The Missive
Interior design by Jeffrey Fuller

Printed in the United States of America

First Edition

ALSO BY TODD GRANDE

The Psychology of Notorious Serial Killers
The Psychology of Notorious Church Killers
The Psychology of Notorious Celebrity Deaths

CHAPTER ONE

IS THIS ALL
I'M EVER GOING TO BE?

IT WAS A COOL OCTOBER NIGHT in 2007, the twilight heat of summertime having given way to the bite of autumn. Jenny Ocean was 28 years old and driving north on US 13 in the direction of Wilmington, Delaware. Over the dashboard of her noisy truck, she could see the storm clouds moving her way as she approached her destination: a hardscrabble lumberyard set pretty much squarely in the middle of the red-light district in the south part of town.

A familiar feeling of dread came over Jenny as she parked and turned off the ignition. The first drops of rain from the forecast storm patted almost silently against her windshield.

She jingled her key ring quietly as she looked at the building and contemplated what was inside. There was a detailed and colorful painting, almost a children's-style graphic depicting a gazelle right inside the front door, which would have been a little odd for any business not called Gazelle Lumber. She wondered every time she went inside why someone would choose to name their business after that particular animal. A gazelle was skittish, always in a state of startled reaction, constantly scared.

She liked the painting, or at least the feeling of familiarity it gave her. But it also made her wonder: *What kind of self-respecting gazelle would want to be seen in this dump?*

Jenny sighed. She was running a little ahead of schedule. It was a Wednesday, about 7:35 p.m., and Gazelle Lumber had long been closed for the day. Jenny parked in the boss's spot right next to the door that led into the front office. She always took the owner's space. It was her small way of rebelling against the world that she intuitively knew looked down on her job as a cleaner, her barely scraping by day to day.

OK, the truck didn't help her public image. It was ancient, and her father had given it to her years ago. It was a far cry from the owner's pristine Lincoln Town Car, which Jenny always saw parked in front when she came to the lumberyard to pick up her twice-a-month paychecks (as well as, more often than not, a slightly lewd comment from the owner, or a joking question about whether she had found a boyfriend yet). The truck was a 1978 Dodge D150, with a three-speed on the column and not much in the way of features. It had belonged to her father before he gave it to her when she turned sixteen. When he had handed over the keys, he joked that it was a luxury model—it had doors, didn't it? The truth was, Jenny didn't really mind how spartan and dilapidated the Dodge was. If anything, it discouraged anyone from trying to steal it from outside her apartment or when she was working.

The job was to come in after hours three Wednesdays a month: vacuum, dust, clean the bathrooms, and take out the trash. Standard unskilled cleaner work. Jenny got the job through a cleaning company, and another worker from the same outfit, Sarah Solomon, would come by every fourth Wednesday to strip and wax the floors. Jenny didn't think she was strong enough to handle the heavy floor machine, so she was happy to let Sarah take the glory—Sarah, a few years older and married to a delivery driver named David whom Jenny had only met in passing, was stocky and gave off an intimidating impression of competence, as though she had seen it all before and dealt with it to her advantage. Jenny wasn't sure anyone would describe herself that way.

The job at Gazelle was strictly part-time, but it paid some of her bills and wasn't her primary source of income. She also worked days as a receptionist at a mental health clinic near her apartment in New Castle. It was also pretty low-paying, but it was steady, and it was within walking distance of her place.

Jenny heaved herself out of the truck. The office wasn't going to clean itself. She had her key at the ready as she crossed the small patch of blacktop—this was definitely a rough part of town, and her heart always quickened when she made her way to the door of the darkened building. She got pelted with thick raindrops, and, as soon as she got inside and bolted the door behind her, saw a flash of lightning and heard a rumble of thunder not long behind.

A little startled, she shook her head as she turned on the lights. The place was the exact same dump it always was, with outdated computers on cheap desks and piles of paper spilling over everywhere. She decided to first go to the warehouse to clean the bathrooms there in order to get it out of the way, as it often involved hand-to-hand combat with the local cockroaches. After achieving victory, she would then work her way up to the front office. While her chronic anxiety tended to wax and wane, it was flaring up in that moment. She felt a little safer in the middle of the large building, rather than up in front where the windows made her feel exposed.

Hanging her coat on a rack just outside the warehouse, Jenny felt inside the pocket for something she carried that made her feel safer: a Smith & Wesson Chief's Special five-shot, .38 caliber revolver.

She had stolen the gun from the man who supplied her with Xanax after her physician wouldn't increase her dosage. Steve lived about a ten-minute's drive from Jenny, and he was clean-cut and nondescript—hardly your clichéd picture of a drug dealer. But he had just about anything a user might want to buy, and he had left her in his dining alcove to go outside to make a deal in the parking lot of the McDonald's down the street (Jenny was one of the few customers granted the privilege of going into Steve's house) when she rifled through his coat and in his desk looking for drugs.

When she found the gun, she stuck it in her purse without thinking. She told herself she was merely keeping herself safe in the moment—she didn't entirely trust Steve or his intentions. After that, a convenient time never arose for her to tell her dealer that she had stolen his gun. He never mentioned it to her. Maybe he racked it up to the cost of doing business, not wanting to accuse any of his steady customers, of which Jenny definitely was one.

She ended up carrying it around with her all the time. Even though she didn't know a lot about firearms, she took it to the local range a few times and learned how to shoot it. It was loaded with ".38 plus p" hollow points recommended to her at the gun shop. The weapon had such a powerful recoil that she would get a blister on her hand from the grip rubbing against the inside of her thumb. She could barely hit the target at seven yards away, but she reasoned that in a life-or-death situation, she would be firing at close range and would only have to hit her mark once to make it count.

Jenny got to work. As she almost always did during the cleaning job, she drifted mentally and became lost in a web of interconnected thoughts. Since kindergarten, she had been told that she was intelligent, creative, and an unconventional thinker. One teacher had told her that she was prone to get too invested in fantasy, an observation that stung and that had stuck with her. She also prided herself on being a problem solver, and as she scrubbed the bathroom sink, she thought about a time in high school when she had helped her mother figure out how to deal with a conflict at work.

Jenny knew people. She liked to think about this and contemplate her other strengths; this is when she felt the most adequate and resourceful. This job cleaning up after the messes of workers at a lumber yard was far from consistent with how she liked to think of herself—and perhaps worse for her, how she would like others to think of her.

Running water in the bathroom sink and squeezing out a dirty sponge, a thought crossed her mind, uninvited: *Is this all I'm ever going to be?*

A picture arose in her mind's eye: her parents, side by side, with fixed and unyielding gruff expressions of judgment. Part of Jenny was always puzzled whenever this visualization came up. Her parents had always been quite supportive of her in many ways, but as she grew older, she increasingly thought of their interactions with her as passive-aggressive. Her parents never acknowledged how hard she worked, or how she might be good at her day job in particular—they only talked about where she was now as though it was some embarrassing stage on the way to something better.

They'd say things like, *Someday, you'll get your life straightened out.* As though that helped. Next was, *Are you still thinking about going back to college?*

The latter sentiment was repeated over and over, at some point almost every time Jenny saw them. The pressure had intensified after Jenny's one-year suspension from the local university had elapsed. She had been caught several times with alcohol in her dorm room. Even though she had been underage at the time, this was a violation that typically wouldn't come with any kind of suspension. But Jenny had found herself taking a strongly acrimonious and defiant tone with the administrators, and it seemed that she had tested their patience beyond its limits.

Sometimes when she got angry, it felt like someone else was talking and that Jenny, the reasonable part of her, was merely watching.

She started cleaning the toilets, which entailed a lot of effort. Her mind drifted to her disappointed parents, which then led back to the circumstances of this job. Scrubbing with the brush, she thought of the euphemism: *lower level*. The job was certainly lower level, and she was the one doing it.

It was amazing for Jenny to observe how reliably this set of thoughts would always come in sequence; it was almost as monotonous as the various repetitive cleaning motions she was performing on autopilot while her brain cycled through various angles on her inescapable inadequacy.

In her mid- and late teens, Jenny struggled with alcohol and benzodiazepine use. She had been prescribed Xanax when she was 15 years old for what was then occasional anxiety. It didn't take her long to develop a dependency on the deceptively addictive drug, and soon she was taking three or four milligrams a day. She tried to stop on her own several times, but the rebound panic and anxiety were unbearable, easily three or four times as severe as the original symptoms she had been trying to address. She'd feel overwhelming panic just sitting in a movie theater or going out with friends, things she had easily been able to enjoy in the past.

This was when she started adding alcohol on top of the Xanax, a highly dangerous practice that worsened the situation. After her unexpected "vacation" from college, she found herself feeling emotionally crippled from her chemical dependency and financially hobbled after her student loans started coming due. She had been caught stealing a couple of times and booked by the police—mere petty theft, shoplifting a watch and a phone, just for petty cash—and even though she had been released with time served, having a misdemeanor record wasn't going to help.

So Jenny had to take whatever work she could find.

When she went to apply for jobs, she knew she looked exhausted and strung out. This didn't open doors for a lot of positions, which she found somehow surprising every time it happened. Like so many people struggling with addiction, Jenny thought she could get some kind of job counseling others dealing with the same challenge—but she soon discovered that the educational requirements for that line of work were substantial. Still, that was where she placed her dreams for herself: of one day becoming a mental health counselor.

Jenny finished up her work in the warehouse, only half noticing what she was doing, and moved to the office. As she came out of the fog of her thoughts, she heard the rain pounding hard on the roof of the building.

I swear, it sounds like this building is made of cardboard.

It sounded as though the storm was going to rip through

the walls of the building as a gust rose up outside with a noisy roar. She didn't look forward to sprinting out to her truck in the downpour after she was done, even if she was parked in the best spot in the lot.

The truth was that the scope of her worry went far beyond the prospect of getting wet. In the previous two months, there had been two rapes and two more attempted rapes within a few miles of Gazelle Lumber. No one had been caught or charged. Jenny didn't feel particularly afraid, but she felt the need for caution. She always felt she had more experience than most with the violence of the world because of her history with substance abuse. Using and especially obtaining illegal drugs puts a person in contact with all kinds of unsavory characters—yet Jenny had dealt with all of them and had never been the victim of assault of any kind. Getting ready to leave the building, Jenny allowed herself to think she was streetwise, tough even, and the security of the .38 caliber revolver only deepened her feeling of confidence.

She had been in the building for close to two hours.

Well, it's as clean as it's going to get.

She reached for her keys. It was only about twenty-five feet from the door to her truck. The building didn't have an alarm to activate. She went through what she had to do: step out into the storm, close the door, turn the deadbolt with the key, and run for it.

She took one last look out the window at the sheets of rain coming down out there and mustered the courage to go out. The rain and the wind hit her hard, and she gasped as she put her key in the deadbolt and turned it.

Then something happened very quickly.

There were two hands on her back, pushing her into the metal-framed glass door. Her left temple slammed into the hard glass and she was dazed, though she remained aware enough to hear a man grunt, then the sound of him falling forward next to her and smacking with a thud into the metal door frame.

Her vision was blurred by the rain as she heard cursing and started flailing with her fists against a dark figure in the night. In just one instant, she had gone from thinking she was totally alone to being in a life-and death struggle with this attacker. He was bigger than her, and fast.

Is this going to be what happens to me?

It was all a terrible blur of violence, happening too fast to understand. Once or twice, she thought she had made contact with her wildly swinging fists, but she was dazed, seeing flashing lights in her field of vision and feeling a powerful rush of adrenaline. Her body bumped hard into his—it was a man for sure—and Jenny twirled and fell to her knees on the hard pavement. She groped inside the pocket of her coat and felt the metallic reassurance of the gun.

She got up quickly, ready to face her assailant. But looking around frantically, she was stunned to see no one.

Cars were passing by on the street on the far side of the parking lot, splashing through puddles with their headlights cutting through the rain as though nothing had happened. Then she gazed down and saw on the ground what looked to be a long kitchen knife at her feet. Even through the rain, she saw it was smeared with something dark that had to be blood.

An involuntary sound came out of her as she panicked and started running her hands all over her own abdomen, neck, chest, and arms to see if she was the source of that blood. There was a rip in the coat sleeve of her left arm, and when she put her fingers in it, it hurt. It *really* hurt. She knew she'd been cut, but she mustered up the courage to pull up the sleeve of her coat and saw that it wasn't too deep.

What the hell just happened?

Jenny didn't have long to enjoy her relief over not being killed. A dark figure came into her field of vision, tall and stocky, backlit by the lights of the nearby street that made her unable to make out his features.

"What are you doing?" the man asked. "What's going on here?"

He reached down to pick up the knife off the ground. He almost made it when three shots rang out in rapid succession.

Jenny realized she was the one who had done the shooting, through the pocket of her coat, seeming to hit the man. Firing three rounds from the revolver would have normally hurt her hand, like it did on the range, but she felt no pain. Her ears were ringing as the man dropped to his knees with a loud groan.

"Jenny. Why the hell did you do that?" he asked her with amazement, his voice strangely calm.

She screamed, "Don't try to come any closer or I'll do it again!"

She stopped. How did this bastard know her name? She wasn't completely certain that any of her rounds had actually struck him. Everything was surreal and confusing, whipped up by the wind and the lashing of the rain. She did know, however, how many shots she had left.

The man lurched forward from his knees and fell toward Jenny with a long, rasping breath. As he fell, he landed on her feet. She panicked, half pulling and half kicking to get away. She stumbled, her knees hitting the wet pavement, then got back up to her feet as a wave of trembling and nausea overtook her.

Jenny stood over the body for a moment, her shaking growing more intense, then decided to go back into the building so she could use the phone to call the police.

She knew she would be in trouble for possessing the stolen firearm, but there was a rapist on the loose. Maybe she would be granted some mercy, or understanding, for feeling the need to be armed. Maybe she had killed a monster and would be forgiven.

Reaching for the door to turn the key to go inside, she saw the key wasn't in the lock.

Oh no. Where did it go?

She started looking around with panicked urgency. She was simultaneously afraid that her attacker would rise up and come for her again, and was concerned about how all this was going to look to the police. She needed to find the keys and call the police before someone else did. This was her best chance of getting some type of deal and maybe avoiding going to prison herself.

Frantically, she searched in the grass, all over the blacktop, under her truck, and even in her pockets. No keys. All of a sudden, she realized the one place she hadn't looked: under the body of the man lying in the rain.

He was face down in a puddle, totally motionless. She didn't want to touch him, but she was growing increasingly desperate by the moment about her own future. She was less and less concerned about him still being alive, however—she got closer, knelt, and saw a spreading pool of dark thick liquid all around him.

With a grunt, she turned him over partway. He was a big guy, with a square jaw and stubbled cheeks. If it was even possible for the rain to beat harder, it did in that moment.

It looked like she had hit him with more than one bullet. Blood was coming out of his chest. She saw the edge of her key ring beneath his side and reached under his body, only to also feel the handle of the knife.

She grunted again loudly as she shifted him. Jenny weighed about 130 pounds, and this guy had to be about 250. She pulled the knife from under his body and tossed it to the nearby grass as she fished for her keys. She got a finger in the ring and pulled it out from under him. It was amazing how heavy he felt.

Then Jenny remembered something from the newspaper accounts: two of the rape victims had escaped by outrunning their attacker. They described him as seeming youthful and very physically fit. They were barely able to get away, even though both of them were young and one described herself as a daily runner. Both had described being chased for more than 200 feet before the attacker gave up and started running away in another direction.

This guy doesn't look like he could chase someone fast for 20 feet, much less 200.

She let him roll back over onto the ground and looked in the back pocket of his soaked jeans for his wallet. She pulled it out and found a Delaware driver's license. The first time she read out the name, her voice sounded angry.

"David Saunders."

But when she said it again, it was in a more somber tone. *David Saunders.* Her co-worker Sarah's truck-driver husband.

I don't understand. Is he the rapist? Did he come here knowing I was working tonight?

Her arms drew back against her chest in a fear reflex; as they shook, the wallet flew through the air and landed near David's body, not far from the knife. It felt like those inanimate objects were looking up at her, mocking her. Every moment that passed, she seemed to be creating more evidence that could be used against her.

She had murdered this man.

Then the pieces started to come together. She had been working early that night. She had finished up just a little while before the time when Sarah would start working on the floors. David must have been there to see his wife, since sometimes when he wasn't on the road, he would come to help her stripping and waxing.

Jenny shook her head. That wasn't right. Sarah wasn't working that night. Maybe David had simply gotten confused and thought his wife would be there.

But why on earth would he attack me?

One of the few details that Jenny remembered about the assault was that the man had seemed strong to the point of athletic. She looked down at David's inert body and saw once again that he was far from fitting that description.

She whispered to herself, under her breath, barely able to form the words.

"I killed Sarah's husband. I killed an innocent man."

CHAPTER TWO

WILMINGTON COULD BE A DANGEROUS PLACE

JENNY UNDERSTOOD that she had a life-changing decision in front of her. David was dead. She could enter the building and call the police. Or she could simply get in her truck and drive away. The consequences of either choice played out in her mind like alternate universes.

The moment her attacker pushed her into the glass door, she felt she was in a struggle for her life. But now she felt like the perpetrator of a crime rather than its victim.

So many questions ran through her mind. Why didn't who-ever attacked her also go after David? Had David seen the man who had pushed her into the door and smacked his own head against the frame?

And even more immediately: was the attacker still nearby?

That last thought motivated Jenny to shield her eyes from the rain, open up the building, and lock the door behind her again. Within a few moments she was in the bathroom, heaving into a toilet and shaking with cold sweats.

What have I done?

She flushed the toilet with her head spinning. The obvious option was to call the police. She reasoned that if she notified the authorities, they would be skeptical of the notion that she had been attacked by an unknown man only for David, whose wife she happened to know, to show up mere moments later. It was the truth, after all, but she became convinced no one would believe her. She had a bump on her head and a shallow cut on her arm—hardly evidence that she had been fighting for her life. And she had killed David with an illegal weapon she'd been concealing. Considering her history of substance abuse and those couple of arrests for petty theft, she didn't feel confident that the law would be on her side.

That thought led her back to her second option. David was dead, one way or the other, and nothing was going to bring him back. It was possible that she could save herself by simply walking outside, getting in the truck, and driving home. Even though the parking lot was only about forty yards from the road, a row of unkempt hedges blocked the view of the ground where David lay. He might not even be discovered until Sarah became worried that he hadn't come home. It was possible that no one would discover his body until morning. Because she had been in the building that night, she would almost certainly be questioned, but she might be able to say that she hadn't seen anything and there would be nothing to contradict her. With the storm raging all evening, the scene in the parking lot could conceivably be washed clean by the rain.

Her thoughts were starting to run in agitated circles. She had hit her head, and it occurred to her that she probably was in a state of trauma, perhaps shock. She felt high, and not in a good way. It was increasingly hard to think clearly at all.

She rubbed her forehead, trying to force her thoughts into some semblance of order. She could tell the police that she had come into the building, cleaned, and left without seeing or hearing anything out of the ordinary. The police might decide that after she left, David had come to the building's entrance and been the victim of a botched robbery. It was even possible that David had the kind of secret that made people enemies— he could be cheating with another man's wife or be a drug user. There was no way for Jenny to know.

Wilmington could be a dangerous place—this she *did* know. Things could happen to people.

Then she started thinking about the evidence: the wallet, the knife, the revolver. David's wallet was lying next to his body from when she had removed it to check his driver's license. It didn't make sense to put it back in his pocket, because she might have left a fingerprint on it that the rain didn't wash away. The knife had her blood and fingerprints on it, so it needed to disappear as well. Of course, the gun itself was a no-brainer. It would be insane to maintain possession of a murder weapon.

I can take the wallet, the knife, and the gun, and put them all in a garbage bag. I can drive to the Christina River, throw them in, and my problems are solved.

The very thought crystallized her plan of action. She dashed to the supply closet to grab a translucent garbage bag and made her way back to the front door. The she stopped herself, realizing that the bag might not be the best for concealing the items that could take away her freedom for decades—maybe for the rest of her life.

Get it together, Jenny.

A black garbage bag made a lot more sense. She ran back down the hallway to the supply closet where they were kept, grabbing a pair of latex gloves and a rag for good measure, then paused a moment before going back out into the rain. She tried to catch her breath, which was coming in jagged gasps. She could barely believe she was going through with this, but images of prison cells and years of confinement ran through her mind. Rationalizations spiraled, keeping her moving on the track she had chosen.

I'm a decent person. Maybe David was up to no good. Anyway, none of it matters. This wasn't my fault. Why should I pay the highest price because no one will believe me?

She unlocked the front door, pushed outside into the rain, and locked up again. She clenched her fists and closed her eyes for a moment until she felt ready for the sight of David. He was still face down, rain pooling around him and diluting the puddle of blood. Then she stopped, alarmed.

The wallet was nowhere to be seen.

She remembered seeing the knife and the wallet on the ground together, and how she had thought they were making fun of her. The knife was still there, but no wallet. She felt completely defeated.

"They were right there together," she whispered aloud. "I *saw* the wallet. What the hell happened to it?"

She looked around, but it was no use. She knew she needed to take the knife and go, if she was going to have a decent chance of claiming not to be the shooter. The only thing she could imagine was that someone wandered by, saw the wallet, and took it. She doubted herself, glancing around frantically as though it was going to magically reappear.

With deliberate motions, she put on the gloves, wiped down the gun and knife thoroughly with the rag, then put them in the plastic bag. Then she stood there rocking back and forth on the balls of her feet, staring at her truck and trying not to look at David.

I'm so sorry.

She wiped at the moisture running down her cheeks. The choices were paralyzing. She needed to take off immediately to have a chance, but that might mean leaving the wallet for someone to discover. If she stayed and kept looking, it was possible that she might somehow find the wallet, but that increased the chances of being caught.

The rain was still falling, not as hard as before, and the static nature of the scene before her wasn't granting any new information on which to base a decision.

Jenny's mind whirred and spun until it came up with an idea. A couple of months earlier, she and Sarah had been at Gazelle Lumber at the same time on a fluke because Sarah had to juggle her schedule around. David had dropped by to help Sarah with the floors, and Jenny had talked to him for just a few minutes—but the important thing was that Sarah had seen them talking and then gone into the back for supplies. If the police found the wallet and found Jenny's fingerprints on it, she could say that David had handed her his wallet to show her pictures of Sarah and David's two young girls. It wasn't a great explanation, but it was plausible, and that's all Jenny needed to break the deadlock in her mind.

Now it was time to run as fast as she could. She sprinted into her truck and started it, her teeth chattering as she backed out of the parking spot and briefly saw David's body illuminated in her headlights. She drove toward home, slowing down on the South Walnut Street Bridge long enough to hurl the garbage bag over the side. It disappeared into the darkness.

The next morning, Jenny was getting ready for work when she looked out the window and saw a blue Ford Crown Victoria driving past her apartment building.

They found something. It's over already. I'm going to prison.

She sat at the plain wooden table in her kitchen and tried to breathe calmly as she waited for a knock at the door that never came. Finally, she locked up the apartment and started her ten-minute drive to work. It was sunny and brisk, the sky clear blue, all the rain of the night before forgotten except for a squish under her feet when she walked through the grass to cross the street.

The Sunrise Mental Health Clinic appeared through her windshield at the end of the block when she also saw a man standing out in front. The first thing she noticed was that he lacked any kind of discernible fashion sense. He was wearing a brown corduroy jacket, glasses, a thick green tie that looked as though it depicted a variety of single-celled organisms, and a pair of black slacks that looked in need of a trip to the dry cleaner.

Who is this clown?

Then she saw the same Crown Victoria that had slowly driven by her apartment earlier that morning, now parked in a visitor's slot. Her concerns about this man's style of dress were immediately assigned a lower priority.

He intercepted Jenny when she was halfway to the building, pulling back his jacket to expose a police badge.

"Are you Jenny Ocean?" he asked in a deep voice.

"I'm Jenny," she said, amazing herself with how casual she sounded, with a note of curiosity. "Can I help you?"

"My name's Detective Sam Longford," he said, looking directly into her eyes. Up close, he wasn't as ridiculous as he had seemed from a distance. He could even be described as handsome, if you only looked at him from the neck up and ignored his tacky clothing. "I'm with the Delaware State Police."

There was something apologetic in his manner, as though he felt sorry about wasting her time and accosting her outside of her job. Jenny didn't say anything by way of reply, concentrating on keeping her smile relaxed.

"I tried to catch up with you at your house," he added. "But I got a call. Sorry to bother you at work. Your neighbor told me where to look for you."

"It's fine," Jenny said. "What can I help you with?" "Can I ask you a few questions about your job at the Gazelle Lumber Company?" he asked. His expression was flat, hard to read.

"There's not much to say about it," Jenny told him. "Unless you're fascinated by taking out trash and cleaning toilets."

Am I flirting with this guy?

Longford let out a quiet chuckle, then got serious again. "Look, something bad happened last night at the lumber company."

"Last night?" Jenny asked. "But I was cleaning there last night. I didn't see anything happen, other than the storm."

"A man's body was found outside the front entrance of the building. It was a homicide. He was shot. Do you know a David Saunders?" Jenny blinked. "You mean Sarah's husband?" Longford nodded.

"I've only met him once or twice," Jenny said. "You're saying he's dead?" Jenny put her hand over her mouth, acting shocked. She had been up nearly all night, rehearsing and preparing for this conversation. Longford took out a small spiral notebook and jotted down what she told him: the times she had arrived and departed from the building, the way nothing had been out of the ordinary. She said that she had rushed from her truck into the building and back out again when she was done cleaning, both times because of the severity of the storm.

From her time working at the mental health clinic, Jenny had learned that the police often used information against people who thought they were saying something innocuous. She could recall several conversations with clients who were sitting in the waiting room who told her that when they were dealing with the police, officers would read meaning into every little thing they did or said. So Jenny didn't elaborate on the bare facts, which were all true, and she allowed herself to show shock and distress over David's death—which she felt, but for reasons she obviously wasn't going to share with the detective.

Detective Longford didn't seem outwardly suspicious. If anything, as he closed up his notebook and put it in his pocket, she suspected that he was interested in her for other reasons.

"Can you share with me your relationship status?" he smiled slightly, almost blushing. "For the investigation, you know."

"Of course," Jenny said. "I'm not married or anything. And I don't have a boyfriend."

"That's difficult to believe, but OK." He smiled at her differently. They were just a man and a woman talking. Police business was concluded. "Thanks for your cooperation, Ms. Ocean. And . . . if I need to follow up with you, can I give you a call?"

She smiled and recited her phone number. "You can call me any time," she heard herself saying. "For any reason at all, really."

He was a bit older than her, which she liked, and she found herself lingering on his green eyes as he turned toward his car. He wasn't particularly tall, but he was muscular, and in their brief meeting, she decided he was smart, tough, and inquisitive.

That didn't necessarily mean she needed to ever see him

again. She hadn't dated anyone in more than a year, which was fine with her.

A few months went by without any more contact from the police, from Sam Longford or anyone else. Nobody even asked to search her truck or her apartment. Sarah quit her job at Gazelle, and Jenny's contact with her was limited and curt. One day, Jenny saw a headline in the paper that said David's murder remained unsolved. The police hadn't been able to collect any usable DNA or fingerprints at the crime scene.

It seemed the police were hesitant to declare the case closed, but they had more or less reached a dead end.

Jenny continued cleaning at Gazelle Lumber for several years. Her boss there said he would understand if she needed to quit after David's murder. Even though she hadn't seen anything, he said, it would make sense if she didn't want to work any longer at a place where someone had been killed.

Jenny said it was OK. Things happened in life, and you couldn't always run away from them.

CHAPTER THREE

SIMPLY IN THE WRONG PLACE AT THE WRONG TIME

OVER THE COURSE of the next several years, Jenny kept moving, trying not to look back. She continually reinvented herself, spending time with different kinds of people, changing her style and her looks, dyeing her hair, changing jobs and apartments, but it was like trying on a succession of disguises with none of them feeling quite right.

She always felt like she was dragging a heavy weight behind her.

That evening in October of 2007 would haunt her. At first it would occupy her mind from time to time, but paradoxically, the more she tried to escape from her past the more it would haunt her until it took the form of an obsession.

A familiar and repetitive cycle started to take shape. It would start with feelings of guilt and shame. She would replay the events of that night, like watching a horrifying film, and she would begin to believe that she was a fundamentally bad person for what she had done. Her rationalizations—that she had been attacked, that she was acting on reflex, that she was only trying to create less suffering by not turning herself in—would fall away like the leaves on autumn trees.

I'm a terrible person. I'm going to burn in hell. The world would be a better place without me.

This would go on for days, weeks, and months. Even when things started looking up in her life, it would exacerbate the suffocatingly negative feelings. Anything positive that happened would feed the shame and the guilt. She started calling the shooting "the Big Deal" in her mind, a sore that wouldn't heal and a place she feared to go.

Why are things going my way? I don't deserve it. I don't deserve success, or love, or anything.

The anguish would sometimes grow so powerful that Jenny would actually wish that good fortune would pass her by. She wanted to be permanently punished for her actions, believing in some superstitious way that it would help her avoid arrest, conviction, and incarceration.

Hand in hand with these feelings was intense anxiety and sometimes panic. She would work herself up and become convinced that the police were going to crash in and arrest her when she least expected it, the moment she let her guard down.

She was always awaiting their arrival. In her mind, every knock at the door was a prelude to a SWAT team raid. Every car that happened to follow her through two turns in town had to be tailing her, getting ready to make the big arrest. She felt special sympathy when she watched the news and saw that someone had been arrested by surprise.

"That's going to be me someday," she would say to the television screen. "I know exactly what you're going through."

She came to believe that the least she could do to maintain her dignity was not to be surprised when they came to take her to prison. It was a way of maintaining at least some illusion of control. But still, the panic attacks were so intense that Jenny often didn't feel she could go to work. She learned to push through with more self-punishing thoughts.

I need to go to work anyway. I don't deserve the luxury of missing work. Being anxious and panicked because of something that I did isn't reason enough to close the shades and stay inside forever.

The anxiety and panic were worse than anything Jenny had ever experienced in her life. It made her dysfunctional, and it kept her from getting close to people. She contemplated suicide several times to escape.

This phase would then blend into a nightmare of obsession. She would replay the events of that awful night over and over, like someone with a remote control freezing and replaying a video. She would visualize how the police might have reacted when they discovered David's body, and wonder if they were still collecting evidence that would lead them to her.

Certain compulsions developed that temporarily helped

alleviate, or at least slightly ease, that web of obsession. She would ceaselessly search the internet for stories about the death of David Saunders, reading the few details of his life that were reported in the media, looking for any new developments in his case. The wallet had never been found. It was assumed that this family-man truck driver had simply been in the wrong place at the wrong time and had been killed for the contents of his pockets.

Once in a while, she would reach out to Sarah, who had gone back to work at the janitorial company, and she would ask her if she had heard anything new about the case.

"Nothing new to speak of, honey," Sarah sighed into the phone the most recent time they spoke. "I don't want to give up hope that they find the bastard who did it, but it's hard. It's really hard."

Jenny felt relieved when she hung up the phone, along with a wave of guilt when she realized she had been mostly faking empathy for Sarah's situation. Jenny couldn't bring herself to fully empathize with Sarah, because she knew that might lead her in a weak moment to tell the truth to the dead man's wife. The revelation of the truth was something that Jenny kept firmly in the category of the unacceptable. Coming clean was not an option. She was trapped in a cage of her own devising, and the only way out was to step into another one.

Sometimes she would sit at the table alone in her apartment, take out a legal pad and pen, and write out in longhand her fabricated story for where she was that night and everything she had done. She would read it aloud, repeating her false narrative with precision and in a totally calm voice. It was a simple enough tale: she got to work a little early that evening, cleaned the building, then went home. The entire time passed without her hearing or seeing anything out of the ordinary, other than the rainstorm. It was a lie that she had practiced so many times that she almost started to believe it. She *wanted* to believe it, but before the narrative could concretize, the anxiety and the obsessions would cycle back and return.

The last phase of this vicious cycle of mental health symptoms was powerful rationalization. Jenny would gather all the scattered thoughts from anxiety, panic, obsession, and depression, and then convince herself that there was no way she was going to be arrested. Sometimes she brewed up anger to assist in the adoption of this rationalization. Jenny felt that she was truly innocent of any crime, even if that would be difficult to prove. She had been attacked by someone she thought to be a serial rapist, defended herself, then found herself in an impossible, unpreventable situation.

I'm a victim here. I don't have to be afraid of anything. I have no reason to be disappointed in myself.

Jenny kept working at the Sunrise Mental Health Clinic after that night in 2007, and she was such a good worker that in 2010, she was promoted to a higher position. The new job carried the responsibility of connecting clients to external resources such as homeless shelters, medical clinics, legal aid providers, and various other community resources as needed. She enjoyed the work and the sense of helping others that came with it, and after getting to know a few of the mental health counselors better, she started to think that she would enjoy doing what they did—and that she could be good at it. It rekindled her ambition from years before, when she had always been daunted by all the requirements for entering the profession. But around the end of 2010, she applied to a counseling program administered by Iron Hill College, a local school that had affordable tuition, financial aid, and classes that could be taken in the evening.

She had to undergo both group and individual interviews conducted by several professors in order to be accepted into the program, as well as an aptitude exam. Applicants weren't given their scores afterwards, although Jenny was pretty certain that her performance on all the tests had been at least above average. So it was with shock and disappointment that she opened up the email from the college telling her that she had been rejected.

Those old images of her parents—stern, disapproving—came back into her mind. It felt like she was always running, but never getting anywhere.

Applicants to the counseling program were encouraged to reapply the next year, but there was no feedback given to help them increase their odds of being accepted. But even with the sting of rejection and the uncertainty of trying again, Jenny was determined not to give up.

She applied the next year and was rejected again. Only on the third try was she accepted into the program.

Jenny knew she should have been happy without harboring any reservations, but the initial rejections had created a feeling within her that didn't subside. It was a nagging fear that she wasn't quite professional counselor material, and it stayed with her for many years to come. In addition to this self-doubt, Jenny harbored seeds of resentment and distrust for the counseling faculty and the way they went about things.

What kind of people are these professors? Is this all some kind of game to them, not even explaining to failed applicants what they need to change or get better at? And who are they to judge, anyway? This lingering distaste for the gatekeepers of her profession would never really go away. It was part of the foundation of what compelled Jenny to forge her own counseling style and philosophy. She looked upon authority figures with skepticism. Her distrust became a fundamental part of how she related to the world.

Despite that rocky start, Jenny found herself doing well in the counseling program. She felt she earned the respect of both her classmates and her professors. The fact that she had years of experience working in a mental health clinic seemed to persuade her peers and teachers to overlook some of her rough edges: her tendency to be combative, her prior substance abuse issues, a growing tendency to "tell it like it is" in conversation.

Jenny progressed through the various required courses in the curriculum covering theories of counseling, psychopathology, and appraisal, and it felt as though she was also learning more and more about herself.

Maybe, she thought, she was growing up. She was able to better exercise discretion, keep her potentially irritating thoughts and views to herself, and deliver her points more tactfully. At the core of her development into a counselor was the emergence of the ability to see herself as others saw her—a significant insight and a major turning point. It was a "light bulb" moment when all of her training seemed to come together into harmony.

Toward the end of her training in the counseling program, with her sights set on graduation, Jenny took advantage of a benefit through the college that gave her ten free counseling sessions. It seemed like a good way to transition from college student to counselor in training, and she was also eager to get a professional view on her mental health and well-being—the few counseling sessions she'd taken part in years earlier had been more or less disasters, mostly because of Jenny's defiance and rejection of authority.

Jenny's excitement turned out to be short-lived. There was nothing wrong with the counselor herself: Madeline was about ten years older than Jenny, had a calming gaze, and wore a black turtleneck like something out of a French art film. The therapist asked open-ended questions about Jenny's past, her family, and her path to becoming a counselor. She was empathetic, engaged, quick-witted, and even funny at times.

It didn't matter.

The Big Deal was like an insurmountable moat around her truest feelings and perceptions. It was a secret only she knew, and it had to stay that way—no matter the effects on her mental state.

Jenny had studied and knew well the ethics a professional counselor had to follow. The counselor technically wouldn't be able to share a secret such as the Big Deal unless Jenny posed some kind of current risk. But this didn't make Jenny feel she could trust Madeline. All the ways that information could be leaked crackled through Jenny's mind like distant lightning. Madeline could die and someone might go through her notes. And what if the counselor didn't follow ethics? All kinds of un-imaginable trouble could ensue.

How can I ever know that my secret will be safe once I speak it?

Unable to talk about the one thing that she desperately need-ed to get out into the open, Jenny found that her counseling sessions became stilted, artificial, and superficial. Jenny would joke and deflect, complain about her parents and men she had dated, but nothing got anywhere near to the core of what Jenny was carrying. She dropped out after only four sessions, tired of the therapy pointing out to her that she would always be alone with the truth and that she was living a lie every day.

As she walked out of the fourth session, knowing it was the last one, even though she didn't inform Madeline, the feelings of nervousness, restlessness, and anxiety felt as though they would be with her every moment for the rest of her life. The depression would ebb and flow at times, but never truly dissi-pated. It was like a cloud that never entirely lifted, a burden she carried that she could never put down.

The days started, the days ended—whether she liked it or not. She just kept moving forward, almost out of instinct, even though it felt as though she was slogging through quicksand.

Graduation day arrived. Jenny didn't really want to attend

the ceremony because of her depression, but she allowed herself to feel some pride. A decade earlier, she wouldn't have thought she'd be the holder of a master's degree, and yet there she was. But her journey to becoming a licensed counselor was just beginning. Regulations in the state of Delaware required that an applicant work for 3,200 hours under supervision before she could then become a candidate for the title of Licensed Professional Counselor of Mental Health (LPCMH). It would take Jenny two-and-a-half years as a counselor-in-training at the agency to rack up the required hours.

Even though she was grateful for their support, and Sunrise was eager to keep her on staff, Jenny went into private practice within four months of receiving her license—the amount of time it took her to get credentialed with the insurance company.

A friend of Jenny's had just left her own counseling practice for a teaching job, making her office available for rent. The office was in an older commercial building on the Kirkwood Highway just outside Newark, a pretty town less than a half-hour's drive to the southwest of Wilmington. The rent was affordable—in fact, because of the location and the age of the building, it was almost half what she might have paid elsewhere. Jenny laid down a deposit before she was fully credentialed, just to make sure she held onto it.

It was a long, one-story building, plain brick with mostly standard boxy windows. There were seven other offices in the building, all accessible off a single indoor hallway. Jenny's office was at the end, toward the back of the building. It was considered one of the best offices in the building, because it was the farthest away from the waiting area and bathroom that served all the office tenants and their clients and guests. It also had a very nice floor-to-ceiling window looking out on the forest of White Clay Creek Park.

When Jenny arrived there on the first day, with a box under her arm, she opened up her office and found a woman sitting behind her desk. Jenny paused.

"Um, I think this is my office," Jenny said, thinking that her tone of voice reflected a textbook case of Imposter Syndrome.

"It is," the woman said brightly. She was wearing a pants suit and had a curly mane of black hair. "I'm Sally Green. I'm also a therapist, my office is Number Three. We're all counselors here, except for Ken the dietician. And he needs a therapist, in my professional opinion."

Jenny just stood there blinking. Sally laughed.

"I'm *kidding*," she said. "Ken's cool. It's a pretty decent bunch here overall. We'll get you into the coffee fund and make sure you have the takeout Thai menu. You'll love it."

Jenny put her box on her rented desk, allowing herself to take a deep breath.

"And you got the killer office," Sally added.

"Thanks," she said. "But I'm worried that it's going to be available for rent pretty soon if I don't get some clients. It's my first day, but I only have two on the calendar."

Sally nodded. "Don't worry. Keep at it, and in six months you won't have a single opening on your calendar." Sally got up and motioned for Jenny to take a seat behind her desk. "There simply aren't enough counselors around her to keep up with the demand. Maybe it's not the greatest sign of the times, but it works for us."

"How long have you been at it?" Jenny asked as she sat down and started opening her box of supplies: some books, eating utensils and a coffee cup, some notepads and pens.

"Six years," Sally replied. She leaned against the wall and peered out the window, where a curious squirrel had walked through the leaves and was staring at them. "Been practicing down the hall here for four of them. It's good work. Now and then, you get the feeling you're actually helping."

Jenny was already happy to have an outgoing person down the hall who might be able to provide advice about the mental health counseling profession. With her anxiety and depression, she didn't feel that she could manage the complexities of a friendship, but having someone to chat with might be a big help.

Jenny's regard for Sally turned out to be well-founded. After just three and a half months of being in practice, just as Sally had predicted, all of Jenny's appointment slots were booked solid.

Jenny worked for eight hours a day, four days a week. She booked a client every hour between 11 and 7 for 50-minute sessions. Inevitably, at least one client would miss their appointment and Jenny used that time to eat, although sometimes all of her clients would show up and she would have to squeeze in just a few minutes for lunch. It was a good routine, and the days passed by quickly.

To take care of her billing, Jenny used a service that charged a few dollars per invoice. The insurance companies usually paid within thirty days, so the first couple of months were financially tight, but Jenny soon started to hit her stride. Most of her classmates weren't even licensed yet, and Jenny was already running what promised to be a successful private practice.

The part of her that was a trained counselor did her job well. Sometimes, just for a few minutes, she was able to take refuge in her profession and the fear would at least lessen. But then the Big Deal would return, and she would have to concentrate harder on what her client was saying lest she lose her train of thought. It was a daily struggle.

CHAPTER FOUR

I ONLY DO WHAT
THE LORD TELLS ME TO DO

IT WAS IN MID-DECEMBER of 2016 that Jenny's life changed forever. When it started, there was no sign of anything momentous happening: Jenny drove into the office in her used Prius, poked her head into Sally's office and said hello, filled her coffee cup at the urn in the lobby, then settled down behind her computer screen in anticipation of the day's clients.

A day like any other day. Routine. Stable.

Looking over her client-management app listing the names of the people who could be coming in that day for counseling, she saw a new one. And since almost every one of Jenny's clients had insurance, it stood out that her noon appointment didn't.

That meant this client was going to pay in cash. Jenny's rate for private pay was $135 an hour, so she figured that this person named Rio Winston had to be at least relatively well off.

When he came through the office door just before noon, she was surprised to see he was wearing blue overalls and work boots. Just below one collar was a small sewed-on patch with his name on it.

Jenny reminded herself that a lot of blue-collar jobs paid decent money. In her line of work, it was important to resist stereotyping people whenever possible.

Jenny introduced herself to Rio in the waiting room. He carried himself like someone who worked hard for a living. He was about average height, with a wiry kind of muscularity. He was clearly strong without being bulky, and his dark hair curled around his ears. He had a pleasant-seeming smile on his face, though Jenny observed right away that his eyes were somewhat dull as he looked at her.

"It's nice to meet you," Jenny said. "Come on back."

They went into Jenny's office. Rio sat down on the small couch against the wall and Jenny took a seat in her black office chair. Jenny's digital clock on the shelf across the room let out a single beep, as it did every hour, to signal that it was noon. Whatever brought Rio into therapy that day, he was very punctual.

"I hope you're comfortable," Jenny said. "If you don't want to sit on the couch, there's also this." Jenny pointed to the small wooden "back-up" chair that clients never opted to use.

"I'm comfortable where I am," Rio said. "This couch is soft."

He seemed slightly hesitant, which was understandable for someone on their first day speaking to a new therapist. She noticed that he wasn't wearing a wedding ring. His work boots were greasy, but they had new shoelaces. He rubbed his hands together and she saw that all his fingernails were ridged with dirt, and that he had a number of scratches and scars on the backs of his hands.

Jenny pulled out a blank paper chart that contained a variety of forms that she had to fill out as part of her obligations as a counselor. Usually the first session, and sometimes part of the second, would be made up of what was essentially an intake interview. During this assessment process, she would ask a variety of questions to better understand the client's history, symptoms, and goals in order to form a treatment plan.

"If you don't mind my asking," Jenny said, "who referred you to me?""Nobody," Rio said, his dark eyes looking somewhere just behind her. "I just found you on the internet."

"Do you remember what website?"Rio looked around the office, then let his gaze rest on the woods outside.

"Couldn't say," he muttered. "I guess the important thing is that I'm here now. Wouldn't you agree?"Jenny was a little put off by what she considered Rio's evasiveness. She pulled up a computer file to start entering information, and when she glanced at him in her peripheral vision, she saw he was staring under her desk at her legs.

Trying to make it sound like she hadn't done it hundreds of times before, and probably failing, Jenny reviewed and recited some of the perfunctory policies and caveats related to being treated by a counselor. Rio nodded that he understood, just like most other clients did at their first appointment, and he seemed a bit bored, like most of them did as well.

"Is this the first time you've seen a counselor?" Jenny asked.

Rio stroked his chin. "First time," he said quietly. "First time for everything. I know that's the saying, anyway"

The session reached the part when Jenny explained about confidentiality. Jenny was racing through the standard legal regulations, as she usually did, because most people didn't take much of an interest and figured out that this was just procedure.

"The confidentiality requirements are pretty standard wherever you go," Jenny explained. He cocked his head slightly. "But let me know if you have any questions about anything. Otherwise, let's get to work."

Rio held up his hand.

"Wait," he said. "Is this the part where you can't tell anybody else what we talk about? Like, you have to keep things confidential?"

"Yes. Sort of." Jenny felt a strange feeling in her spine. "Everything that is said between you and me will remain a secret. But there are exceptions. If you threaten to kill or harm yourself, or somebody else, of course. And if I find out about abuse of a child or an elderly person, for instance, I have to speak up. If I receive a court order requiring me to reveal confidential information, I have to comply and give the court what it wants. And if you give me permission to talk to a third party about information coming from our sessions, I can do so—but only under the terms that you set. Any questions?"

A long silence. Almost thirty seconds.

"Go back and tell me more about that hurting other people exception," Rio said carefully.

Jenny felt her eyes widen. She usually was able to hide any sign of surprise or dismay during therapy, but this was the first time she could remember that a new client wanted to dig deeper on this perfunctory ethical mandate. She was happy to go over the rules with this man, but she certainly wondered why he needed to stop everything to explore this particular guideline.

"Well, if I found out you were planning on causing harm to somebody because of something you said," she explained, "I would have to warn the authorities. This is called the Duty to Protect."

"Duty to Protect," he repeated thoughtfully. "So, what if I was just having thoughts about hurting somebody, but maybe I wasn't really going to go through with it?"

"I'm not sure—"

"Or what about this?" he interrupted. "What if I used words to describe something that I was going to do, but maybe, I was actually in real life meaning to do something a lot worse. Does that make sense?"

Jenny found herself laughing nervously and shifting uncomfortably in her chair.

"Do you mean like a euphemism?" she asked him. "Like, you would tell me you were going to slap somebody, when you really mean that you're going to run them over with your car?"

Rio's eyes stayed the same. He didn't respond with any sign of levity to her burst of laughter; instead, he was utterly still, watching her.

"Yeah," he said. "What if I did that? Could you tell anybody?"

"Well, no, technically not," she said. She was choosing her words very carefully. "But I would appreciate it if you would tell me if you hurt somebody, or if you planned to. We could talk about how to deal with those feelings."

What in the world is he hiding?

"You don't have to worry about me." His mouth curled at the edges, like a pantomime of a smile, but his eyes remained unchanged.

"Good," she replied.

"I only do what the Lord tells me to do," Rio added. "Keeps things nice and clean."

Jenny looked at him, waiting to see if he was going to say anything else. He sat back on the sofa and crossed his legs, letting his gaze settle out the window, into the woods, where the sun beamed through the gaps in the trees and illuminated the forest floor.

She kept up with the standard intake questions, trying not to let her anxiety take hold. She asked him to review, as best he could, a number of key moments and influences from his early life.

"Any spouse or partner?" Jenny asked.

Rio frowned. "No, never."

Rio was just a few years older than Jenny, nearing his fortieth birthday. His father, Ricardo, had passed away 28 years ago. Ricardo Winston had been the owner of a paper mill right there in the town of Newark until his accidental death.

Rio had been still living with his mother, Eileen, when his father died. Even though several members of the senior management team at the paper mill ended up buying it from her for a considerable sum, the bulk of Eileen's estate came from an inheritance she had received when her own father had committed suicide when she was 16 years old. Eileen's mother had also passed away two years earlier from an overdose of heroin.

Eileen herself would meet the same fate as her father, committing suicide several years ago. She had told Rio several times that she intended to kill herself.

"She wanted me to know what was coming," Rio explained, deadpan. "She was preparing me for living without her. It was very considerate."

Jenny took a deep breath. "I know this must be very delicate," she said. "But did your mother give you any idea of her reasons for taking her life?" Rio stared at her, then looked down at his dirty fingernails.

"I don't talk about that," he said.

Rio had an older half-sister named Stacy. Stacy was the child of Ricardo and his first wife, who got divorced not long after Stacy's birth. Stacy and Ricardo had never been particularly close. She rarely called or visited.

"Do you have a sense of why that is?" Jenny asked.

"Who knows with people?" Rio shifted in his chair, his body language suddenly growing uncomfortable. "They do what they do. I don't try to explain it. Maybe if I went to school like you did, I'd have an idea." He motioned at the diploma on her wall.

"We'll work together and hopefully get to some better understanding of things," Jenny offered, lending a note of optimism to her voice.

"So you say," Rio muttered.

In the course of her work, Jenny dealt on a daily basis with people who were in emotional and mental distress. That was the work. She didn't tend to see people at their best, and she encouraged people to let their guard down and be themselves when they were in her office. It was the only way they would be able to make progress.

But Rio was different. He had come to Jenny, he was paying in cash, and yet his reasons for being there were extremely hard to read.

For the rest of that first session, whether he meant to or not, Rio kept pulling the gravity of their conversation back to his mother Eileen. He was gradually painting a reasonably familiar picture: he alluded to a strained relationship with his mother, who, from his descriptions, tended to be extremely dominant and perfectionistic. Rio said something about his mother disliking nearly all men, and Jenny asked to dig a little deeper.

"What was it about men that bothered her?" Jenny asked.

Rio held up his hands as though the answer was self-explanatory.

"She thought men were disgusting in general," he said bluntly. "And she wasn't shy about letting me know."

"How did that affect you?" Jenny asked.

Rio shook his head, as though saying *no*.

"I loved her," he said. "She was wonderful. Perfect."

As they talked, Rio kept speaking of Eileen fondly, almost defensively. It emerged that Rio had been a very troubled youth, and that Eileen had wielded her power to protect him from the police and then the courts.

"What were you arrested for?" Jenny asked.

"How much time do you have?" Rio did his flat-eyed smile. "Shoplifting. Vandalism. Burglary. Underage drinking. Drugs."

He paused. "And sexual assault," he added.

Jenny jotted down a note, trying to appear as neutral as possible. Rio's affect seemed locked away, as though covered in plastic. His defense mechanisms must have been considerable, she realized. It was going to be quite a while before she could get a read on him—if ever.

Rio told her more. Eileen's wealth and influence—not to mention her personality—had earned her the nickname of "Porcupine" from local law enforcement and the high school administration in Newark. Most of the powers that be in town had long ago written him off and thoroughly disliked him, and wanted to see him pay for his range of crimes. But they simply couldn't match the tenacity or viciousness of the continual protective attacks from Eileen. Every time Rio got in trouble, she used her connections and financial resources to apply pressure to local officials, to intimidate witnesses, to fabricate testimony, and to repeatedly hire a prominent defense attorney who was formerly a state prosecutor.

"How did you feel about all this?" Jenny asked.

"Feel about it?" Rio shrugged. "It worked. That's how I feel about it."

Jenny flashed back to her coursework in psychopathology. Rio had been damaged somehow, that was certain. There was no real trace of remorse or contrition in his voice, no sense that he understood that all these things he had done were wrong— and that his mother had perhaps not really helped by protecting him from the consequences of his actions.

But then how am I so different? Have I accepted responsibility for what I did?

"When was your most recent arrest?" Jenny asked, jotting in her pad.

"When I was 24," Rio said evenly.

So, more than a decade ago. Maybe he had made the shift that so many others did, transitioning out of a lawless life after adolescence passed. Rio clearly worked for a living. Maybe, on some level, he had come to Jenny to process what he had done in the past, perhaps even reconcile it with an overbearing and overprotective parental presence. It was possible that they would do some excellent work together, moving Rio toward a more psychologically healthy state of mind as he aged into his forties.

"Can you tell me about it?" Jenny asked.

"Well, I got taken into custody again." There was a dry wryness to his tone. "Cops got a complaint from a 19-year-old neighbor of mine. She said I grabbed her breast with one hand and her hip with the other and tried to push her down on the couch. She had come to me first. She came running next door to where I lived with Eileen to ask if I could fix a faucet in her bathroom that had blown out and was making a mess everywhere. Now, people know I'm good with my hands, and that I have one of the best tool collections in town. So out of the goodness of my heart, I said yes, I would come over and help her out. Look where it got me."

"Walk me through it, please," Jenny said in an even voice. She knew there would be a lot to learn from hearing him describe this event from his particular point of view.

"First of all, I fixed the faucet," Rio said. "I did what she asked me. But then it was time for payment, if you know what I mean."

"I don't know what you mean," Jenny said. "Helping a neighbor is not something you do in exchange for sex."

Rio looked at Jenny. She thought she could see him shake his head, just imperceptibly, as though she was hopelessly naïve.

"I didn't mean any rough stuff," he said. "When I reached out for her, she thought I was joking or something. She started laughing. I didn't like that. I was serious. When I put my hands on her—gentle, you understand—she started screaming like a damned fool. OK, I said. I'll stop. I let her go, easy as can be, and I went outside like a good boy and just stood there waiting for the police to show up. I took some deep breaths, you know, because she had blown things out of proportion and I needed to make sure the cops didn't take it to the next level."

"The next level?" Jenny asked.

"Haven't you been listening?" Rio said impatiently. "The police in this town had been harassing me for no reason since I was about twelve."

Jenny processed this. It certainly didn't sound as though Rio had attracted the attention of the local police for no good reason.

"Now, I wasn't new in town, and I was aware of how the police operate." Rio tapped his forehead. "Rule number one: don't talk. And I didn't deviate from policy. I knew this was going to be inconvenient, but that was about it."

Jenny watched her client, trying to hide her growing fascination.

"Inconvenient," she repeated.

"At first, they thought they really had me this time." That flat smile, now with a tone of satisfaction. "They said, *Rio, we have a credible complaining witness who has no reason in the world to make a false accusation against you. She says that before today, you were always friendly and helpful.*"

He flipped his hand open, palm up, as though to indicate that he was really a nice guy after all.

"But the battle was far from over, especially after Eileen got involved." Rio shifted slightly in his seat, clearly noticing Jenny's interest in his story and playing it up, almost performing. "She turned the tables on everyone. She found a 'witness' who was willing to testify that my neighbor had tried to blackmail him with false accusations. And my goodness, the story she threatened him with sounded a lot like the tall tale she told the police about me. Now this 'witness' wasn't great—he told his story the same way every time, like a damned robot who had memorized it. They said his story was too simple, didn't have enough details, sounded like a lawyer wrote it, and that he didn't show any feeling when he told it. But think about it: if he told it the same way every time, couldn't that simply mean that it was the truth? That's what Eileen argued, anyway."

"So she got in there and made things go away," Jenny said.

"Well, not right away," Rio admitted. "The district attorney who handled the case put on a lot of pressure for me to plea bargain down to a misdemeanor unlawful sexual contact. But Eileen wasn't having it. The lawyer she hired for me pretty much overwhelmed the prosecutor's office with motions, day after day, until they just got so tired they dropped the charges. They just wanted us to go away."

Jenny stared down at her notes.

"But Eileen wasn't done." Rio chuckled. "She called that district attorney every day for the next two weeks, telling him he had to file charges against that woman for trying to blackmail me. Eileen was never satisfied with winning. Boy, she had to grind her opponents into the ground until there was nothing left of them. The police were smart, though. They just kept interviewing our witness over and over again, trying to trip him up, and he got scared and came running to Eileen for more . . . well, he came running to Eileen, let's just put it that way. She finally just had to let it be."

To say this wasn't a typical therapy session was an understatement. Rio had his hands folded in his lap, a picture of peace. Light streamed in through the floor-to-ceiling window.

"Do you have bad feelings around that event?" she asked him.

"Bad feelings? Hell, yes." He slapped one palm against his thigh. "That girl had a lot worse coming than what I did to her. But I guess she got away with it. It happens sometimes. Why, you got something to say about it?"

Jenny willed her face to be still. "This isn't about judgment," she said. "Let me put it this way—do you regret attacking her?" "I had a job to do and I failed," Rio said very matter-of-factly. "That girl was no angel, believe you me. She slept with a boy from my street that I know about, and still another one from the neighborhood across the way. For some reason, I wasn't good enough for her to touch, or good enough to be with. God has rules about how to deal with people like that, you know."

Jenny was going to ask about these rules, but she was startled and let out a gasp when the clocked beeped to indicate that it was already ten minutes before one o'clock. She had completely lost track of the time, having been so engrossed in Rio's narrative.

This might end up delaying her next session by a few minutes, but Jenny needed to know.

"What's the current status of your criminal record?" she asked.

He smiled.

"Don't have one," he said.

"How—"

He held up his hand to silence Jenny. "I had some juvenile convictions," he said. "But I applied to have them expunged when I was back in my early twenties, and expungement was granted. So here I am, innocent as a newborn baby."

She looked down from his smile.

"Will next week at the same time work for you?" she asked.

"It will work for me." Rio reached into his back pocket, pulled out a wallet, and peeled off the exact payment for the session.

"If you ever cancel, you have to let me know twenty-four hours in advance," she said, relieved to be able to move the conversation back to logistics and procedures. "Or more, if possible. I lose money for no-shows that I can't get back.""Don't worry about me being a no-show," he said. Then he paused, looking at her with a pensive, almost reflective expression. "Unless I'm dead, of course."

"I still expect twenty-four hours notice," Jenny said lightly, trying to be funny, trying to break through his implacable calm.

She received only the blankest of stares in return.

CHAPTER FIVE

FAMOUS
IN HIS OWN MIND

RIO BECAME a steady, punctual weekly client—part of the flow of Jenny's weeks. She saw people troubled by anxiety and phobias, people in troubled relationships unsure whether or not to leave, individuals coping with decades-old trauma, and long-term depressives looking for a lifeline to understand their experiences.

In the middle of the week was Rio—a truly unusual client, and a fascinating person whose shell of self-protection made his subjective reality extremely difficult to catch a glimpse of, like a room in shadow or a clouded landscape. Jenny wasn't sure how much counseling was going to help him. To start with, he wasn't at all clear about what he considered his problems to be, and what he wanted from the sessions. And he was so slow and deliberate in his words and expressions that sometimes it felt the hour had passed with very little ground covered, if any at all.

A few months went by. Rio did open up about a broader range of topics, even if he wasn't particularly insightful about them. Sometimes, he would seem to relax and almost become talkative, only to catch himself and go silent after making some cryptic remark.

There was a lot of that—Rio had a tendency to talk about his work, his home life, and his inner world with almost vacuous phrases that he would deliver as though they had some sort of very profound deeper meaning. He spent almost an entire session droning on about the precise dates he'd worked at his various jobs, as well as the full names of his bosses and coworkers—at times such as this, it was almost as though he was giving an interview, assuming that anyone listening would be rapt with interest in these mundane details.

Once he seemed fully relaxed around Jenny, he seemed to start carrying himself with an air of importance that shaded on grandiosity. It reminded Jenny of times she'd seen on TV an older celebrity, like a musician or an actor, speaking of mundane interactions in their past with other famous people with a self-conscious air that assumed anyone listening had to be fascinated by the details. The main difference with Rio, of course, was that he wasn't famous, and he didn't know any prominent people. But his manner, once he was familiar with Jenny, convinced her that if he should become famous by some accident, he would have the mannerisms down pat.

He'd fit right in. It's like he's already famous in his own mind.

During one session, Rio started talking about how a few years ago he had towed a car owned by the actor Nicolas Cage. Apparently, Cage's Dodge Viper had broken down on Interstate 95, and Rio had been the one to get the call, meet Cage, and bring his car into the shop.

Over the next few weeks, Jenny brought up the story a few different times. She wasn't entirely sure why, but something about the incident in Rio's telling seemed strange. She noticed a couple of inconsistencies in how he recited the story, and one day she decided to push back a bit.

She spoke in the softest, most nonthreatening tone she could muster.

"Rio, you said a few weeks ago that Nicolas Cage owned the car that you towed, and that you took it into the shop. But just now you said that after the car was repaired, it was delivered to a house in Newport. Maybe I'm not tracking. Does Nicolas Cage have a house in Newport? I've never heard anything about that."

"I didn't mean he owned it *currently*," Rio said with an air of impatience, as though talking to someone who wasn't very bright and who wasn't keeping up with the conversation. "He owned it at one time. But he was still related to the car."

"How can somebody be related to a car?" Jenny asked.

"Oh, you know, maybe that's not the perfect word." Rio frowned, as though dismissing the entire topic.

"Are you saying you never actually met Nicolas Cage?" Jenny asked.

"A man can't forget about a car like that," Rio said, as though delivering a profound lesson. "I'm sure he felt very strongly about it, and was very happy and grateful that I was able to take it off the highway shoulder safely and take it somewhere it would be fixed with care."

"You never actually talked to Nicolas Cage?" Jenny repeated.

"Not in the most literal sense." Rio paused, looking at Jenny closely. "Look, the car's owner showed me an old registration card with Nicolas Cage's name on it. I'm sure he called Nicolas after speaking with me, you know, to let him know what a great job I did and how I was looking after something he prized very much."

Jenny backed off. She felt herself slipping out of the counselor role and into the interrogator role. Rio wasn't going to admit that he lied, and in a sense, Jenny couldn't have said for sure if she thought he *was* lying.

Is it a lie when the person seems to have convinced themselves that it's true?

It wasn't entirely sure to Jenny which reality would be scarier—Rio believing in his ability to deceive so fluidly, or his believing something that was almost certainly not true.

With her daily schedule almost always booked with a steady stream of clients, Jenny found a more spacious condominium than her previous apartment. Her new home had a fireplace, which she rarely used, and a dining room looking out over a row of furry pine trees, where she always ate alone. She invited her parents over once and they had takeout from the Italian place down the block, but it was the only time they visited her there.

The Big Deal continued to isolate her from others, making her pull away from those she knew and making her shy away from closeness with anyone new. She started eating alone in the living room, watching Netflix, and going to bed early.

Finally, she went to the animal shelter and adopted a cat, which she named Tom (a nod to the hours she had spent watching Looney Tunes as a little girl). Tom was gray, with intense staring eyes and a loud meow. He was always happy when Jenny came home from work, making a racket and following her around until she fed him his dinner.

Some nights, she would look on the internet for any word on David's murder. Other than a short brief saying there had been no progress on the case, there was nothing. She would take a moment's relief in this news, but then the dread and the guilt would descend again.

It's just a matter of time until you get what you deserve.

On those nights, it would take hours before she could get to sleep, and her dreams were filled with being chased by unknown pursuers until the alarm clock would ring out and she would see the sun streaming through the curtains and know that it was time to face another day.

"You've worked your whole adult life as a mechanic and a contractor," she told Rio one morning at his weekly session. "I've thought about that. It seems like you have a passion for fixing broken things."

Rio grinned. Between his first session and this one, he had bought a new pair of bulky work boots.

"That's right," he said, as though speaking to an astute student. "I like restoring systems to working order, bringing things back to the way they should be."

Rio's current employer was an auto garage that also offered towing services. It was called Brandywine Newark Repair, but everyone locally called it BNR. It was well-known, particularly because its logo could be seen on tow trucks all around town. Rio worked in the shop once in a while, but for the past few years, had spent most of his time in the towing service.

Jenny asked Rio why he had to work, since his mother had been so wealthy. He darkly insinuated that she had managed to waste away a great deal of the family money, leaving him with the house he lived in and a sum that he kept in savings and jealously protected. He craved stability and order, which was unsurprising, given his upbringing—although in his younger years he had certainly sowed enough chaos. Today, though, he seemed to be law-abiding and fastidious in his life.

To hear Rio tell it, he enjoyed a good rapport with the owner, managers, and the other employees at BNR.

"I take my work really seriously," Rio told her. "And people appreciate that. They know to expect it from me."

"That gives you satisfaction," Jenny observed.

Rio paused and looked out the window. "*Some* satisfaction," he said, almost to himself.

"What does—"

"Look at it this way," he said with sudden intensity. "Take a tow, for instance. Now, a tow isn't just about a busted car that somebody needs moved from one place to the other."

Jenny jotted down a note. Rio saw this and nodded appreciatively. It was as though she was a celebrity journalist writing down his pearls of wisdom.

"It's an opportunity to restore order to the roadways," Rio said. "It is a chance to rid the world of something flawed, to break down an obstacle to harmony. Do you follow me?" Jenny nodded. She wasn't sure she did.

"It's like this," Rio explained. "Broken vehicles, flat tires, appliances that don't work—anything that isn't functioning to its optimal level is wrong. It's out of place. It's *disgusting*. My desire is to restore the system back to balance, back to perfection."

This tied into what Rio had said about his religious beliefs. From an early age, Rio had been exposed to and indoctrinated into a very harsh, fundamentalist kind of Christianity. His father and mother had initially met in Bible study at a Baptist church where they both attended services—and which they both eventually decided was too worldly and wicked for them and for their increasingly idiosyncratic views on morality.

Rio's parents had switched churches many times over the years, moving from one fundamentalist Protestant denomination and community to another. Eventually, Ricardo had essentially started up his own sect, inviting people from the paper mill and from the nearby area over to the Winston family house every Sunday morning and Wednesday evening.

Ricardo focused his preaching and his teachings on a very

literal interpretation of the Bible, underpinned by an emphasis on what he called the "infallibility of the Word." Eileen shared Ricardo's fixation on sin and wickedness, although she had an additional emphasis.

"Disgust in general," Rio summed up his mother's view of life. "And to be specific, the disgusting nature of man's sex drive. It's a wonder they ever made me."

Although it wasn't apparent at first, Rio had a very high degree of scrupulosity to his religious beliefs. He read the Bible daily, often scouring the Old Testament for tales of punishment and condemnation. He kept these fixations close to the vest, but they emerged the longer he spent time in counseling. Interestingly, he didn't think there was much out of the ordinary about his background or his spirituality.

Jenny had begun to suspect that Rio had obsessive compulsive disorder (OCD). She noticed that he arrived at her office at the same time to the minute every week, for instance, and that he had a way of tapping on the arms of the sofa in her office that seemed to be made up of ritualistic counting.

In addition, he seemed entirely lacking in any understanding of how to process beliefs, especially theological ones, on any kind of continuum. He never showed any sign of thinking in shades of gray. Everything was an absolute—in black and white, in inflexible binaries.

"Do you ever have intrusive thoughts?" Jenny asked him delicately.

He looked over her shoulder.

"What do you mean?" he asked.

"Thoughts that you don't want to be having, but which you can't make go away."

Rio pursed his lips as though he had bit into a lemon.

"Since I was little," he said. "I had these thoughts like voices. They've been hard on me. They tell me that I'm going to burn in hell if I make any mistakes. There's no leeway."

"What kind of mistakes?" Jenny asked.

The woods outside her office window were dark and gloomy, the day overcast. It felt as though the two of them in her office were somehow sealed off from the world.

"Maybe I obsess over it, but that's the way you have to be when you come up short in so many ways," Rio explained calmly. "Ever since I was little, it haunts me when I tell a lie, even a little white one. Or when I'm insensitive to someone or lose my cool and don't act polite. Or when I have sexual thoughts."

This hung in the air between them. Rio seemed as sincere as Jenny had ever seen him. His air of arrogance was gone for the moment.

"My religion is very important to me," Rio added. "You might not understand it, but it's mine. I have high standards. And every violation is a mortal sin."

Jenny took notes. Rio's obsessions were emerging as part of a mental disorder, and it seemed that he had no control over them. For much of his life, he had been tormented and haunted by the prospects of eternal damnation.

"And you still feel this way?" she asked him.

He nodded solemnly. "I knew you would understand," he said. "You have to understand, I've come a long way since the days when every waking moment was caught up in that hell-fire."

Rio unfolded deeper dimensions to his story. Even though Rio's father Ricardo had seemed stricter about his religious beliefs, more dogmatic and inflexible, he had been the one to first suggest that Rio be sent for mental health treatment. Eileen wouldn't hear of it. She had insisted that Rio was, in fact, actually fighting off literal demons—that his troubles were the mark of some grand, exalted spiritual conflict.

For Eileen, Rio's OCD was actually a sign that he had been chosen by God for a higher purpose. She reasoned that this had to be the case, because otherwise their God wouldn't have allowed the demons to test Rio's faith. Eileen instructed Rio to shield his mind from evil thoughts, particularly those about sex. Predictably, Rio had no way to turn off or control his obsessions, and his use of compulsive behavior increased through adolescence as he tried to save his soul. He developed a complex system of rituals that he explained to Jenny in broad strokes—he seemed not to want her to know the details, but they involved prayers, numbers, and visualizations.

"I used to spend about two hours a day asking for forgiveness," Rio added, "and to be spared from eternal torment."

"Thank you for explaining this," Jenny said.

"It's a good deal better now," he said. "Most of the time."

Rio went on. Eileen had been ill-equipped to recognize and understand Rio's mental health issues, but even she eventually came to entertain the possibility that something outside of spiritual forces was causing his distress and pain. As a result, she came up with what she believed was an ingenious way to alleviate his suffering while remaining consistent with her own religious dogma. She subjected adolescent Rio to a series of "lectures" over the course of several months, explaining in detail how the evil thoughts meant Rio was special rather than ill, and that he had indeed been chosen for a higher purpose. Yes, Rio would need to atone for his evil thoughts, but he could do so in ways that didn't involve ritualistic prayer.

Essentially, Eileen tried to create a way out for her son. She devised and then delivered to him another set of behaviors. These behaviors as a whole were what she called "the Cleansing." As soon as Rio spoke those words, he suddenly went quiet.

"The Cleansing," Jenny repeated. "What does that mean? Cleansing away the obsessive and intrusive thoughts? How was that done?""My mother was pretty smart," Rio said. "She knew I needed to get out of the hellfire without losing the Lord. She's the only one who really got it. It wouldn't work for just anyone, to be honest with you. You have to be in a special place with God."

Jenny noticed that Rio took the conversation away from the specific and back into the theoretical. She had an insight: he hadn't meant to tell her all of this, but perhaps he had actually been drawn into an aspect of the therapeutic process that he hadn't anticipated. She felt a glow of accomplishment. Maybe they were getting somewhere, and she might have the opportunity to do more with this client than anyone had before.

She knew she needed to be patient. He was like a gazelle, ready to run away if she got too close—

Why was I just thinking of a gazelle?

She snapped back into the session. She needed to keep facilitating the discussion to his degree of comfort, all the while refraining from sharing her potential diagnosis of him for the time being. She was well aware that Rio might be resistant to her observations about his OCD.

"We're doing great," she said calmly. "Can you tell me anything more about how this 'cleaning' time affected you?" She had deliberately used the wrong word in order to gauge his response.

"Cleansing!" he said, flashing anger. "Not cleaning!" "Of course," Jenny said. "So sorry."

"The way my mother put it to me," he said, instantly calm again, "it's like an alternate way that I can atone for my sins. Like so many other things, it's a gift from a kind and loving God."

"So, it's basically prayer?" Jenny asked, although she sensed it wasn't. While she was trying to stay neutral and practical, part of her was increasingly rapt and fascinated. Rio's pathologies seemed as though they might be totally original and unique in their manifestations. For just a second, she allowed herself to think that her work with him might be a professional coup. She imagined herself as the author of a book, detailing this compelling case and how she got through to the patient and saved him.

"No, it's different. You have to keep up," he said emphatically. "It's things that I can do in the world to balance my evil thoughts. The way Eileen taught me, if I cleanse away the evil things then I would bring balance to the world. The world needs balance. And that would also mean that my wrongdoing will even out."

"What . . . what did you have to cleanse?"

"That's the good part," Rio said with a smile. "I could cleanse anything as long as it was bad. I could fix anything as long as it was broken. I could give order to that which was disordered."

His speech had the pattern of prayer, but he was describing something else. Jenny took notes.

Rio gave her a series of examples that fit the concept: washing his clothes, learning to fix things that were broken around the house, learning to fix cars, organizing his room and his things, keeping the yard tidy.

"Sometimes I'd sin so much," Rio laughed, "that I'd have to clean just about everything in the house."

It turned out that Eileen had essentially channeled Rio's inner pathology of obsessive thoughts by converting him into a sort of mythical handyman-workhorse who could accomplish everything his aging father couldn't. And after Ricardo's death, Eileen not-so-secretly emphasized even more the ways in which Rio's sins were increasing—thus upping the need for him to keep the house immaculate and the chores always done ahead of time. Eventually, Rio had virtually restored the house they shared—he replaced all the windows, redid the siding, upgraded the plumbing and electrical wiring, and laid down new floors throughout the entire first story of their 3,000-square-foot Colonial.

"I was proud to turn those evil thoughts into cleansing action," Rio said. "It's like rechanneling energy. It's what the Lord does every second of every day."

This unusual dynamic remained in place all the way up until the day when Eileen committed suicide. Jenny noted her opinion that the relationship between Rio and his mother had simultaneously helped and hurt both of them. Up until that point in his counseling, Rio had declined to speak about the circumstances around his mother's death. Now, she sensed he might be thawing.

"Do you want to talk about Eileen's suicide?" Jenny asked gently.

Rio stared over her left shoulder, blinking.

"It's OK if you don't—"

"I guess it was me," Rio said flatly. "She gave me the lectures and she invented the Cleansing. But I had a lot of work to do around the house to compensate for my sins. She had been telling me for a while that it was all too much for her to handle. The sins, the Cleansing that came after."

Jenny paused. Something didn't add up.

"I thought the Cleansing was all about dealing with your thoughts," Jenny said. "Now it sounds like you're talking about a different kind of sin."

He gave her that look, as though he was the teacher and she was the dullest student in the class holding everyone back.

"Who knows what we're talking about?" he chuckled.

All throughout Rio's counseling sessions, there were more and more inconsistencies in both what he said and how open he seemed to be when he was saying it. He would never share, for example, what he did with his free time, and he was still coy about what had motivated him to seek therapy.

At the same time, on other matters he would blurt out material that most other clients would have considered sensitive. More than once, he'd revert into coarse language when talking about his criminal past, and he could also be borderline misogynistic when he talked about women he knew, such as a receptionist at work—at those times, it was almost as though he forgot he was talking to a woman.

And when he talked about the sexual aspects of his obsessions for redemption and cleanliness, he would consistently lose the normal pace of their conversation. It was the only time he spoke quickly, and his words would blend together. He would be sitting still, but his hands would move about as he grew more agitated.

"I just thought of Sonia again," Rio said with a smile.

It's almost like he can read my mind sometimes.

Sonia was a woman Rio had dated a long time ago, when he was 23 years old. She had come up more than once.

"I was in love with Sonia from the moment I first saw her," Rio explained, not for the first time. "She came into the shop to have her alternator fixed. I wasn't authorized back then to do that repair. I was mostly just doing oil changes and brakes. So I got to just stand around and talk to her while one of the other technicians was doing all of the work."

He was layering on more detail, embellishing.

"Did you get the sense then that she liked you, too?" she asked him.

"Well, I just figured she did," Rio answered. "I mean, my family was a pretty big deal in town."

"She knew your family?""I assume she *did*," Rio said, a touch patronizingly. "Unless she had been living under a rock or something. I mean, OK, maybe it took her a little while to realize who she was talking to. But after that, we went on a few dates."

"Did you develop a romantic relationship with her?" Jenny asked.

Rio had alluded to a torrid affair with Sonia, but he had never gotten into the specifics of what really happened.

"Not really. Four dates," Rio said slowly. "That was when I asked her if she'd be my girlfriend. She said that she didn't want to settle."

"Ouch," Jenny said. "I'm sorry that happened."

"Doesn't matter, it worked out for the best," Rio said, his eyes shifting around the room. "I realize now that she was doing me a favor. I was too good for her."

Jenny stayed silent.

"On top of that, her turning me down let me know that she's evil," he explained calmly. "There's no place for someone like that in my life."

"Evil seems like a strong word, Rio, for someone who just doesn't want to be someone's girlfriend."

"I would agree with you, Rio said. "If I was just anyone."

The session was almost over. Jenny realized that her breathing was shallow, constricted, her anxiety spiking.

"It sure would have been nice to bang her, though," Rio

continued. "Can't pretend I didn't want to give it to her. I guess you could say that I'm still pretty mad at her that she didn't give it up. You know what I mean?" The alarm went off. It was time to be done for the week with Rio Winston.

She lay awake that night, the cat sleeping at her feet. She thought about the things Rio was telling her, sifting through them and wondering if she was doing the right thing by listening to his opinions and viewpoints without strongly trying to change them. She remembered the words of one of her college professors about not erring on the side of being judgmental.

Clients talk about what they need to talk about. And some of them are always going to be rougher around the edges than we might like.

She shouldn't be a snob, she told herself. Rio was rough-hewn and had been through an unorthodox upbringing while saddled with OCD. Maybe someday she *would* convert all her notes into a book, while leaving his name anonymous, of course.

But none of these thoughts brought her deep, unsettled feelings any peace.

CHAPTER SIX

A PUZZLE SHE WAS STRUGGLING TO SOLVE

TOWARD THE END OF SEPTEMBER of 2017, close to six months after taking on Rio as a client, Jenny started thinking that it was time to make some room for love in her life. Tom was an affectionate companion, but he was only a cat, after all. Her colleagues at work were always asking if she was seeing anyone, and she craved something to look forward to at the end of the day other than television and an early bed.

Of course, the primary reason she hadn't made any meaningful connection with a man in years came down to one source: the Big Deal. She still felt as though she couldn't trust anyone with the truth about it. It's not that she never dated—there had been a promising lawyer in town, and a local chef who cooked for her a few times—but the powerful concealment of her feelings was something that quickly became obvious to any man with even a modicum of sensitivity and perceptiveness. The ones who didn't notice her evasive behavior were either narcissistic themselves, only interested in sex, or both—which made them less than long-term partner material, which she felt more and more was something important and missing from her life.

It was easier said than done, it turned out. She had uploaded a dating app to her phone, but as she swiped through a succession of faces, she became overwhelmed. Maybe it was just her anxiety and guilt talking, but each man's face looked like a bundle of problems that she would be taking on by reaching out and connecting.

How does everyone do it? How do they just live?

One Monday, it was unseasonably cold. All afternoon, the trees outside her window seemed to be shivering in the howling wind that pressed against the window with persistent gusts. Jenny went out to the waiting area to retrieve her last client of the day. She pulled her sweater tight around herself, as though anticipating the chill that was waiting when she walked out of the building.

Just one more, then I'll be out of here.

The client was a teenage male named John with a cluster of symptoms: depression, insomnia, what she believed to be a tech addiction, and self-medicating with marijuana (they all went hand-in-hand, in Jenny's observation). She was surprised when she saw him waiting for her with a man whom she thought she recognized, but struggled to place. The two males said goodbye to one another, and Jenny awkwardly motioned for John to come back to the office as she tried not to stare at the older man. As she was walking John down the hall, her curiosity got the best of her.

"Who is that guy who came with you today?" she asked him.

"That's just my neighbor," John explained. "My mom's stuck at work, and I ran into him and he offered to give me a ride. He's a nice guy."

Jenny didn't think much of it at the time. The session went as usual. As was often the case, John's primary goal from the counseling session was to devise strategies for getting his mother to stop bugging him about his marijuana use. Jenny tried to stay engaged, but she had gone through this loop of thoughts numerous times with John and she just couldn't get invested that afternoon. Her mind kept wandering off to think about the identity of the mystery man in the waiting room. She was absolutely positive she had seen him before, and she had a good impression of him, but she couldn't picture where she had met him as context for figuring out who he might be.

With a suddenness that made her physically twitch, the identity of the man instantaneously came to her. He was Detective Sam Longford, the police officer who had met her outside her old job when he questioned her about the investigation into the shooting of David Saunders.

The Big Deal.

Jenny felt herself breaking into a sweat, and her hands holding her notepad began to tremble. Her teenage client luckily didn't seem to notice; he was deeply invested in a long monologue about how terrible and unbearable his parents were, and how profoundly unfair was their treatment of him.

She glanced at the clock, wishing she could make time move faster. She tried to stay attentive and engaged, but it was really no use. She found herself switching into autopilot and saying mindless, insincere things. It wasn't the way she ever wanted to go through a counseling session, but her mind was spinning with possibilities and ramifications.

"That sounds awful, yes, I follow you," she heard herself saying, as though it was someone else's voice. "Please tell me more."

Finally, the hourly chime indicated that the session was over, and Jenny practically leapt from her seat even though John had been in mid-sentence. He actually kept talking for a good thirty seconds before he realized he had no one listening.

Jenny's mind was whirling. If Detective Longford had come to arrest her, she would have been in custody already. The next logical possibility was that he had come around because he had questions for her. But if that were the case, why would he have given John a ride to his therapy appointment? It seemed that they really were neighbors—John had no earthly reason to lie about that.

Jenny walked her client down the hallway to the waiting room, summoning all her strength and focus to project calm, even though her palms felt clammy and sweaty.

This is probably just a coincidence. Don't blow it out of proportion. No one knows about the Big Deal.

Sam Longford was sitting in the waiting area, his gaze focused on the phone in his hand. When he saw them, he stood up with a smile and pulled his keys out of the pocket of his slacks. He was as poorly dressed as Jenny remembered him, in brown slacks and an earth-tone jacket. At least he wasn't wearing a tacky tie this time.

"You ready to go?" he said. It took Jenny a long moment to realize that he was talking to John and not her.

She hoped she was successfully hiding her massive feelings of relief. She also couldn't help but notice that the detective had a nice smile, which made her feel even more awkward as his gaze focused on her and something seemed to click.

"You look familiar," Jenny said, as much to break the silence as anything.

"You do, too," he said. "I've been trying to remember where we met."

"I used to work at the Sunrise Clinic in New Castle," Jenny explained, pleased at how normal she sounded.

Everything is going to be OK.

"Sunrise Clinic," Sam repeated, seeming as though he was piecing things together.

"I think you stopped by there one time," Jenny continued. "You were investigating the death of my co-worker's husband at another job."

She managed to inject a note of concern into her voice, as though remembering something unpleasant that didn't involve her. She figured the next half-minute or so was going to be very important.

"I remember!" he said. "I thought your name was familiar, too. It's been a while."

"Years," Jenny agreed.

"I remember something else." Sam's smile got a bit naughty. "No boyfriend and no husband, right?" John was watching them as though they were some strange species of wildlife.

"That's right," she said, finding herself engaging with Sam's smile. She remembered there had been something appealing about him, something ineffable but undeniable. "In fact, nothing has changed in that department."

The detective seemed to think about this for several seconds. "Well, then," he finally said, "Would it be OK if I gave you a call sometime?"

"I guess that would be OK," Jenny said, feeling her own smile growing broad.

Over the course of the next several months, Jenny and Sam saw each other a few times a week. There was never any official moment when they declared themselves to be in a relationship with one another, but things progressed faster for Jenny than any other relationship in her memory. The little markers accumulated: they made keys for each other's apartments, they started keeping a toothbrush and some clothes at each other's place, they would talk tentatively about future plans for travel together. By Christmas of 2017, it was pretty much official: they were a couple.

Jenny had some misgivings, however. Sam could be witty and fun to spend time with, but part of him was remote. He didn't seem to notice Jenny's own reserve and carefully guarded boundaries, which was both good and bad. There were a couple of times when Jenny talked about maybe slowing down the pace of their relationship, and Sam had seemed more than happy to oblige, but he would want assurances that they would still have an active sex life. She was fine with that; she enjoyed their physical connection and found herself looking forward to his companionship on the days they spent apart.

In their way, they were both emotionally distant, but felt connected. Their relationship settled into a pattern that others might have found unfulfilling or unsatisfying, but it more or less worked for them.

Still, Jenny found herself constantly vacillating. On the one hand, she was excited to have a partner, even if someone else might have found their connection only quasi-romantic. Sam was no Romeo, but at the same time, that wasn't what she wanted.

On the other hand, she questioned her own judgment and wondered if she was being a bit crazy for getting so close to a police officer. And Sam wasn't just any cop: he was directly involved in the investigation of the man she had shot and killed.

Sam's work life directly touched on the Big Deal. The case was still open. He had no idea he was trying to put the person he was sleeping with behind bars.

Psychologically, Jenny embraced the contradictions in her best, most anxiety-free moments. Even though her ambivalence was extremely strong, she also reasoned that maybe it was smart to keep her enemies close—*very* close, in this case.

The part of her that resented authority enjoyed this.

She also thought that Sam's obvious affection for her might hinder his investigative intensity if the trail ever led too closely to her. The longer they were together, the more their emotions were bound. Having the detective on the case biased in her favor was by no means a bad thing.

At some point, she decided, when they had been together a little longer, she might even dare to drop some casual questions about his work. Sometimes, he mentioned small details from his investigations, and she had to admit it fascinated her. She might even be able to ask about the progress in finding the killer of David Saunders. Once the thought took hold, she couldn't get it out of her mind: the man next to her was a walking storehouse of information about the case, where it was going, and how close the police might be to naming a suspect.

Maybe, she thought, dating Sam was her way of hiding in plain sight.

Even though Sam projected an easygoing air when you first met him, the reality was more complicated. He was assertive, outgoing, and very masculine—all traits that Jenny enjoyed. He shared her rebellious streak and distrust of authority, but in his case it manifested differently. He was highly competitive and deeply cynical, to the point of harboring a generalized suspicion about everything. He'd frequently tell her stories about his conflicts with his peers and supervisors, sometimes rising to the level of shouting arguments, to the point where she was actively amazed that he still held a job with the state police.

One night, after a few glasses of red wine, they were sitting together on the sofa in Jenny's living room when Sam said something that surprised her.

"The bottom line," he said, swirling his glass around and watching how the liquid clung to the sides of the glass, "is that police officers are corrupt. That's the main thing to understand."

"Not all of them," she said, trying to strike a conciliatory note.

He wasn't having it.

"*All* of them," he said firmly.

She let him go on. He was in his intensely analytical mode, and she had to admit she found it interesting. And while he could often come across as intensely judgmental, in this moment, he was almost philosophical and contemplative.

"Think about it like this," he said, scratching Tom on the head as he passed by on the back of the couch. "Being a cop means being a part of an elite organization, like a syndicate, that is basically above the law."

"Isn't that kind of an exaggeration?" Jenny asked, taking a sip of her wine. She was playing devil's advocate, knowing that a major part of her agreed with Sam and wanted to hear more.

"Above the law," he repeated. "That's part of the point of wanting to be a cop. For example, I can't tell you how many times I've seen police officers make other police officers' legal problems basically vanish into thin air."

"Give me an example," Jenny said, shifting to face him better.

"OK." Sam paused for a moment. "How about two examples? One of my fellow detective's kids was arrested just a few weeks ago for possession of a controlled substance. Another one's wife was arrested for shoplifting. Know what happened? All of the evidence just disappeared. Neither one of them is going to face any kind of consequences for what they did. And this happens all the time."

Sam had alluded to this kind of thing in the past, but never before had gotten so specific. Tom had crawled into Sam's lap, and Sam was scratching behind his ears as he spoke. Jenny had a moment's thought that they were both predators of a sort, the cat and the detective. Except Tom only hunted the occasional mouse that was unfortunate enough to make its way into Jenny's condo.

"People are sheep," Sam said. "Plain and simple. They turn to wolves to protect them, and then they're amazed to find out that the wolves are going to do whatever the hell they want— that they're going to be wolves."

Jenny had noticed before this streak of contempt from Sam for regular, non-police citizens. He had a grudging respect for his fellow officers, at least when he wasn't embroiled in arguments with them. He also had a good deal of fear and contempt for the higher-level officials and operatives he believed were the real power behind government.

"Well, who's bigger than the wolves?"

Sam smiled at her and took a sip of his wine. He seemed to be following her train of thought in his own mind, knowing how often Sam saw the world as a web of conspiracies, power, and corruption.

"The best conspiracies are the ones that people don't believe in," Sam said. It was a sentence he had spoken to her more than once in the past.

Because he saw corruption at his level as a police detective, he assumed that similar dynamics went all the way to the highest levels of power. Jenny couldn't say she entirely disagreed. If anything, Sam seemed to admire those who took power without regard for the costs to others. Jenny thought that the only thing that angered him was that he occupied a relatively low level in the web of conspiracy.

"How do criminals fit into it, then?" Jenny asked. "They're not sheep, are they?"

Sam refilled their glasses from the bottle on the table. The label had a picture of an idyllic vineyard on it, a far cry from the bleak worldview that the detective was so starkly articulating.

"Well, you see, where people make a mistake is when they think about criminals as somehow intrinsically bad or evil," Sam said.

Jenny felt her pulse quicken. She wondered for the thousandth time what he would think of her if he knew the truth.

"What are they, then?" she asked.

"I guess you could say that they're mostly *disorganized*," Sam said. "At least compared to the police. From a certain point of view, they're in competition with police for victimizing, or at least taking advantage of, regular people. The thing is that both the police and criminals are corrupt and operating outside the law. But the police are the more organized team." Sam had a great passion for mafia movies and TV shows, anything revolving around organized crime and gangs.

These stories drew him like a powerful magnet. He loved the depictions of their codes of loyalty to others inside their out-fits, and the way they coordinated to pull off the highest-level crimes with impunity.

"So there's a thin line between law enforcement and organized crime," Jenny said, relaxing a little, feeling the conversation turning away from territory that might have brought attention to her.

"A *very* thin line," Sam agreed. He let out a little laugh. "But the thing is, the 'bad' guys seem to have a knack for making a lot more money."

Through her experience as a counselor over the past few years, Jenny had developed a strong distrust of law enforcement. Getting closer to Sam had only reinforced that perception. She knew that there were always two sides to every story, but many of her clients who had gotten into trouble because of mental illness or addiction had stories of experiencing injustice or victimization at one time or another from law enforcement. She knew that some of these stories had to be exaggerated, or maybe the product of a troubled mind, but there were too many of them to be dismissed out of hand. There was at least some fraction of police that consistently abused their position of power and used it to take advantage of the vulnerable. She was sure of it.

Hearing Sam's inside viewpoint on law enforcement and policing also gave Jenny a new psychological avenue for easing her anxiety, shame, and guilt.

What would even be the point of coming clean about the Big

Deal? Would it make sense to leave herself vulnerable to police who are corrupt and criminal themselves?

The idea of atonement for guilt and reconciliation with society only had value if there was someone upstanding, decent, and righteous to whom she could confess and who could fairly judge her. Little by little, Jenny's worldview was becoming darker and more cynical, along with her assessment of the nature of the human condition.

Maybe everyone is evil to one degree or another. And if all people are bad, what's the point of one bad person submitting to the so-called justice designed to benefit the strong and harm the weak?

She had her misgivings about Sam, but she was grateful to him for giving her an education in how the world seemed to really work, and a reason to rest better at night. Her anxiety remained, but she was able to morally condemn herself less and less. What had happened had been an accident, after all—just one of many things gone wrong in a world that wasn't set up for justice.

Jenny felt herself changing the longer she was with Sam. Sometimes when she was alone, she could reflect on how, for so long, she had felt as though she was running from something, never getting a chance to breathe or to rest. She had spent years waiting for the proverbial shoe to drop, working days dealing with other people's problems while never gaining respite from her own.

Sam was surely no angel. Sometimes he could be brutish and simplistic, and needlessly harsh to others. He was also highly motivated by sex to the point of fixation.

At the same time, he had a sort of purity. He was consistent to himself, and he was in alignment with his own value system—even if it was one that Jenny was alternately fascinated with and repulsed by. Sometimes when he went on his rants, she would spar with him, and this was a source of sexual sparks for both of them.

He turned her on. She turned him on. For a while it was truly exciting, the kind of attraction that can paper over major differences. But after a while his appetite for sex became like a chore. The thrill of attraction had become almost mechanistic.

"Look, Sam, I like sex," she said to him one night. "But you're wearing me out. It's not really special if it's every time we're together."

Sam's expression soured. He picked at an imaginary piece of lint on his shirt—he had actually started dressing better recently.

"What, you don't love me anymore," he said, more a statement than a question. "Let me guess. There's another guy."

"How could you possibly come to that conclusion?" Jenny asked him, feeling as though she was speaking to a client. "Can you please go back and work through my actual words? I didn't say anything like that."

They went through a few variations on this conversation, and Sam seemed to become more and more morose. One night he responded with something unexpected.

"I get that you want to slow down on the physical stuff," he said. "You told me to listen. So I listened."

"Thank you," she said.

"But you need to know. I'm also seeing someone else." He paused. "I want us to stay together, too, but I have to attend to my own needs. I want you to understand."

Jenny cycled through surprise, hurt, annoyance, and jealousy. But, to her surprise, she came around to finding the situation acceptable. It crystallized for her the fact that, deep inside, she didn't consider Sam to be true long-term relationship material. There was no reason they had to be exclusive. She hoped one day to be in a position to give what it took to a real-life partner, but she wasn't there yet. In a way, it was easier to be with someone who was as far removed from that status as she was.

At the same time, she wasn't ready to give Sam up. The relationship was far from perfect—even after all the time they'd spent together, he seemed to have no idea how much of herself she kept in reserve and hidden from him—but it would do for the time being.

Jenny also admitted to herself, in more reflective moments, how much she liked being on the inside of the law enforcement system. It relieved her anxiety to think that she might have access to information that could protect her and maintain her freedom. Her mind would wander off into scenarios in which she visualized herself breaking up with Sam, perhaps maintaining some level of friendship in which she'd keep the utility of inside information.

It was like a puzzle she was struggling to solve. At certain moments, she would consider what advice she might give to herself if she was her own client. But she'd banish the speculation. Her situation was unique. Her problems were her own. She would solve her own puzzles without any help.

CHAPTER SEVEN

A TRICKY AND DIFFICULT THING TO BE SURE ABOUT

JENNY WAS ABLE to carve out a short break from her practice during Christmas and New Year's at the end of 2017. She had been feeling for several weeks that she was struggling somehow. She found herself zoning out more and more during therapy sessions, and this level of distraction was inconsistent with her professional values as a counselor. One of her primary New Year's resolutions going into 2018 was to try to stay more focused on her clients.

Of course, there was always talk of burnout for mental health counselors—it was no different in that way than a lot of other professions. But Jenny didn't want to give in or admit such weakness. She had carried a tremendous psychological burden for years now, after all, a secret that she could tell no one. Part of her figured she could atone for the Big Deal by continuing to help others as much as possible.

Whatever happens, I'm going to make the best of it. I'm not going to fail.

She spent a few hours on Christmas day with her parents, whom she no longer saw all that often. They were aging, and the gaps in between her seeing them only drove home and accentuated that fact. They seemed generally happy that she had a good career and a nice place, and they asked why she hadn't brought her boyfriend Sam to meet them. Jenny deflected their questions, a skill at which she had become particularly adept since she was a teenager herself.

Something had to be done, though. Jenny realized that her lack of concentration in counseling sessions was an indicator of a broader sense of exhaustion, the effects of constant stress and anxiety, and so she decided she would start scheduling fewer clients during the day and taking more time off in general. This was upsetting for some of Jenny's clients, because she had to inform them that they were being shifted from weekly sessions to once every other week. A couple left for other counselors, but most made the adjustment and stayed on. Jenny hated to see their expressions of disappointment, but she also knew healthier boundaries for herself would make her a more effective and helpful counselor.

Jenny had no such plan to reduce her sessions with Rio Winston.

He was more fascinating by a wide margin than any other client in her caseload. This caused feelings of guilt to wash over her, because she knew she was showing him undeniable favoritism—something she typically resolved to avoid, and usually with success.

Still, there she was. She sat behind her desk in her office, waiting to begin her first appointment with Rio in the new year. She thought about her long conversations with Sam, how she had started to see many ideas of right and wrong as mere constructs in a wider web of human nature. She thought about everything Sam had told her about law enforcement and its place in a corrupt and amoral world that lay just beneath the surface of things. How that fit into Rio's intense, quasi-religious, obsessive, and idiosyncratic worldview was like a three-dimensional puzzle in her mind, the parts seeming to want to fit if she could just visualize precisely how.

At first, Rio presented with some distressing personality traits: his apparent arrogance, his sense of entitlement, his grandiosity. But increasingly, Jenny was starting to view him as just someone who was managing as well as he could. Given his upbringing and obvious biological propensity for OCD, he was maneuvering through a difficult world with the tools that he had been given.

He indeed showed signs of psychopathy, she thought, but that was a tricky and difficult thing to be sure about.

She had worried for a while in their early sessions where Rio's personality might take him, including whether or not he really would ever intentionally harm anyone. Nothing had come up yet, which helped her sense of ease.

As for what was in his heart, what was in anyone's heart?

This was a world in which things happened. It gave her a sort of freedom to allow herself to drift away from such fixed moral concepts as good and evil. It was doubtful to her, at that point, how useful such notions were for treating her clients, or judging them for their thoughts and emotions.

Jenny was now entering a world of moral relativism. It felt thrilling, with a clarity like cold water rushing over one's self on a hot, humid day. As she had done so many times over the years, she attempted to hush the voices inside that were sounding an alarm.

In a sense, this meant coming around full circle to some of the conflicts she'd had with her teachers and other students during her counseling program in college. Many of them espoused a basically morally relativistic stance, a sort of neutral indifference in which human traits were part of systems and not fixed things to be judged. At the time, she had thought this was inconvenient at best—and probably totally unrealistic—in the "real" world, where there were consequences and judgment all around.

Maybe I was wrong about that.

Part of her had always admired her peers and professors' commitment to moral neutrality, to intellectual impartiality. Morality as an inflexible idea, many said, was anathema to understanding clients. It was a hindrance, an illusion. She had argued against their point for years, but now found herself realizing there was great wisdom in what she had been fighting.

By the time Rio showed up for his first session of 2018, Jenny had been reflecting that she felt well-rested. Part of her felt that she had freed up mental energy by not focusing constantly on moral judgment. It was as though the anxiety inside her might be transforming into something else.

She hadn't seen Rio in five weeks, and she had been worried that he might not show up for the session—that happened frequently when there has been a hiatus, with routines changing and new habits forming. Jenny was more than a little relieved when he showed up right on time, like clockwork, in his overalls with his name stitched below the lapel.

"How have you been since we spoke last?" Jenny asked him.

He folded his hands in his lap. "I'm not much for holidays, so I've worked a lot," he said. "Towed wrecked cars and trucks. Changed a lot of flat tires on the roadside. I did a good deed when a family's minivan slid off the road in that Christmas Eve snowstorm."

"I remember that there was a lot of snow," Jenny said. "Did everything turn out all right for them?""Got to play hero," Rio said. "Got the van out of the ditch. No one was hurt. I think the cops really, fully appreciated how well I handled the situation. They were telling me that none of the other tow drivers in town could have done what I did."

"I see. Nice work." Jenny paused. "Did you spend Christmas with anyone? Any family or friends?"Rio looked at her as though she was speaking a foreign language.

"Don't have family to speak of, and you know that," Rio said in a mildly scolding tone. "I don't ever spend Christmas with anyone. It's just another day to me. Let the sheep have their little fruitcakes and presents."Jenny wrote down a note. When she looked up, Rio had an expression she had never seen before: his eyes were dark and narrowed, his lips a thin, straight line. She felt a brief chill. He wasn't so much looking at her as *observing* her, like something in the lens of a microscope or an animal in a laboratory.

"What is it?" she asked. "Is something wrong?"

"I enjoy the time I spend here with you," he said in a monotone. "First of all, I'd like you to know that."

"I'm glad you think it's been helpful," Jenny said. She lifted her chin and tried to meet his cold gaze head-on, but it wasn't easy. He seemed very mechanical and forced, almost as though he had rehearsed this moment.

"I'm hoping you can help me with something more delicate than what we've talked about so far," Rio said. "It's something that touches on the whole confidentiality thing we talked about when I first started coming to see you."

"OK, sure, as long as we're not talking about killing somebody," Jenny said with nervous laughter.

Her laughter died away when he just sat there looking at her.

"We're probably OK," she said. "What do you want to ask me about?""Well, that's the thing." He tilted his head very slightly, just a few degrees. "What if we were talking about something like killing?"Jenny shifted in her chair. This was not where she had hoped for this to go. She started reciting the limitations of counselor-client confidentiality nearly word for word, the way she had learned the regulations in school. He listened patiently for a while, just like he had done on the first day, but then he raised his hand to silence her and she found herself going immediately quiet.

"I may have done some bad things in the past," he said with no inflection in his voice, very matter of fact. "But I can't go back in time and fix anything. Wouldn't you agree?"

"We can talk about anything that happened in the past." Jenny let out a small sigh. It was possible that this was all related to his OCD and his lifelong sense of transgression from his strange moral system.

"In the past," he repeated.

"Is that all you're talking about?" Jenny asked. He didn't reply. "Or are you talking about things you might do, or are going to do, in the future?"Rio rubbed his chin. He seemed to be carefully considering what Jenny had said to him, as well as choosing his own words with caution.

"So let me get this straight," he said. "Let's say, hypothetically now, that I killed someone in the past. You don't have to report that to the police, right? But if I tell you about something I want to do in the present, you have to tell?""Yes," Jenny said. "I have a duty to protect society. It's what I signed up for when I got into this profession."

"Let's say I was planning on hurting somebody," Rio said. "But I didn't tell you and I just did it. Then, if I came in the next day and told you about it, you couldn't call the police? Is it really just telling you about a plan that gets us into a problem?""Rio, I feel like you're looking for a technicality to exploit." Jenny heard her heart beating in her ears. "I don't want you to hurt anybody. Promise me now that you'll tell me if you're ever going to do anything like that."

Rio sat back and folded his arms behind his head. He frowned and looked at the forest outside, as though profoundly disappointed with her.

"Well, in a way, that's what I'm trying to do right now," he said. "But you don't seem too receptive to listening and understanding."

"What . . . what exactly are you saying?" Outside the window, a light breeze blew through the winter trees. There were several inches of snow on the ground. It looked dark, funereal.

"I'm *saying* that I want to talk about times when I feel a need to hurt someone." He paused, making sure she was hanging on his every word. She was. "And I need to talk about things that happened in the past. And I need to talk to you without worrying that you're going to betray me and run off to tell the police."

"I need to think about it, Rio."

She had just been buying time, trying to process what he was asking of her. He was talking about feeling *a need* to hurt someone, which perhaps meant that he was asking for a safety zone in their conversations to talk about malicious or violent feelings without being reported.

Possibly, this was a kind of safety valve. If he was able to express himself without any filter, this could potentially reduce the power of any obsessively violent thoughts he might be having. Giving him an arena of open expression without fear of punishment might contribute to his mental health and make it less likely that he would actually harm anyone.

He was watching her think. When she had looked down at her notebook, he was gazing at the snow. But he had been watching her, very carefully.

"I really had you going." He gave her that humorless and robotic chuckle. "I'm not going to hurt anyone. I just feel like it sometimes."

Over the next fifteen minutes, Rio gave her assurance after assurance that he was all talk, that he might have done some bad things in the past but now he was on the road to recovery—primarily because of her help and influence. He re-told the story of the family whose minivan slid into a ditch, as though trying to convince her of his harmlessness and capacity for doing good.

But there was a weight in the air. Jenny couldn't stop thinking about Rio's mention of future violence. It was all well and good if he was asking to blow off steam. But she wasn't entirely sure that was the case.

The bell rang to end the session. Rio wore a forced smile as he got up from the sofa and they confirmed their appointment for the same day and time next week.

"We'll continue talking then," Jenny said blandly.

She was in her chair, him standing across from her. He gave her that head tilt and squinted at her, clearly calculating something.

"We sure will," he said. "Just one thing I want you to know."

"And what's that?" Jenny asked.

"I don't want police snooping around in my past, or my present." He nodded, as though agreeing with himself. "You know what I mean? I don't want it any more than a scared little gazelle wants to be invited to dinner with the lions."

Scared little gazelle.

Jenny had sat alone in her office for a full five minutes after Rio left, even though she had another client waiting for her. Thoughts raced through her mind.

Why did he mention a gazelle?

Does he know something about Gazelle Lumber?

Does he know something about David Saunders?

In the week that followed, Jenny's anxiety would spike severely whenever she replayed Rio's words in her mind.

She would tell herself it was just a coincidence. It was just Rio trying to turn a colorful phrase, for whatever reason. She didn't have anything to worry about.

Then she would worry. A lot.

This back-and-forth went through her psyche for the entire week until her next appointment with Rio. A few times, her despair and panic reached such a pitch that she considered reaching out to Sam about it, but she simply had no way of knowing how he would react or what he would do, so she kept him at arm's length for the week and declined three separate invitations to get together. She knew this annoyed him, and probably sparked his feelings of jealousy and possessiveness, but she was walking too intense a wire. She didn't want to take a chance that it might snap, and that she might say something she would regret forever.

Then she would backslide, pick up the phone, and look at

Sam's number on the screen. Rationally, she knew that the odds were in favor of things getting worse if she brought Sam into the situation.

What if Rio knows? Maybe he's going to keep my secret.

That would mean she had confessed to Sam for no reason.

The other possibility would be that Sam would support her, and maybe even help her build up her defense. After all, she had shot David thinking he was the man who had attacked her. She had a reasonable defense, if she could only trust the system to hear her impartially and give her true justice.

But I waited so long. I kept it a secret for so long.

Though it was depressing and sad to admit it, in the end, Jenny didn't trust Sam with her darkest secret. Sam told her about how corrupt police officers were, and when he was telling her stories, he didn't take any great pains to explain how he might be different. How much would Sam risk for her? Not much, she decided. Not when his own interests were at stake as a detective and as a cop.

Rio came back the next week. He sat down delicately on the sofa and looked up at Jenny with a hard-to-read expression.

"How have you been?" Jenny asked him.

"Not bad," Rio said. "Busy at work. A lot of breakdowns in the wintertime. I've even pitched in on a couple of repairs. You know, keeping up the old skills. Never know when you might have to use them. I'm a good mechanic, you know. One of the best in town, really. You can ask anyone." A long silence.

"I'd like to talk about where our conversation ended up last week," Jenny said.

She watched him carefully. He scratched his head with obviously feigned innocence.

"Last week," he repeated. "You mean when I was telling you about helping that nice, grateful family out of the ditch?""No," Jenny said. "And I think you know that."

"Well, OK, let's talk then." Rio slid forward on the sofa, looking at Jenny with renewed interest. Their roles had suddenly reversed. He was the one coaching her along with his expression and body language to speak, to open up.

"We can talk about anything you did in the past," Jenny said carefully. She had thought about this moment so many times during the past week. "It doesn't really matter how far in the past it was. But I don't want to know about any plans you have to do anything illegal."

"Understood," Rio said.

"Is this just about wanting to clear obsessive thoughts out of your conscience?" Jenny asked him. "I mean, are you seeing this as part of your therapeutic process, to keep you from acting out on any of your intrusive ideation?"Rio winced, as though they had been getting close to the truth but Jenny had come up regrettably short.

"Now let me make something clear," he said very slowly. "And I don't mean this in any threatening manner. You follow me?""OK."

Jenny's pulse quickened and her vision blurred slightly. She put her hand on the arm of her chair, willing herself to stay upright.

"We both have skeletons in the closet," Rio said. "If you leave my skeletons be, then I won't do anything to cause your skeletons to rattle."

The fear grew to a roar, making her chest feel hot and hollow.

"That sure sounds like a threat," she said, her throat constricted.

He just looked at her.

"How the hell do you think you know anything about me?" she said, her voice rising but sounding raspy. "I don't have anything to hide.""Don't make me say what I know," Rio said quietly, his voice almost mournful now, as though she was hurting him.

"You need to—""Don't make me say it," Rio repeated. "Not even just in this room. Not even just between you and me, with no one else listening."

"What the hell do you know?" Jenny erupted. "Who the hell do you think you are? Get the hell out of my office right now!"She had risen from her chair, her voice stern and commanding, as though some part of her wished that he would back down, that it would all stop. He did no such thing. He sat absolutely still on the sofa with his dark eyes locked onto hers. She felt as though the room was telescoping in her vision.

She collapsed back down into her chair, panting.

"What do I know and who the 'blank' do I think I am?" he asked, refraining from repeating the word "hell."

She stared at him. Her eyes were burning. She gagged and feared that she was going to vomit all over the carpet.

"Here's my answer to both questions," he said. "I know you shot David Saunders to death. And I'm the man who has his wallet, with both your blood and your fingerprints still on it."

Jenny cried for ten minutes straight while Rio looked on. This was it. All of her worst fears had come to fruition. She didn't want him to see her like this, but there was no helping it. The tears were like a flood, the burning in her chest and throat so strong that she feared she was having a cardiac episode. She could barely breathe.

The way Rio had handled this confrontation swept away any doubt in her mind that she was dealing with a psychopath.

She burned with humiliation that she had been thinking of writing a book about this soulless, damaged person. She had thought she could profit from his treatment. Now she was essentially at his mercy.

"I know you must be thinking a lot of things right now," Rio said as she tried to quell the tears and retching that kept convulsing her midsection. "But I want to let you know very clearly now that I have no intention of ever telling anyone your secret." He handed her the box of tissues that she kept on the table between herself and her clients. She pulled out a handful and started trying to clear her breathing.

"The wallet is someplace safe," Rio continued. "It's in a plastic bag where no one can find it."

"Where is it?" she asked, beginning to collect herself.

"Here's the deal. You get it when I'm done with my mission." He leaned forward, watching her intently. "Then you can burn it, bury it, or do anything you want with it."

Jenny tried to breathe deeply to calm herself, still nearly overwhelmed by the surreal nature of what was happening. And then it struck her.

Rio was the man who attacked me at Gazelle Lumber. The man who hit his head on the doorframe and ran away. But he didn't leave the scene completely, did he?

She looked over at her desk. There was a letter opener there that she'd borrowed from another of the building's tenants earlier in the week when she needed to open a stubborn package.

Jenny leapt from her chair, made for the desk in a quick motion, grabbed the opener, and moved toward Rio.

He stared at her, expressionless.

Her hand was shaking terribly.

"Don't try to get up," she said, her voice unfamiliar to her. "Don't make me use this. I'll kill you as sure as you're sitting there."

"Well look at you, ready to murder again" Rio said with a smirk. He remained as relaxed and composed as he had throughout this terrible hour.

"I mean it," Jenny said.

"Well, I know one thing," Rio said. He looked at her, ignoring the weapon in her hand. "If you *do* kill me, at least this time you'll be killing the right man."

"What the hell do you want from me?" Jenny said. She lowered her voice now, realizing that someone else in the building might hear this confrontation and come to help.

What would I do then? What would I tell anyone who walked in? "I want your help," Rio said, his voice level and quiet.

"Why me?" Jenny asked. "Why the hell couldn't you leave me alone?" "There's no need to destroy the both of us," Rio said. He nodded at the letter opener, and Jenny slowly lowered it. Her adrenaline was fading now, and she knew she had lost her chance to attack him.

And what would happen next? This isn't the parking lot of some building in a bad part of town. This is my office. My name is on the door.

"I attacked you," Rio said. "Now I want to defend you, in a way."

"Defend me?" Jenny repeated.

"I could have killed you a thousand different times since that night," Rio said. "I've watched you inside your apartment. I've seen you come and go."

Jenny fell back into her chair, shaking her head.

"Hurting you isn't part of my mission," Rio told her.

He stared at her expectantly. She knew what he wanted her to ask.

"What *is* your mission?" she finally said.

CHAPTER EIGHT

I WAS THE ONE IN CHARGE

EVEN THOUGH Rio's revelation had felt like the end of the world for Jenny at the time, in the weeks that followed an uneasy peace settled in between the two of them.

One fact was undeniable: Rio hadn't told her of anything he'd done that she could use against him—she knew now that he had attacked her that night at Gazelle Lumber, but she had no proof. He, on the other hand, could call the police on her at any time and turn over the evidence of the wallet he apparently possessed. And yet he hadn't.

Rio clearly had some sense of purpose, some unfolding of events, that apparently would be interrupted or voided if he turned her in. There was a delicate status quo that he was invested in maintaining, and this fact was a strange kind of comfort to her.

She saw Sam once in the week that passed after the session with Rio. He didn't seem to notice how distant she was, or how she didn't engage with him when he went on a rant about his fellow detectives.

It was a strange thing to feel so alone.

It was as though she was being held hostage by Rio. Her very freedom was in the hands of who she believed to be a psychopath. Her anxiety went to another level, transformed into a constant sensation akin to a burning, and yet along with that came a heightened level of awareness. She felt paradoxically alive in a vivid way, strangely free. She was absolutely full of fear, and yet in embracing that terror there was also a sensation of curiosity that verged on excitement.

When she was a student in the counseling program, Jenny had read stories of soldiers in combat who were in situations when it was apparent that they were likely to die. Something kicked in for many of them; they simply accepted the reality of death, and it made them much more effective at fighting. Their doom gave them clarity. Jenny reasoned that dwelling on fear in her situation was going to get her nowhere. It was as though she had to accept the worst possible outcome in order to have a chance of avoiding it.

She had never felt so completely alone.

As he sat down one week after his revelation, Rio picked

up where he left off at first, as though nothing had happened between them. He complained about the stupidity of his co-workers, and he told a self-aggrandizing story about a woman coming into the shop who he thought was attracted to him.

Jenny sat in silence, watching him.

Finally, Rio rubbed his hands together impatiently, as though peeved that Jenny wasn't playing along with his act of normality.

"You want to dig into the real stuff," Rio said.

"It's your hour," Jenny told him.

He smiled, clearly appreciating her calm tone of defiance.

"All this time, you've been waiting for me to open up, right?" he asked. "I've seen you. You've been wondering why I came to you. I mean, we've talked about a lot of things, but you still don't know what makes me tick."

She didn't say anything.

"You ever think about your life as something tragic?" he asked her.

Jenny blinked. "What do you mean?" she asked.

"It's all so complicated." Rio looked out the window at the woods, where the snow had melted, and everything was brown and gray. "And lonely. I mean, my folks are both dead. I never really talk to my sister. The truth is that she doesn't really like me. Never did. So what do I have left? A lot of days and nights, that's what, and they're filled up with a lot of nothing except time to think."

"Do you think you're so unique?" Jenny asked him.

It was as though she hadn't spoken.

"I spend a lot of time looking inward, trying to understand myself," Rio continued. "People look at a guy like me and think I'm dumb. But I have a lot more going on than anyone imagines. I have curiosity about myself, and what brought me to where I am."

"Is this part of what you call your mission?" Jenny asked.

Rio held up one hand in a gesture that said, *Not yet*.

"I need you to understand the process," Rio said.

Jenny stared at him, feeling a familiar burning of anxiety in her chest. Her previous appointment had been with a young mother depressed since the birth of her baby. In the next hour, she would be speaking with a man who had been ordered into counseling after an incident of domestic violence. Sandwiched in between was this man who held the key to her ability to wake up tomorrow outside a jail cell.

"My mother taught me how to compensate for my sinful nature, and I'll always be grateful to her for that," Rio said. "It all started way before I was a teenager."

"What did?" Jenny asked.

"I was totally fascinated by women a long time before I even knew what sex was," Rio said. "I didn't even know what it was about them that I liked. But I knew they were going to be a major part of my life. Like a moth to a flame, you know what I mean? Except I also knew that I wasn't going to be the one getting burned."

Jenny wasn't taking notes. It wasn't like she was going to be able to forget anything he was telling her. He was focused now, speaking with intent, even straying from the dull monotone into which he often lapsed. She could have laughed.

Now he's acting like a client who wants to make progress.

"I remember when I first started fantasizing about tying women up," Rio said, looking out at the woods. "Ropes, maybe chains. I didn't even know about getting turned on, but I sure was."

Jenny sat silent.

"Then I learned about sexual intercourse. Man, that's when the pieces of the puzzle started to come together."

Jenny didn't say anything.

"I wanted it *all the time*." Rio made a fist and rubbed it into his open hand. "Couldn't think of anything else. And I figured, if that's how it was going to be, I needed to be the one in control. You know what I mean? Maybe I couldn't make the urges stop, but I could make sure that women knew I was the one in charge."

"Is this what happened with your neighbor?" Jenny asked. "The one who wanted you to help her with a house repair and who you assaulted?"Rio nodded, seeming satisfied that Jenny was understanding him.

"I fully intended to see that situation through until she started screaming," Rio said. "And then I planned to see where things went from there."

"And your mother protected you," Jenny observed. "Anyone else would have paid a price for what you did. But you didn't."

Despite herself, Jenny felt her familiar fascination with Rio. She had never met anyone like him. She hoped she never would again.

"That's right. But she also knew I had a problem." Rio looked down at the floor. "She knew about my . . . sex drive. And she knew about the thoughts that I couldn't keep out of my head. She called them demons, but it didn't matter what she or anyone else called them. Something had to be done."

"The Cleansing," Jenny said.

"Yeah."

"And did it work?" she asked.

She felt as though she was on a borderline that she was terrified of crossing. Despite all that had passed between them, Jenny still had no concrete knowledge of anything that Rio had done that law enforcement wasn't aware of. Every instinct told her that she was being drawn into a web of complicity. Yet she saw no way out.

"It worked fairly well for a lot of years," Rio told her. "It forced me to stay busy. It distracted me when my drives felt like they were unbearable."

"What about normal life?" Jenny asked. "Taking a girl out on a date? Just integrating your natural impulses into something that's not hurtful?" Rio smirked. "Every time I think you're starting to truly understand, you start talking like a sheep."

Or a gazelle?

"That hurts," she said.

Rio winced. "Sorry," he said. She couldn't tell if he meant it.

There was a long silence between them.

"Eileen kept an eye on me for a long time," Rio started speaking again as though nothing was out of the ordinary.

"She was trying to keep you out of trouble, wasn't she?" Jenny asked.

"When the feelings got too strong, she had a way of noticing." Rio paused, seeming to look into the past. "She would tell me it was just another attack from the demons, that it would fade away eventually if I kept doing the right thing."

"But doesn't calling the thoughts and feelings 'demons' represent a way of freeing you from taking responsibility?" Jenny asked.

Rio looked up at the ceiling, seeming to struggle to control himself for a moment.

"Eileen was highly disgusted by men and their ways. Their desires," Rio added. "But I didn't feel like she judged me. She said I had the demon drive. It wasn't something I could completely control. But where it was gross and dirty in everyone else, in me it was a clear indication that I had a magnificent destiny. My demons were the high-class kind, and they don't choose just anybody to torment."

From what Jenny had heard about Eileen, Rio wasn't the only one suffering from inner torment—whether from demons or otherwise.

"And I never really shared this with her," Rio said. "Because not even Eileen could see the full picture. But my drives are uplifting. They are joyous."

Rio was speaking firmly, with total conviction. There was a note of wonder in his voice, a spiritual or religious dimension.

"My drives point me toward a joyous future of rule and dominion." Rio stared directly at her.

She realized that he was finally getting to the truth, after all the evasion, small talk, and circular tales. This was the real Rio.

"I used to think it was my destiny to rule over the world," Rio said. "But I decided that was dumb. Who needs the hassles and the headaches?""So what do you want instead?"

"I want what I'm going to get," Rio replied, with excitement and confidence. "Total control and rule over my female subjects, along with my selected helpers."

Jenny felt as though she was going to float out of her own body. The room seemed strange and dreamlike. It was as though she had stepped through some invisible portal into some world previously unseen and unthought of.

A picture was starting to form as Jenny's therapeutic training kicked in. When Eileen killed herself, Rio must have lost any stabilizing benefit from her conceptualization of how hard work could occupy her son's time, thoughts, and obsessions. His drives must have become insatiable without her diversions, all the hours of the day no longer filled with cleansing assignments and tasks. He had lost his primary mode of compensation, however odd it might have been, and was unchecked and unguided in his pathologies and, she now was sure, his psychopathy.

"I'm going to tell you a story now," he said.

The session was only halfway through. Jenny wasn't sure she could handle this. Every instinct told her to flee, to break the floor-to-ceiling window and simply run as fast as she could away from there. But where was she going to go? Rio had her in a cage, and he was holding the keys tight.

"After Eileen was gone, my sinful thoughts were like a two-hundred-pound rock and I was trying to carry it up Mount Everest," Rio explained. "I kept fighting, but I didn't know how much longer I could last. That was when I saw something that inspired me. It led me to the Mission."

Rio leaned forward and put his elbows on his knees.

"It was a rainy night in January years ago, not long after I started driving the tow truck. I got called to the scene of a car accident to clear a wreck from the side of the road. Turns out a 27-year-old woman had driven her vehicle into a car parked on the shoulder. Neither car was too severely damaged, but she had booze on her breath and flunked a breathalyzer at the scene. You know what that means: a free ride downtown. Now the cops needed her car towed from the scene before there was another accident."

He glanced up, making sure Jenny was listening. Despite all of her fear in the moment, she was spellbound.

"I pulled my truck right up behind one of the police cruisers and turned on my flashing lights," Rio said. "A cop came up to my window, and when I rolled it down, he said that they needed me to wait a minute while they were taking this woman into custody. I watched the police as they were handcuffing this young woman and leading her around the back of one of the cruisers. The rain kept falling."

Rio's voice was hypnotic as he gestured gently into the air, seemingly creating the textures of what he felt that night.

"She had long hair and a pretty face," Rio said. "And the sight of her in handcuffs was *extremely* arousing for me. I couldn't take my eyes off of her, not even for a second. She looked up and she saw me sitting there watching her. I had a brief fantasy about shooting all the police officers at the scene and kidnapping her."He was explaining all this as though it was the most natural thing in the world.

"The temptation was so strong, but I snapped out of it," Rio said. "That same cop was yelling at me over the sound of my diesel engine. He was telling me that it was all clear for me to tow the car out of there. So I got to work."

"That's it?" Jenny asked. She had been tense with anticipation that Rio was going to disclose something terrible he had done.

"Later that night, after I got home, everything became clear for me. I established my true calling," Rio said. "I came to understand why that woman had been so fascinating to me, why I had felt what I did when she looked at me. It was because she was evil. She was trying to drive me to take the lives of those innocent policemen in service to her. She was like so many other women, evil down to their core and deserving of punishment. It's fine if they want to go around causing trouble and distress for themselves, but they don't stop there. They have to lead others into sin. It's their nature."

"Is that what Eileen told you?" Jenny asked.

"Try to keep up," Rio said, all condescension. "We're not talking about Eileen now. She's out of the picture. Killed herself. We're talking about my destiny here."

"How does it—"

"I had to ask myself if I had been making a mistake in my

thinking all along," Rio interrupted. "My entire philosophy was built around the idea that demons caused my sexual thoughts and drives. But I also knew those urges to be magnificent. What if it was all a gift from God, one that made me special—and that all of it was pointing me toward assuming the power to punish these women and eradicate their evil ways from the face of the earth?"

"Punish them," Jenny said quietly. She felt a tingling in the back of her neck, and her stomach gave a queasy lurch.

"I always had a desire to rape and kill women," Rio said blandly. "And I tormented myself for years and years about it."

"Because it's wrong," Jenny said. "You need help."

"Don't say that." Rio raised a single finger.

Jenny went silent. For the first time, she truly sensed the depths of potential malice in the man sitting across from her.

"Now I realized that these desires serve a higher purpose," Rio said. "It's a way of helping them atone for their sins, as well as compensating for my own. It's a paved road to salvation for the innocent and the wicked alike."

She allowed herself for a moment to allow her mind to twist into Rio's worldview. The experience was like vertigo.

"Eileen used to tell me that my destiny was to be a king among men," Rio said. "But I need no throne. My fate is to be a flawed man, but a warrior servant. I will never be hailed in this life as a great leader, but my function is necessary. My reward in this world will be the indulgence and pleasure of my drives, which God will convert with force into what is necessary for the good of humanity."

"I . . . I'm trying to follow what you're saying," Jenny said.

There were only a few minutes left in their session. Rio noticed her looking at the clock on the shelf.

"Cancel your next appointment," he told her.

Almost in a hypnotic daze, Jenny got up and walked down the hall to the waiting room. Her next client, Henry Woods, was waiting alone in a suit and tie, typing something into his phone. He looked up expectantly and started to stand.

"I'm sorry," Jenny said. "Something has come up. I have to postpone our appointment."

Henry looked concerned. "Are you all right?" he asked. "Is there anything I can do?""No, but thank you." Jenny tried to force a smile. "I'm really sorry to have to do this. I hope you'll understand."

Henry hadn't been the most enthusiastic of her clients; he had agreed to a course of counseling as part of the terms of reconciliation with his wife. He slipped his phone in his pocket and nodded at her.

"I hope everything is all right," he said with a concerned expression.

"Things are fine, thank you," Jenny told him. "I'll see you in two weeks."

Will I?

Rio was waiting patiently in Jenny's office, and as soon as she sat back down in her chair he started speaking again.

"There is a life after this one," he said, carefully enunciating his words for emphasis. "And in it, I will be honored for my work. I am doing God's plan behind the scenes. Think of me as a secret operative like James Bond, willing to sacrifice everything for the greater good of the people and the will of God."

Jenny just looked at him, completely unsure how to respond. Now that he had finally opened up to her, she was terrified of him. She sensed she needed to walk a thin line, allowing him to explain his inner life and his visions without challenging him too much or sparking him to violence. The most horrible part was how comfortable he seemed, as though relieved to finally have a close confidant. She was being pulled into his reality by force, and there was nothing she could think of to do about it.

"I'm glad you're coming to appreciate my philosophy," Rio said. "It encompasses so much more than this world of illusions. You see, the women that I take will join me in the glorious afterlife. Their greater purpose will be realized after they are extinguished on this plane. We will share a special corner of heaven, a paradise that God has made just for our enjoyment."

Sounds like Hell's landfill.

Sitting there in his work clothes and boots, his hair swept away from his high forehead, Rio looked like an average, everyday, working-class man whom you might walk past on the street without a second thought. If you met him out in the world, you'd have absolutely no suspicion of the murderous and psychotic ideas rattling around in his mind.

"You should see it," Rio said. "I wish you could see it right now. It would help you understand."

"See what?" Jenny asked.

"A heavenly mansion with rooms upon rooms." Rio waved his hands, as though carving his vision out of the air. "I will be free to come and go, but my women will not be."

"Do you think they'll like that?" Jenny asked.

Rio pursed his lips. "Because of my heroism in saving them, they will be my slaves for all eternity," he explained. "But that doesn't mean we can't have a good relationship. Some of them in time will come to appreciate that I saved them from an eternity of fire and damnation. They will come to love me, genuinely. More than they have ever loved, or could love, anyone else. We will make love forever."

Jenny felt a shiver. She realized that she could have asked Henry Woods for help, told him that there was a psychopathic killer in her office, begged him to take her to the police. But what then? A confession, a jail cell, a trial. She would never have any semblance of her normal life again, and all because of a momentary accident, started by being attacked by this man.

"It was you outside the lumber company," Jenny said. "Were you going to kill me that night?" "It was fun following you," Rio said, as though that should be enough to answer all her questions.

"I was going to be part of the Mission," Jenny said, almost speaking to herself.

"In my mansion, I understand that some of my women will still not be able to accept their evil nature. Those are the ones who are going to need more punishment." Rio's expression turned sad. "I will punish and punish until they change their ways. But I also know that may never happen for some of them. I will extinguish them quickly in this life, but the consequences will be far more severe in the next one, where there is no chance of me being caught. Where I am the agent of God's glory."

Jenny's mind was reeling between fear for herself and fear for whoever was unfortunate enough to get caught up in Rio's mission. An idea flashed into her consciousness: perhaps this was an opportunity to be redeemed for the Big Deal. Maybe she could step into Rio's psychosis and prevent him from hurting anyone else.

If she was able to keep his favor and make him believe that she was on his side, maybe she could succeed in minimizing more harm in the world. In a sense, maybe she had a special purpose of her own.

"So, you no longer believe that you're under attack from demons?" she asked, hoping to unspool his thought processes.

"Not exactly," he said eagerly. "But I realize the importance of balancing good and bad acts and thoughts. I can do good by punishing the evil, and for that I'll be rewarded. I still think of my nature as having a demon drive. I don't know, maybe it just sounds catchy. But it's all part of the plan."

"But how can you improve the world by causing pain?" Jenny asked, careful to keep her tone academic and inquisitive, rather than accusatory or challenging. She could tell she had his trust, and now she was engaged on a project of hopefully coaching him out of his homicidal plans.

"It's like when I was on that kick of fixing everything around the house," Rio explained. "Sometimes you have to break things or rip things out, right? For me to fix women, I might have to break their earthly bodies."

"I can follow that," Jenny said. "But have the bad feelings

ever really gone away? Might there be a better way of dealing with them?"

"I deal with them by turning myself into a machine," Rio said. "And the more I kill, the more I'm going to be rewarded. God has created an incredible system for me. And the more careful I am, the less likely I will ever be caught, the more slaves I will have and the more I will atone for my sins. It is glorious."

"But you could be caught," Jenny said. "You could spend the rest of your life alone in a prison cell. Do you think that is the purpose God made you for?""God made me great," Rio replied. "And I'm not afraid of going to prison, or even being killed. The only thing I fear is failing at my mission."Jenny felt as though she was in a whirlpool in the sea, with her every attempt at reason bringing her back into the swirl of Rio's churning mind. A part of her wished she hadn't gotten rid of that revolver on the night of the Big Deal. She thought then that maybe she would have the nerve to pull the trigger and kill Rio right there on her sofa.

Another part of her wanted to approach this situation far more pragmatically. As of that moment, she was a free woman. If she made a wrong move, it would be her that was sitting alone in a cell for the rest of her days. She was balancing her own self-preservation with a desire to do good, and perhaps even redeem Rio, if such a thing was possible.

I have to ask him now.

"Are you telling me you've already done this?" Jenny asked him. "Have you attacked and killed women already?""Are you speaking as my therapist?" Rio asked with a smirk.

"Tell me the truth," Jenny demanded.

"What I'm telling you," Rio said very slowly, "is that I have already saved women from a fate far worse than our worldly conception of death."

Jenny let out an involuntary gasp.

"Why do you need me?" she asked. "Why are you telling me all of this? What can I possibly do for you?" "Sometimes I have trouble dealing with my feelings," Rio said.

Jenny let out a harsh, barking, humorless laugh. She regretted it instantly, as a dark cloud passed over Rio's features.

"I'm sorry," she said. "Tell me more."

"Don't ever laugh at me," he said.

"I'm sorry," she repeated. "I'm listening."

"I worry that my feelings are going to interfere with my mission," he said, calm again. His way of being could shift in an instant, now that he was no longer trying to hide his nature from her. "I never liked the idea of talking to a counselor like this. But when I found out that you'd opened a practice, I saw it as part of the plan."

Maybe this is my opening. Maybe I can save lives here.

"What kind of feelings are you talking about?" she asked.

"Human feelings," he said with no trace of irony. "That's why I need to ask for help. I can't let my pride get in the way of what I need to do. That's the whole reason I came to you. It just took me a while to figure out that I can trust you."

The kind of trust built on blackmail.

"I need help, too," Jenny said. "Help me understand. Are you saying that you want me to help you control your emotions so you can . . . *save* people?" She had started to enunciate the word *murder*, but changed it mid-sentence. She sensed that she was going to have to make Rio think she shared his vision in order to have any chance of stopping him.

"I know a lot of things about myself that you probably don't think I know," Rio told her.

"Give me an example."

"I realize how people see me. How you see me." He smiled, very slightly. "People think I'm cold. A loner. Disturbed and worthless. I've read books that say psychopaths don't have an understanding of their own nature."

"You consider yourself a psychopath?" He stared at her.

"I want you to help me understand who I am and how other people see me," he said. "I need to maintain my shield. I don't want anyone to ever know how I truly am, because then they will try to stop me."

"Why can't you just leave me alone?" Jenny pled. "Why can't you go somewhere else? All I've wanted for all these years is just to be able to live a normal life."

He shook his head.

"You don't get to have a normal life any more than I do," he calmly explained. "Considering the pickle that you're in, and the fact that only I know about it, that makes you the only person I can trust and who has the training to help me. You're the only one who won't betray me, because you have everything to lose." "And how do I know you won't reveal my secret no matter what I might do to help you?" she asked him.

Rio blinked, as though his feelings were hurt.

"Come on, now," he said. "By helping me, you will have come over from evil to good. I'm bound by God's law not to hurt you or to let harm come to you. In fact, I'm obligated to protect you."

There was a strange note of intimacy in his voice, almost affection. Jenny wondered, though, what it meant that he had considered her evil up until then. After all, she had only been trying to help him in a therapeutic setting.

"I don't know how this is supposed to work," she told him.

"I want help appearing more normal," Rio said. "I know people think I'm strange. I've been watching you take notes on me since the first day I came in here. I can tell you look at me like some kind of interesting lab experiment."

Jenny didn't say anything. It seemed unlikely now that she was going to write a book and get famous on the details of Rio's case.

"I don't want to raise any suspicion, from the cops or anyone else," he continued.

She shook her head.

"I can't be implicated or involved in anything that causes harm to anyone, Rio," she said flatly. "You have to understand that. Why don't you let me work with you? We can figure out how to deal with your thoughts and drives. We can truly convert it all into something constructive once and for all."

"So now you're stronger than God?" he said in a steely voice. "And you know better than the creator of the universe?" "I'm not saying that."

"Listen to me," he said. "I'm going to take people with or

without you. And think about it. You help me, you keep me more normal and regulated, and I'll be less likely to lose control and inflict even more damage. You'll be saving lives."It was as though the very earth under her feet had crumbled and cracked. She looked out the window at the winter sun in the woods, a picture of stability and normality. She didn't think she would ever enjoy either of those things again.

Again, her mind calculated and tumbled.

"If you turn me in, I'll tell everything I know about you," she said.

"You're not going to do that," he said simply. He peered into her eyes with an almost supernatural calm.

She felt completely locked in. There was something about the force of his certainty that made her certain he would destroy her life without a moment's hesitation if she didn't do as he said.

There was still hope that she could get to him, open his eyes to morality and stop him before he hurt anyone else.

She could continue to delve into the undeniably fascinating labyrinth of Rio's mind and see if she could stabilize it, turning him into something approximating a normal person.

And she could finally, after all these years, resolve the issue of what happened to the wallet on the night of the Big Deal. Its very existence had been such a source of torment for her for so long. But now she knew who had it. She had the opportunity to recover it.

In her mind's eye, Jenny pictured herself throwing the wallet into an open flame and watching it burn, her blood and the other evidence up in smoke and gone forever—never to haunt her again.

"We have to keep talking," Jenny said. "We need to work together. I'm going to need your cooperation."

Rio smiled. "That's what I'm saying," he agreed.

Later, Jenny would tell herself that she never explicitly agreed to Rio's extortion plan, and she had never expressly rejected it, either.

From there on out, theirs would be an uneasy peace, uncluttered with an excess of thoughtful communication.

Both of them would need to select their words carefully. The stakes were now clearly high.

CHAPTER NINE

THE MISSION IS LIKE AN IMMOVABLE OBJECT

OVER THE NEXT several counseling sessions, the topic of future homicides didn't come up between Jenny and Rio. He instead stayed focused on trying to establish a foundation, a conceptual framework so that Jenny could completely understand him.

He had been studying serial killers extensively for the past several years. He had stolen books about killers from the library because he didn't want there to be a record of his checking out books on the subject. He figured that if he was ever investigated by the police, his library record might be a red flag, as it had been in other investigations. He wanted to leave behind no pieces of a puzzle that an enterprising detective might be able to assemble.

Rio positioned himself as morally superior to other superior killers, due to his perceived closeness to God and his execution of His will. Still, when he talked about some of the more famous killers, his admiration for their drive and ingenuity was obvious. For each killer that he talked about, he found something that he admired. He also criticized them, but he wasn't overly judgmental. He felt that most of the others were simply misguided and misinformed about what lay beneath their desire to kill. They had all, he explained, been given what the unenlightened considered a curse. In truth, it was a weapon that could be used either for good or for evil.

Rio considered himself to be working for the side of good.

Although Jenny continued to try to steer Rio into comprehension of moral reality, over these sessions, he continually moved the conversation back to what he had learned from each killer. It was a quiet, subtle battle of wills—a contest of who was going to educate whom.

Jenny felt at times as though she was trapped in an endless stream of serial-killer documentaries. But instead of watching them on TV, the narrator was a serial killer himself—and he was sitting on the sofa directly across from her. She felt a mixture of dread and fascination at these times. If nothing else, it was an ongoing education into the inner workings of psychopathy, narcissism, and sadism.

She successfully compartmentalized her mind and emotions in those weeks. She was able to essentially flip a mental switch and work with her more ordinary clients day after day, talking though phobias, fears, and infidelities while knowing all the while that another session with Rio was on the calendar. Still, she was able to go home at night instead of being trapped behind bars with a future that was uncertain at best.

"Take Danny Rolling, the Gainesville Ripper," Rio said in the next session.

"Let's talk about what you're feeling," Jenny said.

"I'm feeling the need to talk about Danny Rolling." Rio paused. "He was amazing with his sheer aggression. But he had a fatal flaw in his lack of control and emotional reactivity. And he targeted women who looked like previous romantic interests. What a disappointment in the end. Rolling did not know how to properly use the weapon."

Later, Rio brought up Harold Shipman, the so-called Dr. Death. Shipman was a physician who was thought to have killed more than 200 of his own patients.

"This one is of particular interest to me," Rio explained. "Shipman was motivated by the death of his mother."

"And how does that specifically relate to you?" Jenny asked. It was as though she hadn't even spoken.

"He seemingly repeated the circumstances of his mother's death as he killed victims who had trusted him to care for them," Rio explained. "And Shipman maintained a high level of popularity with his patients, even though he was described as arrogant and condescending. That's so very unlike you, Jenny. You come across to your clients as very caring and responsive. I admire that about you."

Jenny couldn't tell whether Rio admired Jenny for her kindness or simply for her ability to project it—no matter what might lie beneath. She also felt as though Rio's stale delivery of the compliment was simply something he was saying because he had heard others say it in different circumstances. As if he was just repeating the phrase without any feeling behind it.

"Thank you," she said.

"But, and here's the theme that develops, Shipman found a way to disappoint." Rio frowned as though smelling something rancid. "Shipman seemed to let himself get addicted to substances. And he became greedy. He forged a will that would have left one of his patients' estate to him."

"This seems to offend you," Jenny said. "Is it because he did something wrong?" "It's because he allowed pleasure and material gain to interfere with the mission," Rio responded. "He lost sight of what was important."

Next, Rio continued Jenny's thoughts with a verbal dissertation on Gary Ridgway, the Green River Killer. It was evident to Jenny right away that this serial homicide offender was someone who thoroughly impressed Rio.

"Ridgway was careful and prolific," Rio said, his tone professorial. "And he managed to evade the police, even though he was considered a suspect for many, many years."

"How did he get caught?" Jenny asked, by now used to the arc of these stories in which some small slip-up unraveled what was sometimes decades of unpunished crimes.

"Ridgway was extremely careful about leaving behind evidence," Rio said. "But DNA was his undoing, as is so often the case."

Jenny thought about her DNA on the wallet. She wondered

where Rio had hidden it, and if she could somehow trick him into telling her.

"Ridgway was unusual in another way," he added. "He was actually married during many of his active killing years. Most of us avoid this. Or else we simply can't pull it off. I've pretty much given up on ever having a normal relationship."

"You don't have to give up," Jennie told him. "You know, you could start to turn this all around today. There are always opportunities to change, Rio."

Part of her knew that even as she was speaking her words weren't true.

"A relationship or a marriage would be a liability," Rio said firmly. "And a distraction from the mission."

Even though he called his urges a demon drive, Rio continued to insist that it was a weapon he was using for good, to the point at which he demonstrated deference to it, rather than something he could really control. It was simply his responsibility to satisfy his drive and complete his mission. His worldview was hermetically sealed, self-justifying, and seemingly impossible to breach.

But she had to keep trying.

When he had run through all of his lengthy monologues about the careers and downfalls of the famous serial killers, Rio started talking about how he viewed balancing his demon drive with the stipulations of his mission. As was increasingly the case, at least for now, he seemed to expect Jenny to simply listen and try to comprehend.

"The demon drive and the mission push in two different

directions sometimes," he told her. "The drive is like an irresistible force. The mission is like an immovable object. You would think that the force came from the object, right? But they also collide with each other. They fight. Each one wants to be satisfied."

"Are you talking about the obsessive thoughts?" Jenny said.

"It's a tension," Rio admitted. "I worry it's my weakness. Sometimes it's like a puzzle I can't solve. Is the mission the drive, or is the drive the mission? I can't allow myself to get confused like this. Do you understand?"

At least Rio was attempting to explain something akin to an internal conflict. It was the first time he had deviated from his robotic recitation of his aberrant acts as something that had to inevitably happen.

Jenny was perversely impressed with her own ability to attend to Rio. She understood that something profound had shifted within her, and she had a distance and objectivity that allowed her to keep going with self-preservation as her primary goal. She continued to try to think fast, to calculate what was happening and how she might best serve her own interests while hopefully forestalling harm to anyone else in the bargain.

At other times, Jenny would be overwhelmed with a desire to murder Rio right there in the office where he sat. Hatred would burn in her like an inferno, especially when she replayed the night of the Big Deal and the reality that Rio had been her assailant.

She had taken a sharp kitchen knife from home and put it

in the purse that sat at her feet now during all the sessions with Rio. There were moments when she almost gave the command to her muscles to reach into the purse and stab him while she had the element of surprise. But those moments were becoming less and less frequent, and this disturbed her all the more.

She worried that she was already becoming accustomed to this arrangement.

This was not normal, and she did not want to feel normal at any point. This man was a serial killer who had almost certainly planned to rape and kill her back in 2007. The only thing that had saved her was probably the wet ground, which made him slip and hit his head on the door frame. Now he had the gall to sit and lecture her, even at one point suggesting that he was her protector from the consequences of her dirty secrets.

She made a commitment to herself.

Remember he is your enemy. You can appear empathic, caring, and understanding, but only in order to defeat him.

In between sessions, Jenny decided that she was going to start carrying a gun. The knife went back into the kitchen drawer. It was a difficult decision for her, because after the Big Deal she never wanted to hold a gun in her hand again, much less point one at somebody and pull the trigger. But her time with Rio and the range of possible threats he posed to her persuaded her to reconsider her stance.

Ironically, the notion on which gun to buy came from Rio himself. He always carried a small semiautomatic pistol in his pocket—a Glock 42, which was chambered in .380 ACP

(Automatic Colt Pistol). Normally, any conversation about firearms would have turned Jenny away, but given the circumstances, she had hung on his every word when he talked about his weapon. She figured she should learn as much as she could, and she was drawn to the Glock because of its small size as well as the fact that the .380 was a low-pressure cartridge, suitable for a shooter without much hand strength or experience firing semiautomatic pistols.

She thought of the gun she had stolen from her former drug dealer, how by then it must have been rusting away at the bottom of the river, having participated in the killing of an innocent man.

Even though she initially felt out of place in a gun shop, when she asked for the Glock the worker she was speaking to seemed immediately impressed and took her for a firearms enthusiast. Because she had asked to see such a small weapon, the clerk seemed to intuit that Jenny was intending to hide it on her person and reminded her that a permit was required in Delaware if someone wanted to carry a concealed weapon.

Initially, Jenny dismissed the need for a permit—after all, she felt as though her freedom hung in the balance every single day as it was. But then she realized that if she did need to use the gun, she didn't want the additional trouble of being charged with an extra crime. Fortunately, Sam was more than happy to introduce her to a firearms instructor who ran safety courses that met Delaware state requirements.

"I like you getting a gun and a conceal permit," Sam said with a kind of grim satisfaction. "Makes me feel like you've been listening to me when I tell you the kind of world we're living in."

After she filled out the necessary paperwork, collected references, and went through the training course and other bureaucratic requirements, the permit was on its way. Unfortunately, it would take several weeks to arrive. In the meantime, Jenny decided to go ahead and carry the gun anyway. She rationalized that carrying the kitchen knife was just as illegal, albeit much less effective.

Weeks went by. Jenny saw a full slate of clients in addition to Rio. She found herself getting almost bored, lulled into a routine, going through the motions with her regular clients and talking in circles with Rio. She felt as though she was keeping him from committing any more crimes, at least for the moment, but he wasn't changing in his psychopathic view of the world. And she wasn't getting any closer to gaining possession of that wallet.

"If I'm really going to help you," she finally said one afternoon, "we need to talk about the real things."

Rio had been rambling about a young woman on his block when he was a teenager toward whom he'd had murderous sexual feelings. At times, it felt as though he was using these sessions just to have a captive audience. He still paid, meticulously, in cash at the end of every hour they spent together.

"The real things," he repeated.

"I had honestly been dreading it, but now I think we just need to get it over with," Jenny said. "Talk to me about the murders."

"I think you mean to say the times I've saved people," Rio said matter-of-factly. "Not murdered."

"Right. Saving." Jenny tried to hide her mixture of horror and annoyance.

Who knew a serial killer would be so pedantic?

"Let's talk about it for real," she said.

She braced herself. She sensed the very real fascination she had with Rio and the workings of his psychology—this was a feeling that never really went away. But whatever the case, she couldn't be forever stuck in a holding pattern with him talking in loops about how the past and present merged in his mind.

"I know it's both things," he said. "Saving and murdering."

Jenny stared at him. In that moment, he seemed to make some kind of an internal decision. They were entering new territory. As careful as they had been with one another until then, words were going to be exchanged that couldn't be taken back.

"The first time I . . . started the mission, I was twenty-six," Rio said, so calm that he might have been talking about a vacation he took more than a decade ago. "She was a prostitute. I intended to kidnap her and have my way, but I ended up killing her sooner than I'd expected. She started screaming, even though I'd warned her not to. So I ended up strangling her in the passenger seat of my truck."Jenny flinched. He was so casual. A feeling of sickness suddenly came over her, partly like a chill from the flu and partly an urge to violently vomit. Rio didn't seem to notice or care.

"I killed four more," he said. "But I don't have a perfect record. Some others I attacked, some I had my way with, but I didn't get to the kill. It's taken a lot of learning, a lot of deepening my understanding of my purpose."

"Are you counting me as one of the women you attacked?" Jenny asked.

Rio snorted and gave a smile.

"Still sore about that, are we?" he said, almost warmly. "I told you not to worry about that anymore. You get things all turned around."

"I was there," Jenny said.

"OK, maybe I was going to kill you that night." Rio looked right into her eyes.

Jenny put her hands on the arms of her chair to stabilize herself.

"But it sure worked out that I didn't," Rio explained. He smiled again, seeming to be trying to approximate some kind of expression of affection.

She sat back in her chair and leveled her gaze at him. She felt something come over her, cold like steel.

"Don't think for a second that I'm afraid of you, Rio," she said. "So you can destroy my life. Fine. But I can destroy yours, too. And if I do it, that's all said and done for your mission. That's it for your heavenly mansion and the approval of God."

Rio gave her a disdainful look that was inconsistent with his next statement.

"Fair enough," he said.

They stared at each other for almost a full minute.

"There's still time in the session," Rio finally said to break the silence. "There's something else I want to talk about."

"It's your hundred-and-thirty-five dollars," Jenny said. She felt suddenly exhausted. With each minute that passed with Rio, she felt herself growing more and more complicit in his evil, more ensnared in the trap he had created for her.

"I can't tell you how strong the urges are that tell me to kill," Rio said.

"Why don't we start there?" Jenny said. "We can find ways to address this at the root, strategies that don't have to involve such extremes of looking at things."

"I have to target only those who are evil," Rio said. "That's my way of dealing with the urges."

As earlier, it was as though Jenny hadn't said anything. Maybe he was going to evade her every attempt to help him stop killing. But that didn't mean that she was going to stop trying.

"Sometimes when I pick someone out, I follow her around so I can find evidence of her evil ways," Rio said. "But sometimes it's not so easy. I can follow someone for weeks and not see any clear sign that she's despicable enough, or so immoral that she's worthy of death at my hands."

"Isn't that a sign to leave her alone?" Jenny asked. "How is it up to you to decide who is worthy of living or dying?"

"Not me. God," Rio said. "But what happens in these situations is very difficult for me. I have the urge but can't act on it. My whole body shakes. The anger is so strong that it feels like it's going to overwhelm me, like I'm going to have a heart attack or a stroke or something. Like I'm going to die."

We should only be so lucky.

The coldness of the feeling behind her thought shocked Jenny.

"It's a good thing, Rio. It means that you saw through the urges and did the right thing. You should feel good about it."

"I don't feel *good*. But I need to know how to cope when this happens."

Rio was clenching and unclenching his fists.

"There have been a few times when I followed through with it anyway," he said in a quiet, hollow voice. "I just couldn't resist."

"You mean you—"

"Every time I kill a woman who I shouldn't, I have to make penance," Rio said. "I have to save one more woman to make up for it."

Jenny felt her stomach clench up.

"Let me get this straight," she said. "Do you mean that when you've killed someone you don't think is evil, you have to kill another person who is evil in order to balance the scales?" "Yes. Exactly."

His dark eyes gleamed. He pulled his wallet out of the back pocket of his overalls and started counting out his fee for the session in a stack of bills, still talking as he meticulously unfolded the money.

"I call it a strike when that happens," Rio said without looking up from the money. "The person I kill after that is a makeup. When I compensate for a strike with a makeup, neither one of them will become my possession in the afterlife. I don't deserve them, because of what I did."

"Do you want me to help you avoid committing strikes?" Jenny said, suddenly making the connection in what he was saying. Part of her was almost giddy—he was actually going to enlist her help in reducing the amount of pain and mayhem he was inflicting on the world.

"You see, Jenny, this is why I'm grateful I came to you." He put the money down on the coffee table between them. "Your work with me can save lives. Every strike means two people die. There's no way around that. But if you can help me prevent a strike, you'll have saved two women. That's more than most people do in their entire lives."

"How many strikes have you had so far?" Jenny asked. She dreaded knowing the answer.

"One so far," Rio said. "That makes two more people dead than was strictly necessary. I would like to avoid that happening again."

It was madness. They were sitting there talking about murdered people in calm, dispassionate tones, as though working through some mild disagreement or other event that might bring someone to counseling.

They only had a couple of minutes left. Jenny didn't want to ask, she didn't want to know, but she had to.

"How many women have you killed, Rio?" He leveled his gaze at her.

"You really want to know?" "I need to know, Rio."

His gaze drifted away for a moment, as though he was adding figures in his head.

"I've made five righteous saves," he told her. "Add in the one strike, and the one makeup, and that makes seven."

"Oh, God," Jenny said quietly.

"You said you needed to know," Rio said.

"I do," Jenny said. "I need to know what I'm dealing with."

"I've committed rape and assault as well," Rio continued. "You should know that."

"How many?""I haven't kept track," Rio said. "Sometimes they've gotten away before I could seal the deal. That was earlier, years ago. Since I started the mission, there were a couple of women who got away from me. It takes a while to develop a successful technique."

The alarm went off to indicate that their session was over. She had another appointment, the client probably waiting outside.

For the first time, there was a redeeming possibility to this nightmare with Rio. She felt like a hostage, and one increasingly compromised by what she knew. But she knew that if she used all of her counseling skills, she could save lives. If she was bold and if she was effective, she might be able to stop Rio from killing altogether.

It was a hope that she needed to hold onto.

CHAPTER TEN

EVERYTHING YOU KNOW
COMES FROM TEXTBOOKS

JENNY'S LIFE outside the counseling sessions with Rio took on a cast of unreality. Constantly hiding the truth about the Big Deal had alienated her from those around her for so long, and now there was another surreal, terrible layer to her experience that she didn't dare share with anyone.

During the weekly sessions, she felt at times as though she was in some kind of awful play, like the one about two people waiting for someone who never arrived, or the one in which people were never able to escape the room they were in.

The alarm would sound at the end of the hour, but she knew that she would only be half-alive until the next session began.

Still, in more optimistic moments, Jenny held out hope for a resolution to her dilemma. She planned all week with arguments and logical points that she could use to detail Rio's thought processes and how he could potentially change them.

Rio was a psychopath. She was sure of it. But he was also pragmatic, intelligent, and someone who was always looking for solutions to problems. She felt he might be open to being convinced to stop killing if she could only land upon the right argument. Their dynamic would shift from minute to minute, each assuming the role of teacher or student, or questioner and subject, depending on where their roaming dialogues took them.

"Just so I understand," Jenny said at the beginning of the next session. "Your killing—pardon me, *saving*—makes up for bad things you've done in your life and for the nature of the thoughts you have?""It more than makes up for them" Rio said patiently, with a trace of pride. "It's my purpose. The mission is necessary to save souls. It's not within your previous conception of life. I thought you understood that by now."

"I get it," Jenny said encouragingly. "But bear with me for a second here. I've been really thinking about this a lot. There might actually be a way out of this that doesn't involve any more . . . saving."

"You say you get it, but you obviously don't," Rio told her. "Sometimes I think you're just playing dumb. You should know that you can't manipulate me. You realize that, don't you? There's no point."

Now, sometimes it was Jenny who would go on speaking as

though her interlocutor hadn't said a word.

"What if there was a way that you could balance out or compensate for what you call evil—but something other than *saving*?" Jenny asked him. "Is it possible that instead you could just let nature take its course with these women?" "We've been down this road, and it's a dead end," Rio said flatly. "It's crucial that I make these women pay. I was chosen to do it. I have special talents and gifts, and God gave them to me so that I could be an effective servant." Outside the window, a squirrel had skittered up to the edge of the small clearing by the side of the building. It had a dark patch on its back. Jenny had come to recognize it. She thought about feeding it but wondered if that would upset the balance of nature. Perhaps it was best simply to let it forage on its own.

"But does it have to be *you*?" Jenny asked. "Isn't it possible that these women would suffer on their own if you didn't save them? Maybe something in their lives would catch up with them. Maybe they would pay for their bad acts even if you didn't come along."

"Like if they got hit by a bus or fell or something?" Rio asked.

"Sure, life is dangerous," Jenny said. "Maybe God has a different fate in mind for them. If nothing else, living in evil is its own kind of punishment, isn't it?" Rio's eyes blazed; his mouth pulled into a tight line of anger.

"The fact that you still have such a long way to go really aggravates me," he said. "Say some evil woman gets hit by a bus. Is that bus killing her or saving her? You're making this all sound simple. It's not simple!"

As was the case at some point during every session, Jenny felt defeated. Rio's self-rationalizations were circular and impenetrable. During these moments, a burning desperation would arise within her. She felt a disgust that deepened when she sensed a part of her becoming more and more fascinated and challenged to win this match of wits—as though it was all some kind of game.

She didn't know which was worse: these moments of feeling so hopeless, or the moments when she felt herself starting to regard all of this as normal.

How the hell did this happen? I'm debating a psychopathic serial killer on his own terms.

Suddenly another tactic came to mind.

"Have you ever considered the possibility that you're simply delusional?" she asked him.

Rio's response to this was a surprise. She had been prepared, even as she spoke those words, for the possibility that Rio might become angry, even violent. At the very least, she had expected him to raise his voice in protest. In that moment, she was acutely aware of her purse sitting on her desk with the pistol inside.

But instead of flying into a rage, Rio looked at her calmly and rubbed his cheek. Nothing in his expression indicated any discomfort or anger whatsoever.

"Sometimes people simply believe things that aren't true," Jenny said, emboldened by his reaction. "It's not because they've been misled or misunderstood anything, but because of organic things that are occurring in their brain. This can lead to stubborn false beliefs. I had a client once who believed that the earth is flat. After a time, he came to understand that his belief was a symptom of something that had gone wrong."

Rio listened to her patiently.

"I'm sure you've had delusional patients," he replied. "And I've considered that in my case, but that's not what's happening here."

"I'd like you to consider all the possibilities," she told him.

"I need to you help me stay on an even keel. Our conversations are working," Rio said. "I'm doing a pretty good job appearing normal, I think, as I carry out my mission. That's what I need from you, to help with my outward personality. Not to tell me I'm some kind of delusional, homicidal nutjob."

"Well, you *are* homicidal," Jenny joked. "So at least on that point we're pretty close to being in agreement."

He stared at her. It had been reckless to tease him, to give him another opportunity to become angry with her, but as usual, humor was utterly lost on him.

"Many great prophets and heroes have been called delusional," Rio replied. "It's just a way for people like you to push people like me to the side."

"People like me?" she repeated.

One side of his mouth curled into a scowl as he remained silent.

"Rio, how do you really know you're right?" she asked. "What if *saving* these women is all a terrible mistake? What if your behavior is just plain wrong, and God doesn't approve of any of it? What if God is appalled?" "How do you know *you're* right?" Rio shot back.

"What do you mean?""Everything you know comes from textbooks." His scowl turned arrogant, almost haughty. "It's all just garbage you learned in school. You know what college is? One idiot who thinks they know what they're talking about explaining nonsense to another idiot who's stupid enough to pay for it."

Jenny bit her lip to stifle her laugh. Part of her thought that he was spot-on, but she didn't want him to think she was mocking him.

"Here's how I know my perspective is right," she explained to him. "You have murdered people. Killing is wrong. Don't you see how serious this is?""It *is* serious," Rio agreed. "It's the most serious thing a person can do. That doesn't mean it shouldn't be done."

Jenny remembered an old saying that she had first heard in grad school: you can't use reason to talk someone out of a position that they didn't acquire through logic.

Rio simply used the language of logic to explain his diseased emotional states and reactions. What came out was approaching delusional, but it held up within his own mind. His emotions and the corresponding pain they caused him came first, with the application of reason coming in a distant second.

Healing him would mean no one else had to die. But he was by far the most difficult client to help that she had ever come across in her practice.

It felt hopeless. Jenny had started to resign herself to the unthinkable reality that Rio was going to continue to kill.

Maybe her only hope was to minimize the harm he was capable of inflicting. She decided to dig deeper into the particulars of his mission, awful though she knew they would be, probing and searching for a potential way out.

"How will you know when the mission is complete?" Jenny asked. He looked up at her with sudden acute interest. "I mean, are you going to keep *saving* for your entire life? That's not much of a plan, if you ask me."

"That wouldn't be a solid plan," he calmy agreed. "I have to reach a fixed number of righteous *saves*, and then I can stop. My work in this world will be done."

Jenny took a deep breath.

"How many?" she asked.

"One for each of my grievous sins," Rio said. He reached down and absentmindedly scratched at the nametag on his overalls.

"OK," Jenny replied. "How many is that?"

"I failed the Lord nine times," Rio said. "So I have to collect nine evil women to take with me to my heavenly manor."

"You've killed seven. Am I right?""I have four more to save from eternal damnation," Rio said. "They don't know it yet, but I'm going to stamp their ticket out of the eternal fire."

"But that adds up to eleven," Jenny said.

"Two were because of the strike," Rio said, as though she were intentionally trying to trip him up. "God and I squared the bill on that one. I don't owe anything more there. Don't try saying that I do."

"I didn't." Jenny paused. "All right, four more. Is that right? Four more and you're done?"The gun was in the purse. She could put a stop to this. But what then?"Four more, and I'm out of your hair," Rio told her. "You get the wallet back, and we go our separate ways. I'll never bother you again. Might want a referral to a new therapist, though. We'll see."

She watched his lips curl into a smirk and realized that he was actually trying to be funny. Jenny had often wanted him to have a sense of humor, but his attempts to express it were somehow more frightening than just remaining humorless.

"What if one of the women you've already killed was extra evil?" Jenny asked. "Isn't it possible that could count as two saves? Maybe you don't need to kill four more people. When you look at it that way, the mission could already be complete."

She knew how she sounded: bargaining, wheedling. But she had to try.

"I see what you're trying to do," Rio said, almost gently. "You think you're doing the right thing."

"Of course I do."

"The problem is that you're forgetting something," Rio went on. "These women are going to burn eternally without me. You're really not helping them by trying to talk me out of saving them."

Jenny kept going for the rest of the session, bringing up one technicality after another, trying to poke holes in Rio's plans and the motivations behind them. She knew she couldn't do anything to help those who were already dead, but maybe she could succeed in some form of harm reduction—a strategy she learned about in school and which was typically applied to drug and alcohol use. She pondered what her professors would think if they knew she was applying it to this life-and-death situation.

Her heart ached. She had fallen so far already, in ways that felt both professional and spiritual. It was feeling as though she had gone with Rio to a place from which there was no possible return.

She had hoped during every minute away from Rio that she could get through this with no one else being hurt. She had fervently wished this could happen with the Big Deal still a secret, with the wallet in her possession, and with Rio rendered harmless and never again crossing the threshold of her office with his psychotic ideation and his maze of pseudo-religious justifications.

She sensed that hope fading away, like the mist of the morning as the harsh rays of the sun warmed some hidden valley. She felt her avenues of escape closing off one by one, stifled by the sheer force of Rio's determination.

Soon enough, after that hope was entirely gone, an unmitigated realism would settle in between the counselor and the killer. All that would be left were strategies and tactics for minimizing the impact of his wrath, and for keeping her own soul as she tried to protect her freedom without losing what she still valued about herself.

CHAPTER ELEVEN

SUCH WAS HER POWER

RIO SAT IN HIS ROCKING CHAIR and looked out his front window. He was contemplating how he would conduct his sixth save—technically, his eighth homicide, but he wasn't counting it that way. He could feel the demon drive swelling up within him, the surest sign that it was time to kill.

He was guided to understand the timing of his kills by more than his intense feelings of lust. The weather also gave him signs. Rio believed with passionate intensity that rain was a sign from God. It meant that it was time to cleanse the Earth of one more evil woman. Each of Rio's previous saves, his Godly killings, had taken place in the rain.

Admittedly, the first two occurred in the rain entirely by accident. Rio had made no plans back then based on rainfall. Instead, both times when he was about to execute his plan, he noticed raindrops striking his forehead like a baptism. It had reminded him of the night when he went to tow the car and saw the woman in her handcuffs. It had been raining then, too. He could just picture that woman, her hands lashed behind her back. It was a cause of inspiration whenever he thought about it.

It was a sin not to recognize when God was telling you something. God was saying that righteous killings had to happen under the cleansing waters of the rain. From the day he made that connection, he would stalk his victims for months, all the while watching weather reports to time his saving with the strongest possibility of a rainstorm. So far it had been perfect. Because it had come from God.

Rio had learned a great deal from studying the lives and work of serial killers. He knew that once the police attributed a string of homicides to a serial killer, they started focusing on discerning the killer's pattern. There were movies and TV shows around this process because it was fascinating to everyone.

Not wanting to end up the subject of some crime documentary, Rio meticulously varied his method of killing each time to keep the authorities from making a connection. With every catch and kill, even with the strike and the subsequent make-up, Rio had made an effort to frame someone else by planting evidence somewhere on their person or property. It had never been enough to convict an innocent man or even lead to a trial, but it had been enough to keep the police plenty busy.

Investigators and detectives had tunnel vision. They would tirelessly chase after their first suspect, blind to the wider world of other viable alternative suspects. They would become slaves to their own narratives, and their pride would become a factor. It was a common human tendency, and Rio counted on it to protect him. Thus far, his efforts had been rewarded. He had avoided being a suspect for any of his work.

This was, of course, how God intended it.

The geography and local characteristics around Rio's house were a big help with eluding detection, both from the police and from his nosy neighbors. A primary and crucial concern for Rio was making sure he wasn't spotted when he left his home to claim a victim.

At first, it seemed like an unsolvable problem. Rio's place was an old Colonial once owned by his parents and where he had lived with Eileen during the Cleansing. It sat at the end of a cul-de-sac in a neighborhood with almost all newer homes. The next home over from theirs was on a farm that, at one time, took up more than 150 acres. A developer had approached the farmer who owned the land and negotiated an asking price for it, but the farmer wouldn't sell without first securing Eileen's permission.

Such was her power that the farmer needed her blessing before he sold his own property.

The farmer had been concerned that a new housing development would impede access to the Winston family property, and he didn't want to make them angry. Furthermore, Eileen owned several acres adjacent, two of which the developer wanted in order to gain access to a secondary nearby public road.

Initially, Eileen had agreed with the developer's plan, but a few months into the grading of the land, before any homes were built, she had a bout of antagonism that led to a slight re-negotiation. She was fine with a new development road and the cul-de-sac that was planned to go in front of her house, but she wanted her home to be the only one on the cul-de-sac.

At first, the developer had said the suggestion was outrageous and that he refused to even consider it. But when he went back to his plans, he saw that pulling out would mean he couldn't build eleven of the planned 250 houses in the development. That was a major chunk of his profit from the deal, but he didn't want to sacrifice the entire project, so he capitulated before too long. That meant what was now Rio's house was an odd duck in what was otherwise a cookie-cutter neighborhood on the edge of town. His place was a lone Colonial, methodically restored, and essentially on its own private road within a very modern development.

When they were building all those other homes, they placed a drainage ditch alongside the road behind Rio's house. This ditch cut off access to that road, which had been the primary way to get out to the highway since the house was built. From Rio's place, he would ostensibly have to use the cul-de-sac and drive through the neighborhood, adding time and distance to the trip every time.

At first, this wasn't something that particularly bothered Rio until he gave it some thought and realized that at least some of the new homes in the development came installed with security cameras. He would have to drive by any number of them on a daily basis in order to get to the highway, and that would leave a digital record of his journey—making for a potentially uncomfortable situation if investigators ever got curious about his whereabouts on the night a target went missing. He could hardly claim to have been spending a quiet night at home, which was his preferred alibi, if half a dozen security cameras had captured the image of his truck driving through the neighborhood around the time of the crime.

He realized that he needed a way to drive off his property and onto the main road without driving through the neighborhood. Simple as that.

Rio looked to the old access road, the one he was cut off from by the drainage ditch. It was his ticket to anonymity when he needed it. He figured he just needed to figure out a way to cross that ditch in his 1996 Toyota Tacoma—and if he did, he could leverage all those security cameras to work in his favor. If the police started investigating his whereabouts, they'd pull video from all those cameras and be unable to find proof that he had left the neighborhood the night of the crime. By then, they'd have some other theory to chase like a dog with a bone, leaving Rio to continue his mission.

The drainage ditch was in the middle of a patch of trees about 200 feet wide. The trees ran parallel to the ditch on either side. One day, Rio had been replacing the fuel line in the pickup and wanted to drive it around a little without getting too far from his house in case the quality of his repair hadn't been good enough. He decided to drive around the back of the house and cruise right up to the tree line.

He noticed then that he was able to maneuver the truck through the trees and pull all the way up to the ditch. The trees were spaced in just such a way that he could weave through them without a scratch on his paint job. He wasn't able to cross the ditch, but he pulled around off the road on the other side and discovered that he could drive through the trees on that side as well. Again, he pulled all the way up to the ditch, looking at his house on the other side.

A couple of days later, he had been just walking around the ditch and contemplating the arrangement of the trees when something occurred to him: there were two concrete encasements for sewer pipes directly across from one another on either side of the ditch. They had been there in plain sight, waiting for Rio to notice them. They were only about half a foot below the edge of the ditch, and only about four feet away from each other. And they looked extremely sturdy.

The Tacoma weighed about 3,400 pounds. Rio reasoned that he could easily fashion two ramps made out of 2 X 10 boards that could easily span that four-foot gap. For each ramp, Rio screwed together a pair of boards and cut them into the exact lengths necessary to fit into the grooves on top of each concrete encasement. He could place the ramps in the bed of his pickup, which was covered by a cap. He now had the perfect way to cross over the ditch and to avoid the cameras.

It was extra good luck that the entrance to his garage faced away from the rest of the neighborhood. This would allow him to pull out, maneuver through the trees, pull out the ramps and place them on the encasements, cross the ditch, and make his way to the highway without being seen. Of course, he would have to take the usual precautions once he was out of the neighborhood, but at least he wouldn't be spotted and recorded at the very beginning of the save.

Rio let his thoughts wander back to the next victim. She was 24 years old. Her name was Karen Concord. She worked as a cashier at a grocery store about twelve miles from Rio's house. He had been intermittently monitoring her for the past six months.

He had learned her work schedule. Then he had followed her around in his truck a few times, looking for evidence of her evil. He was on the hunt to justify his sexual and homicidal desires, which were usually blended together into one insatiable drive.

I am just as God made me.

Even after watching her all this time, though, Rio was struggling to find signs of her treachery. He'd go buy groceries at the store, which was on his way home from work, and carefully listen to each perfunctory phrase she spoke to him when he got to the front of her check-out line. She had pretty, clear skin, and green eyes that seemed kind but which he knew were hiding something from him.

Nothing incriminating revealed itself right away. He carefully observed her choice of clothes—her modest dresses and jeans and blouses—and found nothing of use. She was actually a conservative dresser who seemed to live a fairly ordinary and uneventful life. She attended the local community college one night every week, but Rio hadn't been able to figure out what she was studying.

He started to grow weary of these surveillance trips, tiring himself out installing and removing the wooden ramps each time he went out to watch her. He knew there was something that he was missing. If only he could see through the veil of her spell and witness her being revealed for what she was.

Rio started making inferences based on how Karen Concord interacted with the customers at the store. He would watch her from the Tacoma through the plate-glass window, making conversation sometimes and smiling, but he couldn't hear what they were saying.

Look at her go.

Rio began to fill in the blanks, making up dialogue that was suitable for his purpose. He made himself hear her launching sexually suggestive remarks at the married men who stood in her line. She invited them to come back to her place so they could use drugs together.

Even though she was almost surely telling the customers to have a good night, or making small talk about the weather, Rio believed he knew better. There was meaning underneath even the most innocuous words. And if the words weren't there, someone with Rio's special talents and purpose in life could read the very thoughts beneath them.

Her thoughts are so dirty. Hell, she's probably even killed on her own. She's probably planning another kill right now.

A sense of urgency grew within him. He needed to stop her

from doing whatever unholy thing came next.

Killing her would be righteous. He started to fantasize in detail about having his way with her, which he intended to do in the back of the pickup truck, before he killed her and dumped her body.

He worked to fine-tune the plan and considered how much of this he could share with Jenny, his captive audience. He knew she had to cooperate, but he also knew she was adamant about stopping him from killing. She just didn't understand.

Forgive them, Father. They know not what they do.

CHAPTER TWELVE

EARLY SUMMER, 2018

JENNY WAS INCREASINGLY EXHAUSTED by her excess of ambivalent feelings and thoughts. On the one hand, she was encouraged because Rio hadn't killed anyone that she knew of during the time period in which she had been treating him. On the other, the stress of living under the proverbial Sword of Damocles pushed her to her emotional edge with distressing regularity. In order to cope with the anxiety of her existential uncertainty, Jenny tried to distract herself from her own painful emotions with coping mechanisms such as denial.

She was in denial of her own moral failings. She vacillated between thinking of herself as a victim in her situation and holding herself accountable as, at least, an unwilling perpetrator. The moral ambiguity around killing David Saunders more than a decade ago remained something that she couldn't reconcile. She wondered if she was no better than Rio—more or less a psychopathic, narcissistic, remorseless killer who had fooled herself into believing she was doing the right thing.

Maybe everybody is delusional, and the only difference is the content and the intensity of the delusion.

Jenny knew that she had made one major mistake, other than the Big Deal itself. She should have immediately called the police as soon as she learned that Rio was a killer. Every moment she waited would make her look more complicit and would almost surely sway investigators or a jury against her once the Big Deal became known. As far as the outside world was concerned, she would no longer be seen as a mental health counselor, a concerned citizen, or even a decent person. She would be a conspirator.

She couldn't accept it. She had to hold onto the last remnants of hope that she could be redeemed and freed from this trap. Then the anxiety would ratchet up still higher, her mind racing in search of whatever dwindling odds that this would ever really happen.

A lot of the time, she simply felt numbness. Nothing Rio did or said really had the power to shock her anymore. She was sitting in her chair across from him, one of his hands raking through his hair. The flowers and trees were in full bloom outside the window. Even the beauty of nature seemed to be mocking her at times such as these, when all was darkness within the walls of her office.

"What did you say?" she asked him, even though she knew full well exactly what he had just told her.

"It's time for me to continue my mission," Rio said. "And you know what that means."

"I'm . . . all too aware."

Her own voice sounded slow and sluggish to her. She had known this moment would come, and she had struggled and circled around in her mind to come up with a plan. The sheer cognitive load on her thought processes made her head feel heavy and thick.

Over the next twenty minutes, Rio laid out the details of how he planned to carry out the homicide. Jenny sat there as though encased in plastic, unable to deliver a meaningful response or come up with any counter to his words. She realized that her counseling training was entirely inadequate to deal with something this extreme. Then Rio moved onto the topic of rape, and it was like she had taken a shot of adrenaline to the heart.

"Why do you have to do that?" she shot at him. "Why not just kill the person and be done with it?" Inwardly, she cringed with revulsion at these words. She did not want this sixth victim to die. She wanted to do everything in her power to prevent it. She had adopted a strategy to separate the rape from the murder, hoping to somehow cleave a gap in all of Rio's religious delusions.

"I will have my way with her as part of her punishment," Rio said. "I was designed to cleanse these women of their evil. This is simply part of the process, something that I have to do."

Rio was visibly excited, his face flushed. Jenny willed herself not to be distracted by the wave of fear she felt in his presence.

"What will happen if you don't do that?" she asked.

"Then all I would be doing is murdering them," Rio said, as though the answer was self-evident. "Without their additional punishment, they'll never get to Heaven. And I don't wish eternal fire on anyone."

"What if the plan goes sideways?" Jenny asked. "What if you kill that person without raping her? What happens then?" Rio went somber. "Then I might have to find a replacement."

That realization washed over Jenny: if Rio failed to execute his plan in full, then he was simply going to find another victim. Her own throat felt tight and constricted. Rio was going to kill no matter what strategy she tried to deploy. There was no reasoning with the purity of his hateful, evil drives.

She theorized that Rio's delusional reasoning was just that: a cover for a deep need for revenge against women for myriad perceived injustices, rejections, and his own feelings of helplessness. His sex drive and violence were inextricably interwoven within this lattice of submerged emotion—sheer truths that he wasn't equipped to handle.

"Don't worry," Rio said. "I'm not going to tell you her name."

Jenny involuntarily flinched and her hand shot to her belly, where a lancing pain shot through her midsection.

"I'm not really worried that you would tell her, or that you would get in the way of my plans," Rio continued.

"I don't want to know this," Jenny said in a small voice.

"It's because I'm revolted by her name," Rio said, his eyes

cold and gleaming. "Once someone is at that level of evil, they've become something else. They're no longer worthy of the name they were born with."

"I take it back," Jenny said. "Tell me her name."

This was a desperate strategy. She hoped that if she knew the potential victim's name, she could work on Rio to humanize the woman. Studies had shown that knowing another person's name reduced feelings of hostility toward them—and that Rio's making the woman nameless was yet another of his delusional defense mechanisms he had invented to shield himself from the full reality of what he intended to do.

"Not gonna do it," he said with a smirk.

I was stupid to think I could spark compassion in this monster. What's left? Leveraging his own feelings? Pushing his buttons? "I said tell me," she said with a tone of command. She had never spoken to him in this way, and he was visibly shocked.

"*I said tell me,*" he shot back at her in a simpering, mocking tone.

She contemplated simply going to the desk, pulling out the pistol, and shooting him. It was possible she could get a shot off before he realized what was happening. But then she saw how closely he was watching her, as though monitoring every thought through her features, observing her every gesture, looking like a wild animal on guard for an attack. She didn't think she could kill the killer, not with him looking at her like that.

"I apologize for making fun," he said next. "You've been helping me, and I appreciate that."

Now that the moment of reckless courage had passed, all

she could feel was despair. She didn't have the resolve or the self-destructive capacity to kill him. All that was left was her primal need to find a way out of this. As she felt this need move through her like a wave, she sensed how callous this part of herself was that cared only for her own survival.

She wasn't going to be able to save this woman's life.

Jenny began to cry.

Rio had systematically trapped her and broken down her moral resolve, and there she was. Just like him.

"Hey, take it easy," Rio said, watching her as her head slumped down to her chest and her eyes blurred with tears.

"Don't," she managed to blurt out.

"Look at it this way," he told her. "Four more, and it's over. I'll be nothing more than a bad memory to you. And in the next life, you'll see. You'll understand someday. You'll see that I was a true hero here in this life. And that makes you a hero, too."

"Heroine," she corrected him defiantly, clearing the moisture from her eyes.

He made a disgusted expression. "I never took you for someone who was into drugs. That's a sin, you know."

"Not heroin, you idiot," she spat at him. "A man is a *hero*, and a woman is a *heroine*. If you're going to keep spouting your crazy nonsense, at least get the vocabulary right."

He stared at her as though she was something floating in a test tube in some laboratory somewhere.

"I understand that you needed to do that," he said calmly. "And you should definitely feel that you did everything in your power to stop me. This is all too big for you. I'm glad you got that out of your system. Now you can go back to helping me."

She hated the fact that she was still crying. She had never felt so defeated, not even before, when she had felt trapped and caged. Now it was as though she *lived* in the cage and couldn't remember ever not being a prisoner.

She wished she trusted Sam enough to go to him for help.

"I need you to help me think through something," Rio said. "I need your perspective."

"I can't," Jenny protested.

"You *can*," Rio said. "How about this. If you don't help me, I'll do another strike. That will be the easiest thing in the world for me. Two more innocents. And then blood *would* be on your hands, make no mistake about it."

Jenny tried to blow her nose as she processed this.

"We need to make the most of the time we have left in this session," Rio said. "Come on. Do your job."

She barked out a laugh that dissolved into a sob of despair. She felt ashamed of herself. She should at least have been able to keep her composure, if she couldn't deny him.

"I'm going to disable . . . *her* vehicle, so that it breaks down while she's between her job and her residence," Rio began. "Then I will pull up behind the car in my pickup truck and approach to offer help. When the opportunity presents itself—"

"No," Jenny said.

"I will strike her in the head with the wrench I keep in my truck," Rio continued, his tone like that of someone describing some everyday event. "Now here's the problem: I'm going to have to stall her until we're alone, with no traffic coming in either direction. Naturally, I don't want any witnesses."

Jenny felt gears slipping in her mind. Rio's tone was soothing; he was presenting this situation as something so abstract that he was inviting her in as though it were a simple problem they needed to solve collaboratively. She found herself listening closely.

"This is likely to be a very short interaction," Rio continued. "But I know myself. I have a tendency to come off as cold, distant, and not particularly friendly. I'm especially like this when I'm focused on the mission."

"You know this from experience?" Jenny said, her own voice sounding unfamiliar to her.

"I can manipulate people," Rio said, letting the statement hang between them. "But less so when a save is about to happen. My excitement distracts me. There is always the possibility that I will scare her off. And then she will be doomed to the fire."

Speaking to Rio when he was like this was akin to high-wire gymnastics—up was down, evil was good, killing was saving.

"What do you want from me?" "Help me with my problem," Rio said. "Help me act normal."

Now in the calculus was the prospect of more innocent deaths—two at a time, if Rio decided that a strike was necessary. She was faced with the awful reality of perhaps helping one person lose her life in order that two more might go unharmed. She felt the considerations overloading her moral compass, and that she was crossing yet another border. But this was her fate, wasn't it? "Practice," she said.

"Practice," Rio repeated. "Practice what?""That's the solution to your problem," Jenny told him. "Practice what you're going to say. When you approach her, have a script ready in your mind and go through it like an actor would. Write enough material in advance to last for several minutes, and then memorize it before you leave your house."

This was a terrible perversion of therapeutic advice she had given many times before, for situations ranging from a marriage proposal to confronting a boss who had been abusive and overworking his employees.

"What am I supposed to say?" Rio asked, clearly intrigued. "What's supposed to be in the script?""You have to think about it from the other person's point of view," Jenny told him. It was like listening to someone else's voice. "She's worried about her car just breaking down. You deal with people all the time in your daily life who have the exact same problem. They want to know that you're going to help them. Talk to her about how you're a mechanic and you know how to fix cars. Just come across as though everything is going to be OK, and that you're only there to help."

"That's *good*," he nodded. "I never look at things from other people's point of view. It never would have occurred to me."

"It's called empathy," Jenny said.

"I know that," Rio replied.

"I don't think you have it," she said bluntly.

"Because I'm a psychopath, right?" Rio suggested.

"There's no sense dwelling on the topic," Jenny told him. "But anyone can convincingly fake empathy for a few minutes."

Rio stared at her blankly, seemingly processing something in his mind.

"Any other suggestions?" he said after a long silence.

"Wear your uniform from work," she told him. "The work shirt with your name on it. It will make your stopping to help look more legitimate."

What am I doing?

"That's good," he said. "I can get a patch with someone else's name on it from the garage and put it over mine. That way, in case something goes wrong, she won't know my real name."

"Good idea," Jenny said.

"And nice try," Rio added.

They simply looked at one another for a while, as though they were in a perfectly normal session and had run out of things to talk about for the moment. Finally, Jenny decided to break the silence.

"When is it going to happen?" she asked.

"The next time it rains," Rio said, looking outside at the clear and cloudless sky. "I only do it in the rain. The rain cleanses all the evil from this world."

If only it would cleanse you from the world.

She said nothing.

After the session had ended, Jenny saw two more clients before the workday was over. She got in her car and started driving home, going slow, obeying all the traffic laws as though she was an outlaw hiding from the authorities.

She did an inventory and realized that, at least for the moment, she had no more emotional capacity for sorrow, remorse, or even empathy. She didn't bother to try to rationalize what had happened in the session with Rio earlier that day. She was complicit in his acts, and yet there was a strange comfort in it. It brought her one step closer to being done with Rio forever.

She found herself wishing that Rio would simply kill four people in one night, giving her the freedom that she so desperately wanted.

Nearing her apartment, she looked up to the sky in search of clouds.

CHAPTER THIRTEEN
THE BOYFRIEND'S HOUSE WASN'T FAR

RIO WAS FULLY PREPARED for the kill, but now it was a matter of waiting for the right opportunity. He became tense and apprehensive. He was looking forward with all his being for the pleasure he was going to feel, and the release. And he also didn't want to fail to save Karen Concord.

During July and August, it rained a total of four times. The first two times occurred during the day. The third time, Rio pulled a long shift towing cars. The fourth time, Rio had left his property unseen over the drainage ditch and made his way to the supermarket, only to find that Karen had parked her car in a different spot than usual.

This change made Rio nervous, and his apprehension turned out to be well-founded. Her vehicle was a 2005 Ford Focus. It was parked that night right under a security camera mounted on the wall of the supermarket. He had no choice but to wait for the next rainfall.

In September, a big rainstorm rolled in on a night when Karen was working. Excitement churned through Rio as he crossed over the ditch and made his way into town. His focus on Karen—her long hair, her curvy figure—had become even more of an obsession than usual. He struggled with his violent sexual drive, and more than once had been tempted to simply attack Karen in the parking lot.

But that wasn't the way it needed to be.

He kept talking to himself on the way over.

"Stay focused," he said over and over. "Remember how important this mission is. Remember what you're going to say."

When Rio saw Karen's car parked that night in its usual place, its windshield streaked with the rain predicted to fall for the next few hours, he was filled with joy. It was on the side of the building and there were no cameras there. It was clear that it was his destiny to save her that night.

The shop where Rio worked paid for a website subscription that supplied detailed information on how to repair a wide range of transport: cars, trucks, ATVs, even recreational vehicles. Rio had studied the mechanical schematics for the 2005 Ford Focus and crafted a plan that would allow the car to run for a few miles before the car became disabled, leaving Karen stranded alone on the side of the road.

He parked his truck about 150 feet away from the Ford. He exited quietly and walked over to it carrying a sharpened screwdriver and a cordless impact wrench already fitted with a socket matching the lug nuts for Karen's car. He wore a baseball cap that helped keep the cool rain from falling into his eyes.

He dropped down to the ground when he reached the front of the car and, in a rehearsed motion, thrust the screwdriver through the lower radiator hose. This would cause coolant to leak out at a slow rate.

Karen wouldn't be done with work for another hour, which would be just the right amount of time for the Ford's radiator to lose a sufficient quantity of coolant. He had also planned on loosening several of the lug nuts on the passenger side rear wheel as well (inspired by an abduction attempt attributed to the Zodiac Killer), but he was pleased enough with how well piercing the hose went to simply stand up and calmly walk back to his truck.

Time to wait.

He watched her through the glass, imagining all of the terrible, diseased, wicked thoughts that were passing through her mind as she pretended to be a normal, everyday young woman working at the checkout line. Pretending to be good.

Karen finished her shift at the supermarket exactly on the hour and came out through the automated double doors with her purse over her shoulder. She looked up at the sky, at the falling rain, and quickly made her way to the Ford Focus. She unlocked her car and seemed to pause for a moment.

Did she smell something?

Rio tried to breathe steadily. Maybe she smelled the anti-freeze. She might look down to see it running over the pavement. She might call someone or go back inside the store for help. Then everything would be lost.

But no. She got in the car, started it up, and made her way through the parking lot toward the road. Her red tail lights shone in the falling rain.

As he followed, it didn't take long for Rio to realize that Karen didn't seem to be driving directly home. Along the route to her place, Rio had conducted extensive surveillance to determine which areas would be most advantageous for the attack—basically, places where there weren't many people and where it would be unlikely to have video cameras. He had calculated that there was a greater than 70 percent chance that her car would break down in a suitable area. He also knew the route so well that, if they got separated by a traffic light, he would be able to catch up with her.

If she was driving straight home. But she wasn't.

Now Rio had no idea what the percentage might be of the car becoming inoperable in a favorable place. And because he didn't know where she was headed, he had to make sure to get through every light with her.

He told himself to stay calm, no matter how catastrophic this turn of events potentially was to his plans. He was extraordinary, his talents vast. He followed her, waiting for his opportunity to come.

Karen hesitated at a yellow light, then blew through it. Rio cursed her, forced to put his pedal to the floor in order to make it through before the light turned red, his tires spinning on the wet road. His anger flared deep red, and he contemplated simply ramming his truck into her car.

Rio closed the distance with that thought in his head, trying to restrain himself, thinking that if he caused an accident, he might lose the opportunity to save her. He had to be more compassionate. He had to remember all that he was doing for her.

Then it happened. Karen's brake lights flashed in the rain ahead of him, and she quickly veered over to the side of the road and turned on her blinking hazard lights. Rio pulled up behind her. The rain patted on his window and against the roof of his truck.

He got out of his truck. He walked up to the driver's side of the car, hoping to get her attention before she made a call on her cell phone. He tapped on the glass, startling her, but she lowered her window anyway.

"I thought I saw about a mile back that your car wasn't running right." He smiled and blinked into the rain. "I thought I would lend a hand. I'm a mechanic, you know. I can either get you back on the road or tell you what you need to get fixed."

He was following his script, trying to look relaxed and natural. She looked him over, seemingly wary.

"I can just call my boyfriend," Karen told him. She frowned as rain splattered on the car door. "He only lives about a mile away."

That's where she was headed. Rio had followed her there before, knowing she was going there to sin, but he had been so clouded with anger while following her from the supermarket that he hadn't made the obvious connection.

She was holding a phone, but its screen was dark. She hadn't dialed it yet.

Rio looked both ways, up and down the roadway. No one was around for the moment. He smiled and reached into his jacket.

"Got a tool in here," he muttered. He looked into her eyes. "I wondered where you were going. You usually go straight home from work."

Karen's eyes widened just for a second as she connected the dots.

Rio struck her across the head with the wrench. The first blow didn't knock her out, but the second one did. He looked up—there was still no one around. The rain kept falling, partially blocked by the trees that lined the road. He had to move fast.

Rio opened up the door of the Focus, dragged Karen around to the back of his truck, and threw her in the bed. He made sure the blinkers and the headlights on the Focus were switched off before he got back in his Tacoma and drove away. He didn't bother taking her phone from the center console of her car because his potential plan to make her give him the password required her to be conscious. He had intended to send text messages from her phone to make it seem as though she was fine, but he had to be flexible. She wasn't going to regain consciousness anytime soon.

Rio took her to a secluded place in the woods, put on his

latex gloves and other measures to hide the evidence of his actions, and did his worst to her. He fulfilled all of the desires that
had been building up over the course of the last year. The only
mercy was that she didn't know what happened. Rio seemed to
have mortally wounded her with that vicious second blow from
the wrench. He had intended to drag out and savor the experience, relishing every precious second, but then he realized that
her quick death, along with her change in route, presented him
with an opportunity that he needed to take advantage of.

Every time Rio saved a woman, he tried to change an aspect
of the homicide to prevent investigators from realizing that a
serial killer was on the loose. He had intended after the murder
of Karen Concord to cut her body into small pieces and dispose
of them in a nearby marsh. Disposing of a body this way was
taxing, and though Rio didn't consider himself to be afraid of
hard work, he saw that he needed to work smarter and not
harder in this situation.

It would be better for the police to know that Karen was
dead and have them chase after the wrong person than to make
her into a missing person, with the police checking into all
manner of places they didn't belong.

The boyfriend's house wasn't far. Rio had even fantasized
about abducting Karen from there, maybe catching her in the
act of sinning, but that would have meant that he had to kill
the boyfriend. That would mean an unacceptable elevation of
risk.

Rio didn't like to think about the boyfriend's name, but he
did. *Brian.*

Behind Brian's house were woods that were about a hundred feet deep. On the far side of those woods was a road that wouldn't be heavily traveled that time of the evening. Rio drove along the road for a while until he was able to figure out where the boyfriend's house was on the far side. Rio slowed down next to a small sign pointing to a neighborhood church, then pulled up onto the shoulder.

He got out of the truck, looked around, carried her body into the woods, and dumped her on the ground without looking at her face. She lay on the ground just a few feet past the tree line, not visible to any motorists who might be passing on the road.

Driving away, Rio instantly became dissatisfied with his plan. There was a reason why he put such a premium on extended and tedious strategizing. Whenever he acted impulsively, he would second-guess himself and become so displeased with the results that the nagging doubt was tantamount to torture.

The thoughts started cascading violently.

"This strategy is unbecoming of a hero warrior," Rio said to himself under his breath. His anxiety mounted. "Can't leave her there. Doesn't do anything good. Doesn't further the mission."

Rio turned the truck around and parked in a dark area to the side of the road about 500 feet from where he had dumped her body. He turned off the truck and darkened his lights. The rain patted on the roof. He got out and walked through the woods to Karen, his pace slowed by how hard it was to see in the dark.

He found himself carefully counting his steps. His right hand divided up every moment into two parts. An intolerable sensation came across his chest, seemingly driven by the churning of his mind, by the disordered terror of a severe attack of OCD.

It was hard dragging her body through the woods toward Brian's house, but he was up for the challenge. He stopped about every twenty feet to make sure that she hadn't lost any clothing or left any other traces. He had to switch from one hand to the other about every ten paces, but it felt like something he had to do—he didn't want either arm to become too tired, in case he found himself doing combat with someone unexpected.

Through the rain, in the near distance, Rio could see the shape of the back of Brian's house. An old, dilapidated chain-link fence was all that separated Rio and Karen from the back porch of the brick ranch house. Rio hoisted her body over the fence, then jumped over it himself as he calculated his next move. He was feeling that thrill again, all the possibilities flashing in his mind, but he also knew that his next steps would be among the most important of his life.

Wish I had more time to think it through. One. Three. Five.

But in that moment of confusion came inspiration. He knew that one thing that would work in his favor was a crime scene full of all kinds of contradictory clues and information. Police investigators didn't like to admit that they were confused or didn't have a clear path to solving a crime, so they would increasingly center on the obvious suspect, Brian, and dismiss any indications that the killer could have been anyone else.

After scanning the yard for anything useful, Rio spotted a

rusty rake, a flowerpot, and a garden hose. He stood there in the rain, looking at these items in the dark, searching for the moment of inspiration that could lead him to visualize a disorganized crime scene. Then he realized that he didn't have to use all of these things to create what he needed.

The cause of Karen's death was a blow to the head with a box wrench. Rio had struck her with the flat part, which he believed would leave a wound similar to the handle of the rake.

No lights were on in the house. Either Karen's visit had been meant to be a surprise, or Brian had gone to bed for the night, or possibly, he was out looking for her.

Rio lay out Karen's body in the grass, closer to the back door of the house. He knew she was right-handed from all his time watching her, so he took that hand and scratched at the wooden handle with her fingernails, even breaking one. Then he dropped her arm and ran back into the woods. He forced himself to ignore all the myriad obsessive thoughts running through his mind.

Go back and check. Make sure it's perfect. What about the angle of her body relative to the house? Maybe we should hit her with the rake handle a couple of times, just to be sure? How many steps back to the truck? When he got to the edge of the woods, Rio tried to calm himself and walk at a normal pace as he made his way along the roadside back to his vehicle. He pulled his collar up around his ears and pulled his hat down over his eyes. His body felt strange, as though he was walking through molasses and had to deliberately command every muscle in his arms and legs to keep moving forward. It was as though his body had forgotten how to walk on its own, then how to reach out and grab the door handle of the truck, then how to push in the clutch and put the vehicle into first gear. But he was able to get the truck moving. He didn't think anyone had spotted him, and his anxiety and riot of obsessive thoughts began to lift slowly, but noticeably after he had driven for about a mile.

Now something started to happen in his mind that he enjoyed, and he allowed himself to smile as the windshield wipers beat a slow but insistent rhythm.

He started to fantasize about how various people would react to the crime he had just committed.

A crime in this world, a blessing in the next.

He saw these people in his mind's eye, almost as though they were characters in a play. He pictured one police officer as the voice of skepticism, challenging the more conventional-thinking investigators who were positive that the boyfriend Brian was the killer.

This imaginary skeptic was really the voice of doubt in Rio's own mind, the one who thought a smart cop was going to piece things together and track Rio down.

He watched the drama play out as he drove.

"I don't know, chief," said the smart cop. "I'm just not buying that the boyfriend did it."

"What's your evidence?" said the lieutenant, squinting through a cloud of cigarette smoke outside the police station.

"We're supposed to believe that the victim's car just happened to break down a mile from his house?"

"Cars break down all the time."

"And instead of calling for help, she somehow makes her way through the woods to approach the place from the back-yard," the smart cop said, his voice rising with incredulity. "And then the boyfriend kills her when she arrives?"

"She was killed with the boyfriend's rake, a blunt blow to the head," said the superior officer. "There's no other DNA on her. There's no evidence that anyone else killed her. The boyfriend must be hiding something. Her family said they had fights. If he didn't do it, then who did?"Rio laughed to himself as he steered through town, careful to stay below the speed limit.

"Maybe you're right," said the skeptical officer.

Listen to your boss's wise words.

Maybe it wasn't the greatest frame job in the world, but he pushed away the doubts and reassured himself that it was good enough. The police would be chasing their tails for months, and even if they never charged the boyfriend with the crime, Rio knew that he had created enough of a cloud of confusion to keep them away from his own door.

He was the best in the world at what he did, after all, and he was chosen.

CHAPTER FOURTEEN

SHE STARED AT THE CEILING FOR HOURS

THE RELATIONSHIP between Jenny and Sam Longford had been going through ups and downs for several months. Jenny had been successfully able to continue to hide her anxiety and alienation over her sessions with Rio. She frankly thought that Sam was so self-centered that he wouldn't have noticed if she was showing signs of all the strain she was under. They continued to see each other at least a couple of times a week, and the companionship and company were better than facing every night alone. He was still able to make her laugh sometimes, and that was one of the few spots of relief in her life.

Anyway, it was the kind of relationship Jenny felt she deserved.

The pair started spending more time together after Sam was assigned to investigate the Karen Concord case.

It wasn't long before Jenny thought she knew what had happened to Karen. Then she became the instigator of she and Sam spending more time together, staying up late and talking. She found herself probing Sam for information while trying not to be too obvious about it.

At one point early on, Sam believed there was a good chance that he was going to be transferred off the investigation. Jenny's anger in reaction to this surprised her. But she had committed so much time recently to Sam, and the line between simple companionship and keeping tabs on the case had become increasingly blurred. Hearing updates on the investigation gave her a sense of control.

She was relieved when Sam announced that his supervisor had decided to keep him on the case after all.

Jenny's feelings toward Rio were like a sun that had flamed with unthinkable heat of hatred, but which after exploding, was cooled and dark, simmering in space. She no longer hated him or really cared about him at all. Helping him was a necessity. If Sam was closing in on Rio in any way, she could warn the killer in time to counter the investigation. She could keep buying time, calculating what came next.

She felt that she had been running for her life for so long that she barely understood who she had become.

Sam had excitedly and frequently talked about the Concord case in the early days of the investigation—the murder was frequently in the media, and he was asked to go on camera and explain the particulars of what the police had learned—or at least what he could share with the public. But his sharing started to decrease over time, something that displeased Jenny but which she was forced to hide.

She needed to know everything Sam knew. This led her to a sort of experiment in behaviorism.

Sam was motivated by seeking excitement. In Jenny's observation, this was pretty common in people who worked in law enforcement. Consistent with this psychological profile, Sam was fixated on sex. He sought it frequently—from Jenny and from other romantic partners (it had been some time since there was a pretense that their relationship was exclusive).

Jenny found herself less and less interested in sex, feeling out of touch with her body in light of the daily stress she was under. And considering the framework of the very uncertain level of commitment in their relationship, Jenny didn't feel particularly obligated to satisfy all of Sam's frequent advances.

But one night, when she and Sam were watching a murder mystery on TV, she found herself getting aroused and initiating sex—something she did so rarely that Sam seemed pleasantly shocked. A few nights later, Sam suggested they watch another murder investigation movie, a not-so-subtle ploy for a repeat performance in the bedroom.

Jenny realized that she may have found a way to motivate Sam to keep her consistently in the loop on the Concord murder investigation.

She put her theory into operation by patiently waiting for

the next time Sam made mention of the case. He brought up the fact that he had been reviewing DNA evidence in the case, trying to piece together a better timeline of events. While he was talking, she put her hand on his shoulder and gave him a long kiss.

"This is kind of weird," she said. "But can I tell you something? Without you judging me, I mean."Sam put his arm around her. "Go ahead," he said.

"When you talk about the case, I get turned on." She pretended to be embarrassed. "I'm sorry. I know that's kind of sick."

Sam pulled her tighter. "I can talk about my work as much as you want," he said. "If I only knew all this time about this secret of what does it for you, then my police work is pretty much all I ever would have talked about."

After they were done in the bedroom, Sam fell asleep and Jenny lay staring up at the ceiling.

He thought he was conditioning her behavior. But he was the one being conditioned.

I have to be careful not to be too obvious about this. But this is my ticket to learning about the case in real time. This is how I can make sure that I'm one step ahead of the Big Deal coming out into the open.

She stared at the ceiling for hours before she could sleep even for just a few minutes.

The next time Jenny was over at Sam's house, she told him about how the details of the case kept coming to her mind, and that she had begun to realize that true-crime scenarios were the key that unlocked her libido.

She kind of felt like herself, and in a way she didn't.

Sam was eager to make love and keep talking. After sex was the only time that Sam was ever particularly emotional, as though some barrier in his feelings was temporarily lowered. It was the only time he ever opened up, and as they lay together, she could see that something was bothering him.

"What's going on?" she asked.

"Well, it's the Concord case," he said, stroking the side of her face.

"Did something happen?" she asked, trying to keep her voice level and even. "Has there been some new discovery?" "Anything but," Sam said, shaking his head in frustration. "To tell you the truth, I'm starting to really worry that we may never solve it. The evidence just doesn't point to any one conclusion. I'm starting to feel like I'm just going around in circles."

That was music to Jenny's ears.

More frequent sexual activity between Sam and Jenny started to affect the nature of their relationship. The more sex they had, the more Sam wanted. She had started to try to lose herself in sheer physicality, but things started to change. Sam's level of sexual assertiveness was normally pretty high, but still in the playful range, but the more they had sex, the more he started to push the boundary between being assertive and being aggressive. It was as though a veil was slowly being lifted, and she was seeing him for what he really was.

She wanted to keep the information flowing, so she simply

dealt with what Sam was becoming, but her level of resentment increased as his behavior worsened. Their relationship was outwardly fiery, but inside, she felt completely numb.

The case was proceeding slowly. Sam and his colleagues were fixated on the boyfriend, just as Rio had predicted during one of their weekly counseling sessions. Still, the physical evidence led to more questions than answers—and it didn't all point to the boyfriend.

Some of the theories the police were now entertaining strained credulity. One theory was that Karen Concord had broken down on the road and, after the boyfriend had gone out to find her after she didn't show up on time, they had a vicious argument. Knocked unconscious but still alive, Karen had been driven back to the house by Brian and had subsequently died in the backyard.

The police knew that the lower radiator hose in Karen's car was the cause of her pulling over, but they believed that the hose had simply failed with age and was unrelated to the homicide. They also tended to dismiss the fact that Karen's body seemed to have been dragged prior to being left in the backyard. The assumption was that Karen had tried to run away, but the boyfriend assaulted her and pulled her through the yard.

At certain moments, Jenny was tempted to offer advice to Sam that would throw him even further off the trail, but he was doing such a good job of confusing himself that she didn't see the need.

A couple of weeks went by without any new developments

in the case. Sam had started talking about random news from his colleagues' investigations and even from books he'd read and movies he'd seen in an obvious effort to make Jenny aroused. But Jenny was feeling exhausted, so she started applying the brakes. Sam was hyper-sensitive to her reduced sexual interest, which led to an argument.

"I don't understand," he said petulantly. "You've been in the mood all the time lately. What the hell changed? Did I do something wrong?" "These stories from the movies don't do it for me anymore," she told him. "What gets me going is when you're involved in a case. I picture you looking all confident, with everyone hanging on your every word. That's what's sexy."

"There isn't always something new to talk about," Sam explained. "There just haven't been any new developments." "I know, but we've been getting it on a lot lately, haven't we?" she asked. "We have to slow down a little at some point, right?" "Why do we have to slow down? I'm happy the way things are!" She knew how temperamental Sam could be, and she got in the habit of placating him when he showed up with offerings of other investigations and even theories about famous unsolved cases.

One week, they had sex nearly every day, and when she was having a glass of wine later, a thought occurred to her: how different, really, were Sam and Rio? She had spent what seemed like endless hours alone in a room with Rio, a man who had raped and killed several women, and he had never physically tried anything with her. Yet, here she was with a police officer—a man who considered himself her boyfriend—and she couldn't seem to keep him off of her.

Yet both made their demands of her.

She thought about Sam's theory about how police and criminals were actually very much alike. She wondered if the only real difference between Sam and Rio was in how they expressed their drives and the nature of their delusions.

And she wondered at moments like these about how deluded she herself might be. After all, she was the link that bound the two men together.

Jenny wasn't happy with Sam. But she was glad that she had been putting up with him when a new development in the case gave her the opportunity to put her finger on the scale. Sam was deep in doubt about Brian as the murderer, and he had started to wonder if someone who knew Karen might have killed her and dumped the body in Brian's yard to throw off the authorities.

Brian himself—a twenty-something with a community college degree who worked in an animal shelter—was hardly a classic murderer. Quiet, calm, and extremely upset in the wake of Karen's death, he was a main suspect, but something about the circumstances of Karen's death had started to gnaw at Sam.

"I think it was someone who knew her," Sam said. "It's just a hunch, but I keep coming back to it."

Jenny listened. Rio, of course, had been a stranger to Karen Concord.

"Makes sense," she agreed. "Isn't it true that most murder

victims know their attacker?"Jenny hadn't known Rio the night of the Big Deal. But she had known David.

"Yeah," Sam said. He seemed lost in thought for a moment. "But maybe I'm wrong. Maybe I need to go in another direction entirely."

They were sitting in Jenny's dining nook, having polished off a dinner of take-out sushi. Jenny felt a slight tingle of alarm.

"What kind of other direction?" she asked.

Sam took a sip of water. She knew him well enough to know that his internal cognitive wheels were turning.

"What do you think?" Jenny said carefully, putting a note of doubt into her voice. "Like, there's some kind of killer out there on the loose who Karen didn't know?""I don't know. Maybe." Sam looked up at her. "I guess it's something we have to consider and look into either way."

"It doesn't make sense," Jenny said firmly.

Part of her was listening to herself, observing her actions. She started to clear their plates from the dining table.

"How so?" Sam asked.

"How would that work?" Jenny frowned, wanting to convey that the scenario made no sense to her. "Some random stranger just happens to see her broken down on the road and decides to kill her? I mean, there's no one else's DNA or fingerprints anywhere, right? There's no evidence to support that idea."

"You're right," Sam said, looking down at the table. She could see he felt dejected. "There's nothing. I'm just grasping at straws."

"There's your answer," Jenny said.

She knew she should have been experiencing conflicted emotions, but she wasn't. She was looking for her path to safety, every moment of every day.

It would have been as impossible to resurrect her old sense of moral values as it would have been to bring one of Rio's victims back to life. Both were dead and in the past.

All Jenny could do was desperately try to hold onto her future.

CHAPTER FIFTEEN

SOME LINES SHOULDN'T BE CROSSED

JENNY WAS CAREFUL about what she said to Rio, especially when it came to Sam. She didn't want to seem evasive, so she revealed some superficial details about her relationship, but she omitted the fact that Sam was working the Karen Concord case. She mentioned Sam only as her on-again, off-again boyfriend, and Rio seemed mostly uninterested.

Since the murder, Rio had skipped two sessions, leaving only a to-the-point voicemail saying he couldn't make it, but to hold his usual slot and he would pay her for the inconvenience. When he finally did show up, almost a month since the murder, Rio explained that his mind had been too occupied with remembering and reviewing all the details of the crime to come in for a counseling appointment.

It had been both a relief not to see him as well as a source of dread.

"I'm ready to talk now," Rio said. He was wearing a new pair of work boots and his hair had been newly styled, making him look several years younger.

Jenny nodded, trying to pretend not to be interested. In fact, she was fascinated despite herself, feeling almost a magnetic pull toward what he was going to tell her. She was actually amazed to be sitting across from someone who had recently killed someone.

"Saving Karen was a little harder than I thought," Rio explained. "I got greedy. It wasn't part of the original plan, but I decided to try to frame the boyfriend."

The boyfriend, Brian Armstrong, had been the subject of speculation in the local news as well as with the police, as Jenny knew well.

"What *was* the plan?" Jenny asked.

"To start with, not to kill her so quickly," Rio looked up with a furrowed brow. "That really cut into how much I could enjoy myself."

Jenny looked down at her notepad. She had stopped writing anything down weeks ago, but it gave her a place to look when she was uncomfortable.

"I know that offends your sensibilities," Rio said.

"You're saying you wish you had more time to rape her?" Jenny asked.

Rio ran his hands through his hair. "It doesn't matter, there'll be plenty of time in heaven," he said. "But the plan was to put her body in my freezer for a few weeks, then I was going to . . . let's say *dismantle* it and put it in a marsh."

"Sounds like you had thought it through."

"I did, but with her dying so quickly, it no longer made sense to bring her back to the house," Rio continued. "All risk, no reward. But the obvious shortcoming at that point was that there was no obvious suspect. But I knew she was driving to the boyfriend's house, so it all just kind of fell into place."

"It's a good thing you can think on your feet."

"Yeah, but the counting in my head and the doubting thoughts started up. I got so anxious I couldn't focus on one thing to the next the way I needed to. I got obsessed with making sure nothing came loose on her body when I was dragging her. I got obsessed with all the objects in the backyard."

Jenny understood that Rio had an attack of his OCD during his crime. She imagined with some horror the scene that must have been taking place in his mind.

"The OCD is affecting you in a variety of ways," Jenny said, trying to stay as professional as possible. "From a clinical point of view, your entire rationale for killing is based on obsession, and your acts of . . . *saving* are the result of compulsions."

For a moment, Jenny forgot that she was helping a murderer reflect on his homicidal actions. When a realization of the truth came to her in the next instant, she shrugged it off. Now that she was back in her office with Rio, she felt even more estranged from her own sense of morality. There was no right or wrong: those were just concepts to torture herself with. Best to simply put one foot in front of the other. Rio was just a client, murder was just another consequence of psychological imbalance, and Jenny's job was to offer insights.

She was somewhat surprised when Rio leaned forward on the sofa with a look of genuine curiosity. "OK. Tell me more," he said.

"Obsessions often start with something you arguably should be doing, but then push you much farther than necessary," Jenny said. "Like checking to make sure nothing came loose. It's smart not to leave evidence behind, but you're describing taking being careful to such an extreme that it impedes your ability to think clearly."

"Exactly. It was overkill." Rio seemed not to recognize the dark pun he had just uttered. "I wasn't leaving anything behind, there wasn't a need to keep checking and checking. How do I beat this? I'm not always going to be able to exactly follow my plans, and this could lead to me making a real mistake."

"Don't give into the obsession," she said firmly. It was advice she had given to others in her practice. "Go out of your way to violate its rules. Show it hatred, show it disrespect."

"Disrespect," Rio repeated.

"That's exactly what you do to women," Jenny added without thinking. "Do it to the obsession as well."

"*Evil* women," Rio corrected her. "Not all women."

Jenny remembered her insight that Rio had never treated her badly, while her supposed lover had been treating her rougher and rougher.

"All right," Jenny said.

Rio nodded, deep in thought. "OK, I will disrespect the

obsession."Outside the window, a blackbird had perched on a branch close to the window of Jenny's office. It peered inside with its head cocked. Jenny imagined that it was looking at them with disapproval.

"The last woman I saved took place far behind my ideal schedule," Rio said out of nowhere. "Because I had to wait for the rain to cleanse."

Jenny nodded. She tried to take a deep breath, but it came out ragged and she was only able to get about a half-lungful of air.

"I feel a lot of pressure to keep moving forward with the mission," Rio said.

The muscles in her face felt impossibly tight as she tried not to show an outward reaction. She allowed herself to think that somehow this might all come to an end. A battle of conflicting emotions was taking place within her when Rio aimed an intense and focused gaze into her eyes.

"How are things going with the cop?" he asked.

"Fine," Jenny said.

"Did some looking into him," Rio said. "I didn't realize that he was a detective. Pretty fancy."

"They don't know anything about you," Jenny said through clenched teeth. "They're off on a wild goose chase, just like you intended."

"You two having a lot of sex?" Rio asked bluntly.

Jenny frowned and stayed silent. Rio pursed his lips and looked away from her with dripping disdain.

"You know what angers me?" he said. "When I feel like

someone thinks they are too good to tell me things."

He stayed on the sofa with his body language tight. But he remained still, looking away.

Are his feelings hurt?

"Some things are personal," Jenny said, trying to inject a note of friendliness into her voice. "Some lines shouldn't be crossed."

"All that matters for me is the mission, all that matters for you is being free," Rio said, like a teacher explaining a simple math problem. "And I tell you about my feelings. Why can't you tell me about yours?" *Is he getting off on this?*

"What do you want?" she said brightly. "Do you want to know the details of what it's like when we have sex?" Rio paused and looked at her, seemingly seriously contemplating the question.

"No, I want you to stay with him." He paused, apparently wanting her to understand the undertone of what he had just said.

"I might," Jenny said. "I might not."

"You will, at least for a while." Rio fixed her with a curious look. "But I want to know why you're with him in the first place. I want to know what it takes to get a woman like you. A smart woman, powerful."

"Try not killing people to start with," Jenny said.

"I know you think you're funny," Rio told her. "But someday you'll see that I'm right. You'll understand what makes me a hero."

"I'll bet you hate people like Sam," Jenny said defiantly. "People who try to do good in the world."

For an instant, Jenny wondered if she had gone too far. But Rio seemed to be enjoying this back and forth, breaking down the barriers of counselor and client.

"Not at all. I completely understand why he would want to catch someone like me and shoot me dead," Rio said calmly. "He believes he's working on the side of justice. He simply can't see the truth. It's not his fault he wasn't chosen."

Even though Jenny had been trying to defend Sam, she felt her feelings shifting. Strictly as a matter of who was more dangerous to her personally, she had to admit it was Sam, with his sexual pressure and aggression. With Rio, she at least had a confidant who was keeping her secret. Rio and Jenny were two people who could only confide in one another.

Don't feel compassion for him. He's the one who got you into this terrible thing in the first place.

A good counselor was able to put herself in the position of the client, to see the world through his lens—if only long enough to make constructive observations and give useful advice.

Don't go there. Don't look at the world through his eyes.

Jenny realized again that she had erased her boundaries and redrawn them to the point that she barely knew herself.

But she had to hold on. She had to not let the delusion inside.

CHAPTER SIXTEEN

THAT WOULD MAKE ME MAD, TOO

JENNY'S RELATIONSHIP with Sam, at least for her, was devolving into passive-aggressive feelings and behavior.

From her perspective, their relationship was increasingly mechanical, insensitive, and repetitive. They had fallen into a pattern of discussing Sam's work and having sex, and not much else. Their conversations were devoid of any intimate sharing of emotions because they were using each other for their own benefit.

It had been two months since the Karen Concord homicide. It was also nearly the one-year anniversary of taking on Rio as a client. She worked diligently in her mind and emotions to accept the reality of her situation, but something was changing inside her.

She had always been careful and cautious. Now she felt nihilistic, bleak, and often angry. Rio had taken away any sense of security, comfort, and self-assuredness from her, all in the name of what he wanted with no regard for her own needs. He had also made her determined not to let another person do the same to her.

Sam was making no progress on solving the murder. The trail was cold. There wasn't enough evidence to charge Brian Armstrong and there was no secondary suspect.

Jenny started to pull back from Sam. It wasn't difficult: just deny him sex, she realized, and he would quickly lose interest and look elsewhere.

Her name was Taylor Stolly, a young female neighbor of Sam's who lived with and cared for her elderly grandfather. Jenny and Sam had gotten into a fight as their relationship deteriorated, with Jenny finding herself suspicious and jealous despite herself. Sam had been able to keep the new relationship a secret, but then he got angry and couldn't hide the truth. He confirmed it with callous, lacerating precision, but in the next breath was telling Jenny that he wanted to keep seeing her.

She had known there were other women before, but now she didn't want to go through all the uncertainty of being with him while he was also with someone else. So they broke up, like they had before.

It felt unsatisfying, with both somehow knowing that they would probably slide together again the next time they were both lonely and unattached.

It felt like what she deserved.

The pretense of any professional counseling relationship had pretty much evaporated. Rio still paid in cash at the end of each hour, but now, Jenny was sharing more details about her own life, such as her failed relationship with Sam. She didn't share any sexual details with Rio, though she sensed he would have liked it, but she was able to reveal a great deal about her own emotional turmoil and Sam's insensitivity.

"You're breaking up with him," Rio said.

"I think you're in the clear, if that's what you're thinking," Jenny told him.

"Not just me," Rio pointed out. "But OK. What's the problem, really? What did he do to lose you?" "It feels like he has no idea that I have needs, too," Jenny said. "I want a real partner, someone I can rely on. He just takes and takes. There's no support. It never feels like he wants to be specifically with me."

This was the first time in a while that Jenny had articulated any sense that she deserved anything out of her personal life. It was as though some part of her that had been shut away had flickered back to life.

"Sounds to me like you're clingy," Rio said. He clearly didn't mean to be humorous or offensive, and in fact was getting into the spirit of the conversation.

"Maybe. Sort of," Jenny admitted. "I haven't thought about it in a while. I want to be close to someone. I want to be with someone who appreciates me and connects to my feelings."

Rio just looked at her. "I'm not sure I understand," he said. *I'm talking about my emotional needs with a psychopath.*

"Never mind," Jenny said. "Let's talk about—"

"No, this is good," Rio said. "You should talk about this. Can you describe something that he did wrong?" Jenny thought about it for a while.

"Right around last Valentine's Day, we went out shopping and I found a ring that I liked," Jenny remembered. "It was silver with an amethyst."

"Amethyst," Rio repeated. "Purple stone. Pretty."

"It wasn't an expensive ring," Jenny said. "And I hinted that I wanted him to buy it for me. Valentine's Day came and went. No ring. I was mad but I didn't want to admit it, so I ended up starting a fight about something else. It was a terrible fight."

"Violent?" Rio asked.

"No, but a lot of yelling." Jenny paused. "Two days later, he shows up with a ring with a peridot. You know, like emerald green."

Rio shook his head. "I get it," he said. "You were mad because he didn't follow your orders. That would make me mad, too."

"It's not that he didn't follow my orders," Jenny said. "It's because he didn't care enough about me to buy me the ring I wanted."

"But he bought you a ring," Rio said.

"It was the wrong one!"

Rio stared blankly at Jenny. This was one of the few times she had really tried to speak with him like a normal person, and his look was a textbook example of lack of empathy. It occurred to her that this was why people saw there was something wrong with Rio, how he appeared creepy and cold. In a therapeutic setting, for a time she had thought he was simply repressed or suffering from attachment trauma. But it was definitely something else.

Jenny switched back to counselor mode. She had to try to help him make some kind of change, even if on some level, she knew it was impossible.

She listed a few movies she had watched recently, hoping to find a story they both knew as common ground. But Rio wasn't much of a moviegoer and she quickly became frustrated. She looked around the office and finally saw a book on the shelf. She had had it since college—a collection of the works of Edgar Allan Poe.

"Let's try this," she said. "Just sit still and listen. Please."

She read him "The Raven," the story of a man haunted by the memories of a lost love who is reminded of his grief by a determined, cryptic, and single-minded blackbird. In the story, a raven visits the man on a cold December evening and repeats the word "nevermore," which the protagonist interprets as meaning that he will never see his lost love. When she was finished reading, Rio shifted on the sofa uncomfortably. She couldn't tell if he had been able to follow or not.

"What do you think the guy in the story was feeling?" she asked him.

"Probably pissed off," Rio offered, seeming unsure of himself. "That dumb bird wouldn't leave him alone."

"What did he want the bird to tell him?" Jenny asked.

"Not sure," Rio said blankly. "Something other than 'nevermore,' I guess. It's just stupid, don't you think?" Jenny's reaction was something between shock and disappointment, but she wasn't worried about him being able to read the subtlety of her expression. She wondered what school must have been like for him, unable to empathize with the feelings of another human being. It must have been a matter of constant anger and incomprehension.

"Maybe we can revisit this later," she told him.

She spent the rest of the session trying to work through the concept of empathy with Rio, couching it as something he would need to know about in order to best fulfill his mission.

"All the information you need to empathize is available to you," Jenny explained. "You just need to be able to interpret it."

"I've never been able to do that," Rio said calmly. "Eileen told me it was part of my being chosen. She said I was above the feelings of ordinary people."

Jenny blinked. What a terrible thing to instill in a young man with Rio's psychological characteristics.

"Think about this," she said. "What do you think Karen Concord was feeling right before you killed her?" Rio looked around the room. "I'm not sure she felt anything," he said. "I hit her just about out of the blue."

"She had no clue what was about to happen?" "Well, not entirely," Rio told her. "I gave her one little clue, right before I hit her in the head. Just a little hint that I had been following her and knew her routine." "Why did you do that?" Jenny asked. "Why did you tip your hand like that?" "Well, I knew I was going to hit her pretty hard," he replied. "I didn't think she was going to die right then, but I knew she probably wasn't going to be totally conscious ever again." Jenny stayed silent, feeling a tingling on the back of her neck.

"I guess I figured I wanted her to know that I was there to kill her," he said. "I didn't want her to die and not understand that."

Jenny worked through his logic. "But wouldn't she figure out you had killed her when she awoke in the afterlife?" "I've always figured the women I save will only have their own memories to rely on," he said. "Who's going to tell them what happened on earth if they don't know it for themselves?" "I don't know," Jennie admitted. "Angels?" "I'm sure angels have more important things to do than whisper in the ears of evil women to let them know what happened at the end of their lives," Rio said with exasperation. "Now you're just being ridiculous."

Jenny rubbed her forehead. *She* was being ridiculous. Not the man who killed for sex slaves in the afterlife.

"Back to the point," she said. "Why does it matter if she gives you credit?" "If she didn't know I was the one to save her, why should she fear me?"

That was it, she realized: fear was the only emotion that Rio could recognize, or care about, in other people. He was able to recognize fear states most strongly based on the observable behavior he saw. He was broadly aware of other emotional states, and could even name them, but he wasn't capable of feeling those emotions himself or particularly motivated to try. He demonstrated some cognitive empathy, but with a total absence of emotional empathy.

Ultimately, nothing truly mattered to Rio beyond how he could use it to further his own interests. The subjective experiences and emotions of other people were like raw data being fed into a computer, simply components in a calculation leading to a result. The only factors that limited his capacity for rape and murder were his religious beliefs and the consequences should he be caught. His religion constrained, at least in theory, whom he could assault and murder, and the criminal justice system forced him at least to be cautious. An arrest would mean he couldn't complete his mission, which, for him, had profound metaphysical consequences.

This realization, in a roundabout way, made Jenny feel fractionally more comfortable with Rio. She didn't think he would target her at any point because she didn't think he would decide she was evil. And she also didn't mind the small additional reassurance that their connection made Jenny a potentially unwise target if Rio wanted to stay out of prison because of their connection as counselor and client.

But how strong was that connection? He always paid in cash, after all.

Jenny thought about the people who might have seen Rio coming and going from her office in the time he had been receiving counseling from her. He had an obsessive habit of entering the waiting room only after the client she had just seen had left the building. After each session was over, Rio would immediately head for the bathroom at the other end of the hallway, and he wouldn't leave until Jenny had escorted her next client into her office.

She wondered if he hewed to this habit simply because of his OCD.

Or is it because he doesn't want anyone to know he's here?

"Are you listening?" Rio asked.

"I'm sorry." Jenny rubbed her eyes. "What were we saying?""We're on the clock here," he told her.

"I know," she said. "Please, just remind me."

"If the woman I saved doesn't know it was me before she leaves this earth, how can I expect her to fear me in the afterlife?" he repeated.

As was so often the case, his logic was utterly twisted, but airtight on its own terms. He was watching her expectantly, wanting an answer.

"I think she would fear you in any case," Jenny said simply.

"But you understand my point," Rio said, blankly staring at her. "They *have* to know. Their fear is the basis of understanding their evil."

Jenny, in that moment, questioned her certainty that Rio would never target her.

CHAPTER SEVENTEEN

EXCITEMENT AND CAUTION WERE DOING BATTLE

THE INVESTIGATION INTO the Karen Concord murder stalled in late November, according to the local TV and newspaper reports. With this assurance, Rio felt comfortable contemplating his seventh homicide.

In order to stay true to his strategy, he knew that the next victim to be saved had to be different from all the ones who had come before. He had been thinking obsessively, and even before Karen's murder, he knew that the one after her would probably take place inside a victim's home. He knew this with the certainty of a visionary.

From Rio's point of view, committing a murder inside a private home came with various logistical advantages as well as disadvantages. It would remove the chaos of the streets and the public eye, such as encountering passersby on the side of the road, but his planning and flexibility would be limited by location and the victim he selected to save from evil.

He started looking around. Rio became increasingly frustrated with how good and guileless many of his potential victims appeared to be. It was a considerable obstacle to the mission.

But he knew he could subtly shift his standards of perception as to what he considered evil. It was part of his gift. This made it easier to justify waiving some of his internal regulations, but he was aware of his own contradictions. He would have to deliberately compensate for softening one rule by obsessively adhering to the rest in the strictest way possible.

This was his mindset when he started patrolling for victims at the anchor department store at a mall several miles away. There were plenty to choose from. Though it wasn't yet Thanksgiving, there were already plenty of shoppers looking to get a head start on Christmas. There were twinkling lights and festive decorations, and hordes of people paying no attention to him as he moved through their midst.

When Rio would go on patrol in this manner, he would always shop for everyday items that he actually needed and follow a reasonably normal path through the store. He knew that the store was full of cameras and he didn't want to stand out to any security personnel, uniformed or undercover. He knew it was possible that for any victim he saved, the police might track her activities back to the store and review the security camera recordings. Rio didn't want to be the creepy man walking behind the missing woman that caused the officers assigned to the case to stop the recording, point at the monitor, and say, "That's our guy!"

In keeping with his typical practice of providing the police with a good alternative suspect to direct attention away from himself, Rio ideally liked the victim to have some type of interaction with a suspicious individual in the days preceding the homicide—or, ideally, on the day itself. But this was a goal that was sometimes out of his control. As with all his previous killings, his superior planning had to run hand-in-hand with a degree of luck in order for it to go forward.

The luck was in the woman's favor if Rio was able to save her. There was no escape from the torments of Hell.

Rio expanded his patrols of stores, all of them ringing with Christmas music and the forced cheer of the season. He found several suitable victims during the next few outings after he decided to widen his perception of who might be harboring secret wickedness.

He followed four different women home in the course of a single week, only to find that each of their houses was a veritable fortress. One had a loud security system you could hear being deactivated from the street. Another had the most active and nosy neighbors Rio had seen in a long time. The remaining two seemed more encouraging, but the geography and positioning of their houses were not—one house was on a street with a plethora of visible security cameras on several homes, while the other was on a street where the houses were set so close together that noises would probably carry and alert the neighbors.

These women would not be saved. Rio grimly accepted the torments that awaited them.

Rio was getting concerned about the sheer number of times he had patrolled the same stores. He was running out of items on his shopping list, and he was worried that his sheer appearance on so many security cameras might get noticed and draw suspicion. To adjust, Rio kept modifying his appearance. He had his standard nondescript baseball cap pulled down and his jacket with the collar turned up, but he bought a fake beard at a costume shop and learned how to apply it convincingly after a few tries. When he was wearing it, he looked like a different person entirely. He went to the thrift store and bought a couple of different jackets and caps, and even found a pair of glasses with more-or-less clear lenses. He wondered why he had never thought of this before—it would be another skill in his repertoire.

He had been tired and ready to give up for the night when he was patrolling a Walmart next to the highway. He saw someone who made him glad he hadn't given up on the evening.

Almost on cue, he turned the corner into an aisle of Christmas decorations and he saw her. She was wearing exercise clothes and a puffy jacket, with her sandy hair pulled back from her pretty features with some kind of hair band. Her voice was raised in an abrasive and aggressive tone.

She was arguing pretty fiercely about the accuracy of a sales flyer from the newspaper. Her face was clenched up in anger, and her tone was superior and haughty as she overwhelmed the stammering teenager who had the misfortune to try to help her. Rio thought to himself that he didn't even need that level of bad behavior to see the evil in someone, but he silently thanked her for putting in the extra effort.

He followed her at a distance through the store after that encounter, weaving through the housewares and the haircare products when, to his amazement, he saw her approach another potential victim. This one was even more desirable, but he sensed he would be faithful to the first.

Rio pretended to be fascinated by a display of hair conditioners as he listened to them talk.

"You about done?" the first one asked.

The second one was even prettier. A little taller, with a real wicked expression that she didn't even try to hide.

"Yeah," she said. "Did you get everything on Mom's list?" *So they're sisters.*

He followed them at a distance as they went up to the self-serve checkout. Rio moved silently behind them as he started to bag up his own purchases, slumping his shoulders, his fake beard and glasses making him look like someone at least ten years older.

They were waiting on the sidewalk outside Walmart, purchases in hand, when Rio silently walked past them. He heard a car pull up and the doors open, and he pretended to drop his keys so he could turn around and get a look.

The car was parked in the fire lane. *So entitled.* The driver was a man about the same age as the women. Rio didn't know anything about his first target, her sister, or the man driving the car, but that would soon change.

As Rio followed them home, the car kept turning down familiar streets. It was getting uncomfortably close to Rio's own neighborhood. Even though his excitement was building and the demon drive was barking at him, he remained only cautiously optimistic. It might be a very poor idea to conduct a home invasion in a house so close to his own.

Excitement and caution were doing battle in his mind.

When the car finally slowed down to park, Rio saw that apparently the woman from the Walmart lived with her sister and the man in the same residence. It was a single-family home, and it was only about three miles from Rio's.

This complication initially disappointed him. As he sat in his truck down the street, watching them unpack the car, he started thinking of scenarios in which he lured the other man and woman away from the house so he could save his intended target.

He had thought he would be faithful to the first sister, but now he was having trouble deciding which one to save. They each deserved it so much. He distracted himself by focusing on the house itself. Its position wasn't ideal. There were homes on either side as well as lining the opposite side of the street. There were also houses on the far side of the backyard. But there was good news as well—there was lots of space between the houses and plenty of street parking nearby.

The next day, Rio visited the house again. He saw the mail

carrier stopping at the mailbox and, after waiting a few moments to be sure no one was looking, he stole the mail and swiftly drove away.

He drove home, taking a circuitous route, looking in his rearview mirror to make sure no one was following. Stealing the mail had been a risk, but it was one he knew he could pull off if no one was looking for a total of about fifteen seconds. The reward that came with the risk was considerable.

At his kitchen table, Rio sifted through a stack of bills and junk mail, and pieced things together. His initial target's name was Margaret Tuffin. Her sister's name was Rhonda Bressett, and the man was named Stephen Bressett. It appeared that Rhonda and Stephen were married, and that Margaret lived with them on at least a semi-permanent basis.

Two days later, Rio took another chance and returned the mail to the mailbox. No one saw him and he believed he had enough information to begin to plan his attack. As he got back into the Tacoma to drive away, something caught his attention in the house's driveway: a 2009 Honda Accord with distinctive damage to its front bumper.

The winter sky was dark and cloudy the next day when it came to him: he recognized the Honda. Nathan, one of the newer mechanics at BNR, had recently lost control of an air hammer when he was working on that very car. Nathan had been standing by his toolbox at the front of the car when he pulled the trigger on the air hammer before he properly fit a chisel in it. The result was a scratch in the shape of a circle on the front bumper—it joined up with some flaws already there to make, Rio thought, something like a happy face.

Rio pulled up the file at work. The owner of the car was Rhonda Bressett. It looked like BNR had offered to repaint the bumper for free, but Rhonda hadn't brought the car back yet to take them up on the offer. It was the kind of superficial repair that the mechanics in the shop would sometimes place bets on whether the customer would ever bring it back to be fixed.

As Rio went through his work shift, taking calls and fixing flats and towing breakdowns, he started to feel overwhelmed by the complexities of selecting either Margaret or Rhonda to be saved.

The strategic questions alone were daunting. What, for instance, was Rio going to do with Rhonda's husband and the sister he chose not to kill? Would it be necessary to find a way to justify killing all of them, instead of puzzling over the logistics of accounting for all three of them while saving only one?

Thoughts spun into obsession. He saw maps in his mind, wondering if there was enough distance between his house and theirs, or whether this amounted to targeting someone in his own backyard—a classic mistake. He wondered if the connection to BNR could work to his advantage, conveniently offering an explanation for evidence connecting him to the scene. On the other hand, it might be a liability—a too-obvious connection to the victim. He was frustrated beyond measure.

The demon drive kept its voice in his ears, trying to override the need to be extraordinarily careful.

"Hey, you hear me?" said Stan, his supervisor at work. Rio

had just pulled in the tow truck and was standing in the break-room, thinking, calculating.

"Yeah," Rio said, looking up. "What do you need?""Don't need much," Stan said. "You just looked like you were thinking some pretty deep shit."

"Always," Rio said, and tried to convincingly smile. "You know how it goes. Living the dream."

CHAPTER EIGHTEEN

HER MOTION WAS SMOOTH AND DELIBERATE

AT RIO'S NEXT SESSION, Jenny had to hide her shock at his psychological condition. He was speaking too quickly, skipping over things, talking about three people she didn't know, rambling about surveillance cameras and records at work and the geography of his neighborhood.

He was in a full-blown episode of his OCD, speaking a language known only entirely to him, making references to numbers and mailboxes and things that she could have no possible way of knowing about.

But she knew what he was talking about underneath it all. Another save. She tried to will herself to take a long, deep breath to calm her central nervous system, but nothing was going to calm the burning in her chest and in her ears.

"Are you following me?" he asked, looking up from a rapid-fire recital of local department stores.

She would do what she did for any other patient. Jenny got up and went to her desk, where she found a blank pad of paper and a ballpoint pen. She went back to her chair and handed them to Rio across the table.

"Here," she said. "Write down all these thoughts. Take your time. Try to create some organization. Remember, don't respect the obsessive thoughts. Get control over them."

Rio started to write everything down, frowning, crossing some things out and drawing lines between others. As soon as he finished one line, he was on to the next. She glanced down at the pad, happy that his cribbed handwriting was almost impossible to read, especially upside down.

She started to think through a clinical observation. Now, Rio didn't seem anxious. As his visible agitation started to decrease through the writing exercise, he simply seemed obsessed, perfectionistic, and in a state of heightened excitability.

She knew why.

"I have to cover every angle," he said, almost to himself. "I know you understand that, if anyone does."

Jenny made a noncommittal noise.

"Is it possible to observe that writing everything down is lessening your drive for violence?" she then asked him, putting a sunny note in her voice.

"You know, I really feel I deserve this to be the best saving ever," he said as he looked up from the pad. "I was denied too much in the way things went down with Karen Concord. This one needs to make up for it."

The comment hung in the air. She looked at his angular features, the dark curls of his hair. She had never before been in the presence of such relentless narcissism.

He didn't care that she didn't reply. He started ripping the pages on which he had written out of the notebook.

Jenny took an inner inventory. She didn't know what was there anymore. There was no way to justify her sitting there, no web of rationalization that could justify her continuing to run for her life at all costs. There was a deep, grievous pain inside her, but she was blunting it with ice and callousness.

What could I possibly say now? Who would even try to defend me?

She felt like a mannequin. Maybe she was getting closer to freedom. Perhaps not. At that moment, she couldn't even imagine what that freedom would constitute. Trying to save herself, she was making herself into another of Rio's victims—but instead of going to some twisted afterlife, she was condemning herself to a personal hell.

It felt like dying slowly, with a part of herself being sliced away and cauterized, leaving nothing to feel. Rio had brought her into his twisted labyrinth of delusion and perversion, burning away Jenny's hopes, dreams, and morals like so much fuel.

She sat in her office with him across from her, still engrossed in his pages of written evil, and she tried to hate him. But every attempt she made to dissolve into that hatred, every impulse she felt to lash out and kill him, simply doubled back and ricocheted into destructive energy directed at herself. She had an absurd image in her mind: Rio as made of rubber, and her striking him with all her might with a baseball bat. Every swing simply bounced off him and lashed her with all the force of her own anger.

Why bother swinging the damned bat?

She blamed and excoriated herself, then in her memory whirled back to the night when her act of self-defense led her to this moment, to this intolerable compromise.

"There are two possibilities," Rio said. "Their names are—"

"Don't," Jenny interrupted. "I can't."

A long silence.

"Woman A and Woman B," Rio finally spat out, in a tone that suggested, *Are you satisfied?*

She didn't say anything.

"I saw Woman A first. I saw her bring evil," Rio continued. "The other one is her sister. She's the more attractive one. I fantasize about her constantly."

Is he trying to get me to pick one? "You seem to forget that I think killing people is morally reprehensible," Jenny said slowly. "Why don't we start working together from there?" "The faster you help me choose, the faster we part ways."

This was of course his way of moving the goalposts yet again. At first, Jenny was supposed to help him work through his pathologies to appear more normal. In her hopes, this would have helped him *become* more normal. But he continually compromised her further, drawing her into an ethical maze.

"You keep returning to my motivation for getting you out of my life, and believe me, I want that," Jenny said slowly and clearly. "But is this really something you should rush? Maybe you should think about them more clearly as actual people and not just as objects for your fixation."Rio looked surprised. He seemed to have thought he had Jenny's help as a total co-conspirator. "OK, play it that way," he said. "But if you won't help me pick one, how am I going to figure it out?"

"Do both women really qualify to be *saved*?" she asked him. "Are they both really *evil*?"

Jenny drawled out both words, trying to convey contempt to Rio, but as usual only the literal meaning of her words had any impact on him. He was either uninterested or incapable of any subtlety of interpretation.

"Woman A qualifies," Rio said. "I haven't got anything on Woman B."

"Then why are we even talking?" Jenny asked.

Rio paused, looking out the window at the denuded winter trees. "Because I really want to find a way to save both of them," he said.

"Both of them don't need saving," Jenny blurted out, unsure what she was even trying to convince him of. "If you don't follow the rules you've set up, then what will it mean for you? How could you possibly still be a hero in heaven?"She closed her eyes. Here she was, pressuring a psychopath to follow his own perverted logic. None of it mattered, though maybe she could apply pressure to his tortured reasoning and save a stranger from harm.

"I do get very anxious whenever I break the rules," he admitted quietly. "I end up making mistakes, falling into the counting, all that nonsense and distraction. It's all my punishment for breaking with God's purpose for me."

"Are you implying that God gave you the OCD?""Who else could have?" Rio said with a mirthless laugh. "Nothing else explains it. Those thoughts keep me in line. Why else would they exist?""Because you have a mental disorder," Jenny said, keeping her tone nonconfrontational, speaking like a clinical counselor. "It forces those thoughts into your head and fills you with those drives. You're simply trying to deal with it all as best you can, but you have to understand what you're dealing with."Rio shifted on the sofa, rubbing his hand over his mouth, looking more agitated than he ever usually did.

"I don't have much use for your theories," he said. "And you know something else?""What?" she replied. She felt something cold in the middle of her chest.

"If you'd have just died that night like you were supposed to, there would be one less woman to save." He looked at her triumphantly, obviously realizing that he had shocked her. "Do you ever think about that?"Trying to stay calm and not take the bait, Jenny calmly pulled her handbag from her nearby desk and let it rest in her lap. She unzipped it and reached inside with her right hand. Her motion was smooth and deliberate, and she made eye contact with Rio as she felt the metal and plastic of the gun in her fingers.

Rio reached across the table with the precision and quickness of a snake. He grabbed the weapon before she was able to get it out of her purse. She was stunned by his sheer strength as he wrenched it effortlessly out of her hand.

Without any expression, he sat back on the sofa and slowly examined the weapon, checking to see if it was loaded, while Jenny gasped for air and tried to keep from passing out.

It took her a full five minutes to calm down.

The rage and panic she had felt when she went for the gun were now replaced by a feeling of resignation, and a sense that she didn't care at all if she had gone too far, or even if this meant that her détente with Rio was finished.

"I wasn't really going to kill you," she said, looking down at the floor, her head in her hands. She had broken a sweat all over.

"You weren't going to be able to," Rio said. "There's no round in the chamber."

Rio removed the magazine and pulled the slide back, confirming that there was no round in the chamber.

"The guy at the gun store told me to carry it that way," Jenny explained. "Otherwise, I could accidentally pull the trigger. Like, something in my purse could get inside the trigger thingy."

Rio snorted, his haughty and superior manner returning.

"*Trigger guard* is the term you are looking for. If it was me, I'd worry more about not being able to *deliberately* fire this gun," he said. "Gun store workers know how to sell guns, not how to handle them. Let me give you some good advice."

His lecturing tone suggested that he held no hard feelings at all about her reaching for the pistol in the middle of what was ostensibly a mental health counseling session.

"If you're going to carry a gun, make sure you're ready to fire it at all times," he said. "Get a pocket holster and carry it that way. Nothing can get inside the trigger guard and pull the trigger when you're carrying it right. You'll be safe from a trigger snag."

She stared at him.

"Thanks for the tip," she said.

"I have another one for you," he said.

There was a long silence. "Go ahead," she said.

"If you intend to kill a man, don't hesitate or move slowly," he said calmly. "Draw the weapon and pull the trigger. More importantly, have a plan. Reduce the variables. Don't give him a chance to react."

He looked at her, his mouth a horizontal line, his eyes dead.

"Thanks," she said. "I'll keep that in mind."

The chime rang out that indicated their session was finished. Rio took his payment out of his pocket, put the gun on the folded cash, and silently handed both to Jenny.

CHAPTER NINETEEN

HE WOULD MAKE A PRETTY DECENT DETECTIVE

RIO WENT BACK into the planning stage during his shift at work. That night, he was dispatched to the scene of two different accidents in order to tow vehicles away, but he was able to spend the rest of the shift in the shop. After he helped one of the mechanics change a power-steering rack in a customer's pickup truck, Rio sat alone in the office at one of the company computers.

He had a stack of paperwork next to him, but he wasn't working on company business. His first purpose was to gather information on the geography surrounding the house where Margaret Tuffin lived—this was crucial to planning both his entry and his escape. The second object of his search was finding a viable alternative suspect that would lead the police in a direction other than Rio's.

One of the other mechanics working that evening was logged into the computer Rio was using. All of the searches Rio was making would point back to Paul, who was out in the bay doing a brake job. Paul was also the same mechanic who had damaged Rhonda Bressett's bumper. It wasn't a direct connection to Margaret, but Rio figured the association would be close enough for any halfway-decent detective to start looking in Paul's direction.

The aerial view of the house actually soon helped Rio start to formulate a plan that might not require an alternative suspect—not that Rio cared at all what happened to Paul. Rio was most intent on finding a way to approach the rear of the house without being noticed. He figured that trying to come in from the front was too risky, and that the possibility of being spotted from a neighbor's living room was too great.

Behind the street where the house sat was a service road that belonged to a local utility. On the other side of that service road was another neighborhood. There were trees on both sides of the road that would offer cover, although from the way the house was positioned, it looked like he'd have to cross through three backyards before he got to the rear of Margaret's house.

He was already picturing it, seeing the lights of the house shining through the perfect, godly beads of falling rain.

The next night, Rio drove out to the entrance of the service road and parked his truck on the shoulder of the road that intersected it. The service road seemed to be little used, but it still had a gate that blocked public access. Rio examined the mechanics of the gate and saw that he could easily open it by removing its padlock with a bolt cutter. All in all, though, he would prefer not to cause any damage to the gate. He wanted his means for getting in and out to be concealed from investigators.

He simply hoisted one leg over it, pulled himself up, and, in one motion, easily jumped over the gate. Treading softly, he walked to the edge of the tree line behind Margaret's neighborhood. He didn't like what he immediately saw: one of the three backyards he was going to need to cross was encircled by an old chain-link fence. He carefully made his way up to the fence, though, and saw that it would be easy to climb. It wasn't very high at all and didn't seem to be the product of superior workmanship.

Not even close enough to keep me out.

Rio gazed in the night at the house where Margaret lived with her sister and her husband. He replayed her hectoring voice from that night at Walmart, the way she had just oozed evil.

He was only about 150 feet away. The place wasn't very big, with vinyl siding and a little patio. There was a screened-in porch back there as well that wouldn't offer much in the way of resistance. This kind of porch also had the advantage of providing cover while he was breaking through the rear sliding door to gain access to what was inside.

A sense of peace came over him. He knew what he needed to get in there. Now his thoughts moved to determining the schedules of the house's three occupants. He needed to find out how their lives worked before he saved one of them.

Rio had gained a lot of skill at ascertaining the routines of his targets—so much so that he thought he would make a pretty decent police detective, if he ever stooped to that kind of thing. In a way, he and the police were two sides of the same coin, even if they lacked his higher skill and his pipeline to the divine.

He could afford to be patient and not make any risky moves as he followed the three of them. If he had any suspicion whatsoever that one of his targets might have become suspicious, he would simply disengage and wait another day.

Margaret worked from home. Rhonda and Stephen worked traditional eight-hour days from Monday through Friday, like clockwork. The married couple seemed to enjoy eating out together, and they mostly favored Friday and Saturday nights. They didn't take Margaret out with them once during the time that Rio conducted his surveillance.

The opportunity presented itself with blinding obviousness. He would wait until it rained on a Friday or Saturday night. If Rhonda and Stephen went out that evening, he would save Margaret in the house.

He was just about to consider his surveillance complete when he saw something out of the ordinary in Stephen's behavior. Stephen parked two blocks from the house one afternoon and walked to the house. Looking around, he came around back and entered through the sliding glass door. About half an hour later, he came out the back of the house the same way and returned to his vehicle. Just a few minutes after that, Rhonda arrived at the house in her car. Barely fifteen minutes after this, Stephen came back—this time, pulling his car into the driveway and entering the front of the house.

A few days later, Rio saw it happen again: the same way, the same timing.

Well, just look at that.

It was hard to draw any other conclusion than Stephen was having sex on the side with his sister-in-law, and maybe had been for a while. Parking some distance from the house allowed him an escape if needed, without the telltale sign of his car in the driveway when it shouldn't have been.

Rio tried to stay calm as he drove the Tacoma back to his house, but it was hard to contain his excitement. Stephen was giving Rio a fantastic opportunity to frame him for the murder that he was going to commit. Rio was familiar with cases such as Scott Peterson's, who was having an affair during the time his wife was murdered and was subsequently convicted of the crime. This was an opportunity too good to pass up. The difficulty was in figuring out how to kill Margaret and make it look like Stephen had been the perpetrator.

But as he drove, Rio came up with a better idea. He smiled at the obviousness of it.

He would wipe out all three of them, leaving no one alive to offer their viewpoint on what had happened.

Nice and clean.

Another advantage to this strategy was that Rio didn't have to be concerned about making contact with any of the victims prior to the killings in order to manipulate their stories. No one would be left to recall a mystery man lurking around the neighborhood asking questions. Even though men had never played into Rio's mission and system, and he had never killed a man before, he was more than happy to murder Stephen. He really didn't care what happened to Stephen in the afterlife—he was probably going to Hell for adultery. And if he didn't, Rio fantasized about a conversation with Stephen in the hereafter when Rio would mock him for his sin and generously thank him for making the enslavement of Margaret so easy and carefree.

One thing was certain: it would be important that Stephen knew who killed him before he died. In the afterlife, Stephen would need to know the full truth of how a hero such as Rio took him down for his depraved infidelity. Rio wasn't sure the goal was possible, but prioritizing it lessened his anxiety. He felt as though he was following the rules.

When he got back home, Rio obsessively checked multiple weather forecasts to see when the next rainstorms were on the way, the harbinger of a triple murder.

His planning became even more meticulous. It would be favorable not to have to bring any of his own weapons into the house, so Rio decided that he would need to commit a burglary in advance to see what weapons might be available to him in the residence. There were limited opportunities to pull this off, because Margaret rarely ventured from the house.

But then he got lucky.

One night about a week later, Rio was conducting surveillance when he saw the trio leaving together in Rhonda's car. He followed them for a time, until he was certain that they were headed together to the Christiana Mall.

Perfect. The poorly designed road network around the mall made it hard to enter and exit the place efficiently, even during times when the shopping center wasn't busy. During the Christmas season, a driver would have to count on at least twenty minutes each way to make it to and from Route 1, the nearest highway.

Feeling confident that he was going to have enough time to do what he needed, Rio sped back to the utility service road, parked his truck in the dark, and made his way to the edge of the tree line behind the houses in his targets' neighborhood. He had practiced this routine in his mind over and over.

Rio got to the back of the house without incident. He knew the tools he needed to bring to break into both the sliding glass door and the main door in the rear of the attached garage. It only took a simple screwdriver to pop the lock on the sliding glass door; then he was inside the house and locking the door behind him. He noticed he had scratched the door plate right around the locking mechanism, but he hoped the residents didn't notice before he came for them.

He took a few deep breaths to steady himself, telling the OCD to leave him alone, that he didn't need it in order to fulfill his mission.

The house was a bonanza. Rio found more weapons and things that could be used as weapons than he had hoped possible. There were several firearms—rifles, shotguns, and a single pistol. They all had trigger locks, except for the pistol—a Rossi R462 .357 Magnum. By design, the gun had an internal key-operated locking mechanism at the base of the hammer, which prevented the hammer from being drawn back and the trigger from being pulled.

No counting. No counting.

Rio knew the system well, and he had a few firearms that also sported this particular feature. He was thinking about how he might find a serviceable key to bring for the murders when he spotted one hanging on a ring in the closet, just a couple of feet from where he had found the pistol.

God is watching.

Rio disengaged the gun's lock, removed all six cartridges, returned the key to the ring, and carefully returned the firearm under the small stack of clothes where he had found it. He verified that the other weapons were unloaded and continued to explore the house.

There were family photos running all along the stairs between the ground floor and the second floor. Rio glanced at them for just a moment, uninterested in the details of these peoples' lives. There were a ton of books on a couple of shelves in the living room, but again, these caused him to take no interest.

Over the next several minutes, Rio located the things that interested him. On a small notepad, he recorded the location of several kitchen knives, a baseball bat, an extension cord and rope, and an eight-pound sledgehammer he had found sitting in the garage.

The options were starting to feel overwhelming. He paced around the house, trying to narrow down which weapon would be the best. He checked and rechecked, finding himself making sure over and over that each item was where he had left it. His anxiety started to rise precipitously, his breathing getting faster and his vision blurring.

Why now, demon?

He prayed to God to rid him of the demon. He remembered what Jenny had told him.

Back to the fire with you! I don't respect you. I defy you.

As he blinked and blinked and pounded his forehead to try to clear his thoughts, he entertained the possibility that the OCD might actually be a psychiatric disorder and not something supernaturally imposed. He knew Jenny thought so, and he respected her. But truly embracing this idea would mean the whole house of cards of his belief system would collapse.

With a loud grunt, Rio willed the compulsions away, knowing that they were only temporarily kept at bay. He started moving around the house again, free if only for the moment. Then he stopped.

There was a car pulling into the driveway.

Anger replaced Rio's anxiety. If it was Margaret, Stephen, and Rhonda, then they had made a miraculous getaway through the traffic at the mall. But then, Rio was going to also have to escape. It wasn't raining, and he wasn't fully prepared for saving Margaret, then killing Stephen and Rhonda.

Rio peeked out through the curtains that covered the front window. He was being careful, but he also felt bold and fearless. This was his special calling. This was what he did best.

There was a car he recognized out there, one that he had spotted a number of times in the neighborhood. It was driven by a young man, and he was merely using the driveway to turn around. In a fury, Rio thought about how he could vandalize the car or render it inoperable to make that young man pay for interrupting him during his work.

I can't believe this guy. Doesn't he know how important I am?

But in the next moment, the pragmatic side focused on the mission took over. He decided to be magnanimous and let the young man off the hook. Rio was in the middle of a burglary, after all, and he didn't want to do anything to reveal his presence.

Still, it took a couple of minutes for the rage to subside. The demon drive was getting stronger and stronger.

He made his way to the main door in the rear of the garage. As he reached for the door, he noticed there was a lot of dust covering it and around it, with dusty things stacked all around. It looked like this door didn't get used very often. Rio opened it carefully, trying not to disturb the dust and the dirt, and put a small strip of tape over the strike plate. He'd be able to re-enter the house without having to break in.

Rio tested his handiwork by opening and closing the door a few times. *Perfect.*

Satisfied, he made his way back to the Tacoma. He had left everything as he had found it, with the exception of the six .357 Magnum cartridges clinking softly in his jacket pocket.

CHAPTER TWENTY

DREAMING OF A
WHITE CHRISTMAS

IT WAS A FEW MINUTES past the start time of Rio's regular weekly appointment and he still hadn't arrived. He was almost never late. Jenny had a strange feeling as she gazed at the clock. She was actually disappointed, as she sometimes felt when a particularly interesting client would miss a session.

Jenny knew this was a bad sign. Her boundaries were eroded and fading even more than before. Whenever this happened with another client—such as in one case with an attractive and smart male client her own age—Jenny would take time to reflect on how she could firm up her boundaries. In a couple of cases, she had taken the professionally recommended step of referring the client to another counselor.

But that wasn't an option with Rio.

She was on her own, and she had to supervise her own feelings.

Even though Jenny had every rational reason to hate and abhor Rio, she didn't. Not exactly. She could never be attracted to him in the least, but being forced to spend so much time alone with him had resulted in changes in her attitude.

It would have been difficult to explain to anyone, but she actually enjoyed the strange freedom they had developed, in which she could say basically anything to him and he would react in his strange, emotionless way. It was a paradox: she felt so safe sitting across from someone she knew was so dangerous, even though he was a person who had once tried to kill her.

Then a feeling akin to relief came over Jenny when Rio showed up eight minutes late—fairly standard for some clients, but a rarity for him.

"The traffic is getting really bad out there," he said, taking off his Carhartt jacket and bunching it up at his feet even though there was a coat tree by the door. "What is going on these days?" She couldn't tell if he was joking. "The holidays," she said. "People are out shopping. This happens every year."

Rio rolled his eyes and brushed his hair from his forehead, clearly contemptuous of people's holidays and rituals and ordinary concerns.

"I need to talk about symptom management," he said.

She paused. "What did you . . . decide about the next saving?"

He looked at her directly.

"There might be some collateral damage," he said.

That hung between them for a long moment. Jenny allowed the ramifications of what he had said to sink in. He would be killing more than one person. Automatically, as it had so many times in recent weeks, Jenny's mind went into calculation mode: what she could do to stop him, or slow him, without throwing away her own life at the same time. She hoped if she could get him talking, she could dissuade him from going through with a more extreme mode of killing than his usual mission.

Then the persistent thought: *Just turn yourself in.*

She took a deep breath. She was in deep. Sometimes when she spoke, she wasn't even sure who it was doing the talking.

"OK," she finally said. "Tell me about it."

Rio nodded with, it seemed, approval. She had a sense that he took sport in gradually breaking down the guardrails of her resistance, drawing her closer to him. She observed it, with part of her holding out hope to manipulate and control him, another part strangely held in thrall to whatever he was going to say.

He talked her through his vision for his seventh homicide—although Rio didn't think of what he envisioned as a triple homicide. He focused on the single upcoming murder that would add a slave to his list. He didn't seem overly concerned about what would happen to his other two victims (although he mentioned in passing that he had a very strong sexual attraction to Rhonda, Margaret's sister). He contemplated saving Rhonda still, but he was increasingly resigned to what seemed to be his fate to save Margaret.

Now she knew their names.

"Is that what you think I should do?" Rio said. "I'm having trouble choosing. I think I know, but then my thoughts get confused."

"I don't know," Jenny said quietly.

"You're not helping," Rio said with petulance. "I need help finding clarity. You're just leaving me feeling stuck."

How am I supposed to help? "How is this even supposed to work?" she said. "You're going to break into the house, take Margaret, and then what? Kill Stephen? Are you at least going to leave Rhonda unharmed?"

Rio scratched at some stubble on his chin. "All three will die," he said.

Jenny shook her head. "I don't get it," she said. "Doesn't that break all the rules you follow? Are you changing them now?" "Not at all," he replied with confidence. "Margaret is number seven. I will dominate her in this world and then in the afterlife."

Jenny tried not to wince. She needed to keep some semblance of a counselor's authority in the moment when she might be able to save lives.

"But two more people, Rio," Jenny pleaded. "It feels like you're escalating and not staying close to the parameters of your mission."

She knew, as she said this, that she was consigning Margaret to death. She was getting in deeper. Her mind flashed: to the gun, to the phone, and a confession. She thought, not for the first time, about using the gun on herself. But she felt locked in, somehow more under Rio's control than she had understood until that moment.

She had been running all her life. Now she needed to run and couldn't.

"I'll just simply kill them," Rio said, as though it was the most ordinary thing in the world. "Stephen's actions prove him to be evil, so he's simply getting what he deserves. With Rhonda, well, I've thought about the situation. She probably wouldn't want to go on living if she knew that her husband and her sister were murdered because they were having an affair with each other."

Jenny had a very strange sensation, as though she was floating just above and behind herself—observing, participating but not entirely.

"Isn't there some way to leave Rhonda out of this?" she asked. "I know how you think by now. You're going to try to frame this guy for killing his sister-in-law and then himself, right?" Rio's eyes widened. He gave that little smirk. "OK, here we go," he said to her. "You're learning. It's good to see."

"But killing one extra person increases the chances that you're going to mess up and miss something," Jenny said. "You might leave more evidence behind and give the police a reason to suspect that Stephen was set up and wasn't the killer at all."

Rio threw up his hands. "I wish there was a way, alright?" he said. "You're so smart? You tell me."

"What if you catch them having sex and do it then?" Jenny asked, putting a challenge into her voice. "That way, they're doing the work for you— leaving an obvious crime scene behind, and Rhonda will show up and see what happened and piece it all together."

The words just came out. Some part of her had looked at the situation, examined the angles for a best outcome, and produced that thought.

Rio hesitated, looking up at the ceiling as though doing a complicated math problem in his head.

"That actually makes sense," he said then. "I'm impressed. You know what? You make a better serial killer than you do a victim."

As he smiled at her, a familiar tingle went up her neck. She laughed then. Loudly, involuntarily. He was right, after all—she had survived Rio's attack, she had then killed a man, and now she was helping refine his plans, even if the idea was to do less harm.

Maybe she *was* more of a predator than a victim. It wasn't an idea that she wanted to entertain for very long.

"I'm only going to kill Margaret and Stephen," he announced, as though restructuring his vacation plans. "It's probably not going to work logistically to kill them while they're having sex. Too hard to get the timing right."

Jenny heard a pounding in her temples. "But you'll leave Rhonda alone, right?" she said. "She hasn't done anything."

"I can pretty easily disable that Honda Accord of hers," Rio said, nodding his agreement. "Then I can do what needs to be done before she gets home."

She had won a small victory, following defeat after defeat with Rio. She had gotten him to change his mind about something.

Call the police. Make it stop.

Her heart was beating so hard it felt as though she was running up a hill. A small bead of sweat gathered at her hairline and started to fall down her brow.

"Hey, are you all right?" Rio asked. "Something looks different about you. Are you sick or something?"

"I'm fine," she said. "Just . . . let's keep going."

The weather became unseasonably cold in Delaware as Christmas approached. It rained several times, gray and chilly, and even snowed once, though there wasn't much in the way of accumulation. Still, these developments forced Rio to contemplate questions that he hadn't previously considered.

Did snow amount to the same thing as rain? Was snow also a way for God to enact His cleansing upon the Earth?

He thought about it for several hours as he worked a shift driving the tow truck. After a while, the answer seemed obvious: rain and snow were both God's will. Not only would snow eventually melt into water, washing the ground like rain, but snow was also white and was a symbol of purity.

A snowstorm was forecast just a few days before Christmas. This one was going to be significant, dropping at least six inches. The voices on the radio were all talking about how it was going to be a White Christmas.

Rio reviewed his plan over and over. It was relatively straightforward. He would save Margaret and kill Stephen, framing Rhonda's husband to make it look like a murder-suicide between lovers.

He went through the steps. If the weather forecast was cor-

rect, he would park his car next to the service road right before it started snowing. He'd be dressed in overalls like a utility
worker, he'd walk to the tree line, and quickly make his way
across the backyards to get to Margaret's house. He'd look up at
the power lines as he went, on the off chance he was spotted, as
though he was in the area to make a repair or check on utilities.

When he got to the back of the house, he'd go in through
the door he had rigged to stay unlocked when he broke in. He
would surprise Margaret, who would be home working at the
time. He would tie her up and dominate her.

Then he would wait for Stephen to arrive. Using Stephen's
own .357 Magnum, Rio would kill him. He would shoot
Margaret with the same gun, then untie her before he left the
house. It wasn't the tidiest of murder-suicide scenes, Rio reasoned, but the police would be as lazy as they always were, and
they would find a way to link the two and shy away from other suspects. He assumed Rhonda had some level of suspicion
about her husband and sister, the way people being cheated on
almost always do. Even as they try to push the thought from
their mind.

Rio checked the weather on his phone at his kitchen table.
He looked up. Through the window, he saw the very first flakes
begin to fall. He looked over at a row of china plates on a shelf
high up on the wall. Like so many things in the house, they had
belonged to Eileen. He thought about her. The way she would
see him if she were still alive, if she hadn't needed to kill herself
to escape.

Would she be proud?

He quickly climbed into his truck and drove through the trees behind his house. Sliding the gear shift out of gear and setting the brake, he hurriedly placed the planks across the storm drains so he could cross the ditch. The demon drive was distracting him so much that he started driving to the road leaving the planks behind. They were positioned across the ditch in the gently falling snow.

Go back? Don't go back?

This wasn't necessarily a problem, but he liked to retrieve the planks each time in case someone might wander through the woods and come across them. Every time Rio made a mistake like this, he felt heavy and leaden, with an ache in his gut as though he had been punched. The mistakes, perceived or imagined, piled up and became a competing voice in his mind trying to drown out the demon drive.

Stop before it's too late.

Rio pressed on, driving just below the speed limit on the highway, telling himself that the distracting voices were a compulsion, a weakness, not of God. He would disrespect the voices. But with mistake number one already having occurred, he hoped there wouldn't be any more to clutter up his mind.

He had one stop before he went to the house. He made his way to the office park where Rhonda worked at an insurance company. He found her Honda Accord in the parking lot and parked his truck beside it, obscuring its visibility from the office building. He hopped out, trying to behave as casually and naturally as he could.

With his valve stem tool, he quickly set out to remove the

valve cores from both of the car's rear tires. After he had finished the first one, a pedestrian appeared in Rio's peripheral vision, startling him.

Do I need to kill him?

The pedestrian kept on walking, showing no sign of having seen Rio kneeling by the Honda. Rio climbed back into his truck and drove away, having deflated only one of the two tires. But he wasn't worried about it. Disabling both tires was probably overkill. Anyway, even without tire trouble, Rio calculated that he had almost two hours before Rhonda would pull up in her driveway coming home from work.

The timetable was activated. Stephen would be arriving about 45 minutes after Rio got into the house. This didn't leave Rio as much time as he would have liked to spend with Margaret, but Stephen getting home before Rhonda was crucial—it was the only way he could spare Rhonda's life, which he considered a peace offering to Jenny.

Rio knew Jenny didn't want him to save, or to kill at all. It was just about the only thing he didn't like about her.

He also knew he needed to learn to act more human. He had read somewhere that all good friendships and relationships were based on some degree of give and take. Jenny would have to get her way some of the time. And he was able to work this situation into his belief system, so it didn't even feel like that much of a concession to him.

It was getting close to 5:30. Rio felt an electric energy coursing through him as the day faded into darkness. He calmly drove to the entrance to the service road and parked his truck.

The sky had a peculiar glow from the snowstorm rolling in. He made his way by foot to the tree line behind the house. He needed to cross the backyards in between, the place where he had the greatest danger of exposure, but the dark and the snow were working with him.

Then he actually saw her: Margaret, a small figure in the near distance, pulling a rocking chair into the house, probably wanting to save it from getting covered in snow.

Won't need that chair much longer.

Rio quickly covered the distance he needed to cover, jumping over the final chain-link fence with an excitement that threatened his ability to stay under control.

Slave Number Seven was going to be his, and nothing was going to stop him.

He got distracted, only for a moment, by the sight of his footsteps behind him in the snow. He was going to leave fresh footprints after the killings when he left the house.

But it wasn't a problem. He looked up. God's snow was going to cover his tracks. This removed any doubt that he had been given a sign.

Rio turned the knob on the main door in the rear of the garage. It opened easily with no resistance. He stepped quietly into the house and started going through his checklist in his mind.

He thought to himself that it was going to be a glorious evening.

CHAPTER TWENTY-ONE

NOT ALWAYS A CLEAN AND ORGANIZED AFFAIR

RIO COULD SEE out the window that the snow was falling harder. He felt a glorious stillness, like a sense of comfort. These moments of anticipation were among his favorites in life, and he felt he deserved to enjoy what was coming as much as he could.

He started to move through the house without fear. He heard a TV playing somewhere. There was a string of Christmas lights hanging in the kitchen, and he noticed that some of the lights on the string adjacent to one another were the same color. They shouldn't have been. This offended his sense of order.

Don't think about it. Stay on task.

He came upon Margaret sitting in the living room, watching a TV newscast about the weather. He didn't want to give her the opportunity to scream, so he was coiled and ready to move fast, but he paused when he realized she was unaware he was behind her.

Her hair was pulled back into a ponytail. She was wearing exercise clothes, and she idly scratched her cheek as the TV announcer talked about the snow.

"Could be up to seven or eight inches, more than we had forecast," the weatherman said, standing in front of a map showing snowfall totals across the state. "Things are changing quickly by the hour and we're trying to stay in front of it."

Rio relished the moment as he tightened his grip on the ball peen hammer he'd picked up in the garage. Then he thought back to when he had saved Karen. He had killed her prematurely and didn't get to fully enjoy her.

He carefully put the hammer down on a nearby chair without making a sound.

"The roads are OK for now," the weather person was saying. "But around nine or ten tonight, you're going to want to be inside."

Rio pulled out his Glock 42 and grabbed Margaret around the neck while shoving the gun into her temple. Margaret gasped and tried to bring her hands up, trying to turn around, her face exhibiting a totally confused and terrified expression.

"Stay quiet and you won't get hurt," Rio hissed at her.

She's wondering if you're lying.

Rio walked her into the bedroom and tied her up with her own pantyhose from the drawer by the bed. After he dominated her, he sat on the edge of her bed, just staring at her. His mind wandered to the times when he was telling Jenny that he had the power to manipulate people. He was fighting the strong desire to instill sheer terror in Margaret and to condemn her for being part of Stephen's infidelity, but he thought of what he had learned with Jenny and decided to apply it.

"I need you to stay quiet," he said calmly, trying to sound reassuring. "I already have what I came for. There's no need for me to kill anybody. I know your brother-in-law is coming home, and I'm going to have to knock him unconscious before I leave."

She stared up at him from the bed, her eyes wild and wide.

"Stay quiet and no one dies," Rio said. "Do we have an agreement?"She nodded her head.

A vibration and a beep came from Margaret's purse. It was still on the sofa in the living room, but it was audible from where they were.

"What's that noise?" Rio asked.

"It's my phone," Margaret said in a hushed voice. "Somebody just texted me."

Rio went out into the living room and got the purse. When he returned, she was just as he left her.

"Unlock the phone," he said, handing her the purse. "And give it to me."He took the phone, turning the screen so that Margaret couldn't see. The text message was from Rhonda: *On my way home. Office closing early. Had a flat tire, but Paul from security figured out how to fix it.*

Rio was careful not to react. This meant that Rhonda was

probably going to arrive home before Stephen. It also meant that his plan for sparing Rhonda's life was likely going to disintegrate. Rio left Margaret tied up in the bedroom with a reminder to stay quiet, then closed her door and went out to the living room to contemplate the situation. The TV was still on, so Rio switched it off so he could think more clearly.

There was room in Rio's belief system for the messiness of unexpected events. It wasn't desirable, but being a serial killer was not always a clean and organized affair. Rhonda had just become a logistical problem. She could be dealt with by using deadly force, and she would count as nothing more than an unfortunate, but forgivable strike for which he could atone.

The real challenge was resisting his temptation to sexually dominate Rhonda. From the outset, he had been more attracted to her than to Margaret, but Margaret had presented herself as needing to be saved because of her unambiguous evil.

The excitement of the demon drive was building up inside him. From one moment to the next, he alternately fought it and gave it free rein.

He knew that if he dominated Rhonda, such a deviation from the plan would make the obsessive thoughts become unbearable, and compulsions would follow. His powerful symptoms were best processed as a punishment from God, and Rio kept himself on track by only inflicting them on the evil.

Is Rhonda evil?

Before he could work through the puzzle in his mind, he heard a car crunching through the snow in the driveway, its headlights brightening the living room before they were shut off. He had to make a decision. He accelerated the calculations taking place in his mind.

I can't leave now. Margaret is still alive and would be a witness against me. I don't have time to kill her.

Rhonda had to die.

Just as he finished his morbid computation, Rhonda started to open the front door. Rio stood behind it.

She walked into the foyer and closed the door behind her. Rio put her in a chokehold with the intention of rendering her unconscious and killing her later. As she struggled against Rio's unyielding grip, grunting for air, he could smell her perfume.

"Stop struggling," he said into her ear.

She complied, and he let her drop to the floor. He was able to tie her up while she was still conscious. He took her into her bedroom down the hall from Margaret's, where the door was still closed. He considered what he was going to do. Battling against the horrible uprising of obsessive feelings and thoughts, he remembered what Jenny had told him about disrespecting the symptoms.

This has to end now. Get out of my head!

He built up his courage. He satisfied himself with Rhonda. Back in the kitchen, he saw the Christmas lights with their color arrangement that had so disturbed him such a short time ago.

I don't care about the order of the lights!

Rio knew he had dealt a blow to his horrific OCD, taking away at least some of its power, understanding it as a disorder that afflicted him. It wasn't part of a divine plan, like the demon drive. He vowed never to give in to the symptoms again, no matter how invasive or insistent they became. It was all just stress and genetics, as he had read but never allowed himself to believe.

It was all quiet in the house save for the sound of his heart beating in his ears.

This meant something radical: that Rhonda wasn't a strike. She was something that he simply took for himself because it was what he desired.

There were going to be no more strikes.

He felt strength in every part of his body, as though he was invincible. He eagerly awaited Stephen's arrival. With Margaret and Rhonda both tied up in their rooms and under orders to stay quiet lest everyone in the house be killed, Rio retrieved Stephen's .357 Magnum revolver and loaded it with the cartridges he had taken from the house the last time he had broken in. Looking at the revolver in his hand, he contemplated how loud the discharge from the gun was going to be.

The last thing he needed was some nosy neighbor curious about what had caused the noise. Even if no one was inclined to investigate or call the police, they might take note of the time when they heard a popping sound—which would help the police in putting together an accurate timeline of the crime.

He remembered something and went back to the closet where Stephen stored the gun. Rio placed his .380 in his pocket and switched to Stephen's .357 Magnum, loading it with .38 Special wadcutter cartridges. Even though those were substantially less powerful than the cartridges he removed from it on his prior visit, just about any bullet would do at point-blank range—and they also belonged to Stephen.

Rio heard the sound of a car pulling into the driveway, then a car door opening. He hid behind the front door once again. No sound was coming from either of the bedrooms.

Stephen walked in the front door. Rio held the gun level with Stephen's head as the door opened and, as Stephen shut it, he thrust the revolver forward to within inches of Stephen's head and pulled the trigger.

The bullet entered Stephen's left temple and killed him instantly. He slumped to the floor.

Not good!

Having been concentrating on the shot, Rio realized too late that he had discharged the weapon a moment before the door had been fully closed. The noise of the gunshot would have gone cascading through the neighborhood. He was so upset by this, he did not even realize the rule about Stephen knowing who had killed him was broken.

Motivated by the potential consequences of his noisy mistake, Rio moved quickly to take his other two victims. He opened the door to Rhonda's room, grabbed her, and dragged her out to the foyer where Stephen lay. He punched her once, hard, to stun her, then put the revolver in Stephen's hand and manipulated the dead man's finger into the trigger guard.

He fired a single bullet into Rhonda's head before she could even figure out what was going on. Not even bothering to untie Rhonda's hands and feet, Rio went into the other bedroom, where Margaret lay trembling with a look of terror.

Getting ready to drag Margaret out for her turn with the gun held by her dead lover and brother-in-law, Rio looked down and saw blood on Margaret's arm where he had just placed his hand.

He pieced together what had happened. When he was choking Rhonda, he had pressed his own fingernail through his latex glove and cut himself. He dropped the limp Margaret onto her bed. She seemed to be in shock and wasn't going anywhere.

Furiously, Rio scoured the house in search of any blood he might have left behind. It only took a few seconds to find the first stain—on the wall right by the front door. He pulled a rag from his pocket and found some bleach under the sink, then started trying to wipe the wall clean. He felt pressure mounting terribly when he finished and saw yet another stain on the arm of the couch.

Options swirled through his mind. He could cut the fabric out of the couch and take it with him, but that only solved the problem of the spot he was looking at. The larger challenge was that he couldn't know every place in the house where he might have left his blood. He was going to need a far more comprehensive solution if he wanted to ensure that this mistake led to a minimal chance of his being arrested.

Then he looked up. *No, no.*

There was a neighbor out there in the heavily falling snow on the sidewalk, looking with curiosity at the front door. They had probably heard the sound of the first or second gunshot and had come over to investigate.

This was a major problem because there was still one shot left to be executed. Stephen's gun had to be used to kill Margaret in order for the police to conclude that a murder-suicide had taken place. Otherwise, the investigators would widen their search outside of the three domestic victims.

Running out of time and losing confidence in his ability to identify and properly clean any blood he might have left at the scene, in the next moment, Rio came up with a gambit.

Logistics and probabilities cascaded through his mind.

It might turn out to be a disaster.

Rio was an on-call tow truck driver that night for BNR. He didn't like to be on-call on the nights when he was planning a save, because if a call came in, he would have difficulty responding if he was in the middle of his mission. That night, Rio had originally been off the schedule, but he had gotten a call to possibly be ready to serve as a backup because of the snowstorm. Figuring his chances of actually getting called in were quite low, he agreed to it because it was an assignment he would almost always take. He didn't want to do anything out of the ordinary in case he was investigated later.

Rhonda had been a BNR customer in the past, so it wouldn't be out of the realm of possibility for someone in her household to call BNR if they happened to need a tow. He came up with the idea of having Margaret call BNR and request for Rhonda's Honda Accord to be towed back to the shop.

After all, Rhonda had had trouble with her car earlier that evening and had to be helped out by a co-worker. But the immediate problem was that Ray, the tow truck driver who was the primary on-call that night, would be the first one notified of an incoming request. If Rio was going to be the one dispatched to the house in response to a call from Margaret, then Ray would have to be busy—or else Margaret could somehow request Rio, but that would raise tons of suspicion.

Rio looked out the window at the falling snow, which was starting to accumulate with a great deal of depth. He would have to take his chances.

"Here's what I need you to do," he told Margaret after he had gone back into her room and closed the door behind him.

"What happened out there?" she whispered.

"Everyone is fine," Rio said. "I just need you to follow my instructions and everyone is going to be OK." Rio could see Margaret clinging to her ridiculous hope as she executed his command. She would make a good slave. Her voice was going to be shaky, so Rio ordered her to tell the dispatcher that she was sorry for how she sounded, but that her sister's husband was in a bad mood and they just had an argument.

"No, no, everything is fine," Margaret said, apparently in response to concern from the dispatcher.

The dispatcher worked for a service that BNR hired by the month. They worked for a variety of companies including taxicabs, HVAC repair, and plumbers—anyone who needed to be contacted out of the blue. Rio hit the button to put the call on speaker.

"Can we get someone to come pick up the car tomorrow?" asked the dispatcher. "Looks like the primary drivers are all out on calls."

Rio nodded with encouragement as Margaret looked up with a confused expression. He muted the phone.

"Tell them the car has to be picked up tonight," he said. "Tell them that it's blocking the driveway."

It was working. With the other drivers busy, Rio was going to get the call to pick up Rhonda's car.

"Good job," Rio said to Margaret after she had hung up. She looked up expectantly, her eyes wide with hope.

Rio covered her mouth and dragged her out to where Stephen and Rhonda lay next to each other. His movements were fluid, precise, and focused as he put the gun in Stephen's hand and used it to save Margaret. Rio left the gun in Stephen's hand. Then he unlocked the front door and made his way to the back of the house.

It was important to keep moving. He had no way of knowing how long it would be before a suspicious neighbor, who might have heard the third shot, might decide to investigate. The snow was going to make his journey difficult. There was a lot of work ahead, including driving back home to where the BNR tow truck was parked, checking his phone to get the dispatch assignment, and driving back to the house to pick up Rhonda's car.

You made it too complicated. Count your steps.

Rio gritted his teeth and made himself focus on his mission. He started trudging through the snow outside, which was now inches deep. He was leaving footprints, but the snow was falling hard enough that they would soon be obscured.

His worries were far from over, but he made his way back to his truck without anyone seeing him. He climbed in, pressed in the clutch, switched into four-wheel drive, pushed the gear shift into first, and gently let the clutch up. He was headed home. He felt that God was looking after him.

CHAPTER TWENTY-TWO

THE LIGHTS ARE ON, BUT NO ONE ANSWERED

DRIVING HOME as quickly as possible, Rio focused on not getting in an accident on the snow-slick roads while his mind raced. For years he had looked forward to the snow, because it would mean additional income from driving the tow truck—sometimes he would put in as many as ten hours in addition to his usual eight-hour shift.

This storm was even more special. It marked the occasion of his being able to dominate two victims back-to-back, as well as his power in standing up to his obsessive and overpowering thoughts and compulsions.

But he also feared the tide of OCD returning stronger than

ever, and he questioned the spiritual significance of what had happened. He wondered if there was going to be a price to pay for what he had done to Rhonda. Perhaps God was going to strike him down or allow the police to finally catch him.

Maybe the retribution has already come.

In his frenzy of indulgence, Rio had cut his hand and not even realized it. If he had been satisfied with only saving Margaret, then he would have had more control and at least noticed the cut without spreading blood around.

The snowstorm made everything slower and harder. Traffic was at a crawl, and there were cars spun out to the side of the road. Rio's four-wheel drive was cutting through the snow, but that wasn't making the other drivers go any faster.

He made it to the woods behind his house, turning off into the dirt and driving over the planks covering the drainage ditch that he had left earlier in the night after he quickly got out to brush the snow off them. Once he got to the other side, he removed the planks from the encasement and put them in the bed of the Tacoma.

After he slid the pickup into the garage, he turned on his phone. He was pleased by the message that was waiting for him: a text from the dispatcher saying a Honda Accord needed to be towed to the shop. The address was the home he had just left.

But what he didn't expect was the text that had come just before the one for Rhonda's car. This one was requesting that he tow another disabled car, one in the town of Bear. It wasn't unusual during a snowstorm to get multiple requests, and in his mind, Rio quickly calculated that the distance between Bear and the house where he had just killed three people was roughly eight miles.

Nobody would think much of it if Rio simply went to pick up the Accord first. It was up to drivers to prioritize calls in most cases. Of course, he also knew that he would never make it to Bear after what was about to happen at the house in Newark.

Rio prepared to step out of the door for the next phase of his plan when he remembered his Glock was still in his pocket. As he placed it carefully in an end table drawer by his front door, he tried to slow his mind and consider anything else he may have forgotten.

No mistakes from this point on.

The drive back to the house in the tow truck was slow, but Rio took the time to slow his mind and begin to think about the role he was going to play. Just as Jenny had advised him, he composed lines of dialogue in his mind and practiced them, so that he would seem normal and human.

When he got to the house, Rio backed the tow truck into the driveway, aligning it in position next to Rhonda's Honda Accord. As he stepped out of his truck, he saw that there were footprints leading from the sidewalk to the front door. Someone had approached the house while he was gone.

Rio was visually following the footprints back to their origin when a neighbor clumsily made her way in the snow toward him, her boots crunching on the driveway, a big knit hat on her head and her glasses fogged up in the cold. She looked to be about sixty, and she came up to him talking fast and loudly.

"Did the people who live here call you?" she asked.

"I got a message from my dispatcher saying they need this car towed," Rio said, motioning to the Accord.

"Do you know where they are?" the woman asked. "I heard a bang earlier and came over and knocked on the door. The lights are on, but no one answered."

"I don't know anything about that," Rio said, carefully enunciating his words. "A bang, you say? Let's go to the door and see if they answer this time."

As they walked together up the driveway to the front door, the neighbor slipped in the snow. Normally Rio didn't care about anyone else's well-being, but he knew that the neighbor was going to be extensively questioned by the police, so he took hold of her arm.

"Thank you," she said gratefully.

This also allowed him to control who was going to reach the door first. When they were almost there, Rio considered telling her that he was going to check around the back of the house—this would take care of the matter of any footprints he left out there. But enough snow had fallen since he had first left to completely obscure them, and he didn't trust the neighbor to proceed in a predictable manner.

Rio let go of the neighbor's arm and climbed the three steps to the front door. He opened the screen as he pushed the doorbell.

"I don't hear anyone inside," he told the neighbor. He put

his hand on the doorknob and turned it.

"Is it unlocked?" the neighbor asked. She was by his side.

"Feels like it," Rio said, trying to sound uncertain.

He pushed the door open just a fraction.

"Hello?" he called out through the crack. "Is anyone here? I'm the tow truck driver you called!"He pushed the door open more.

Rio had practiced this in his mind. Trying to simulate the emotions of a normal person, he looked at the three bodies lying in the foyer and let out a high-pitched scream of terror.

He knew it sounded fake, like something a comedian would do on stage. But then the neighbor came around to see what he was looking at and she started screaming as well—and hers definitely sounded like the real thing. Her screaming and sobbing was also a lot louder than his, and he saw porchlights coming on next door and across the street.

"Call the police," he told her as he entered the house. "And don't come in."

He knew he didn't have long to establish his alibi. He stepped over the bodies and looked around, touching the sofa, standing where he had stood before, calling out in a loud voice to ask if anyone else was in the house. He hoped he sounded courageous, willing to confront the monster who had committed these crimes.

Coming out the front door with his face in his hands, Rio called out, "There's no one else in there, but there are three people dead!"

In the driveway, he waited for the police along with the

neighbor and a small crowd that was starting to amass in the front yard. Rio had closed the door behind him and ordered away anyone who looked as though they were going inside.

"You don't want to see what's in there," he said more than once, hoping he sounded authentic to these strangers' ears.

People were crying and wailing. Rio kept trying to simulate human emotions, talking about how upset he was, saying that he was torn up inside. As he described his anguish and loss, he looked into the eyes of the other people out there, trying to see if they believed him. All he could see was distress and incomprehension—whether directed toward him or toward the situation as a whole, he wasn't sure which.

As the minutes ticked by, Rio got a deepening sense that people were looking at him strangely. He decided to change his approach.

"I just can't believe it," he started muttering to himself over and over.

That seemed to help. No one was staring at him anymore. In fact, they were mostly looking away, as though they didn't want to deal with his traumatized behavior. When one of the neighbors came over and put his hand on Rio's shoulder, though, he decided that this approach would be the one he took with the police.

It was several hours before Rio was allowed to leave the property. The house was taped off as a crime scene. Three different covered stretchers emerged at different points as the bodies were removed after evidence was taken.

The police had a lot of questions for him, the neighbor who

had gone with him to the door, and pretty much everyone else who had gathered in front of the house. Rio didn't recognize any of the cops. They probably hadn't been on the force when he was young and getting in trouble.

"I can't believe this is happening," Rio told a sympathetic cop at one point while going through the chronology of his evening after he got the tow request on his phone at his house. "I've never seen anything like this."

During the questioning, Rio pressed hard on his hand to get it bleeding again. He said that he'd opened up a cut from his job getting into his truck that night, and said he was worried that he might have bled on something inside when he was looking around for an intruder. The police took a picture of his hand and seemed satisfied with his explanation. Rio leaned against his truck at one point as he heard a detective questioning a neighbor about the comings and goings of Stephen and the two sisters. They were asking about any jealousy between the three, or any sign that something was going on that wasn't right.

The seeds that Rio had planted had already taken root.

Finally, when dawn was approaching, Rio was driving his tow truck back to his house. The snow had stopped falling. The purification had occurred, but he was still beset by nagging inner voices.

Should never have gone back. Should have taken your chances.

Sitting at his kitchen table as the sun rose over his snow-covered yard, Rio mustered all his will to silence the doubts and the spiraling apprehensions.

He was special, after all.

He had only two more kills until his mission was complete. Two more, and his destiny would be fulfilled.

Minor mistakes were trivial in the eyes of God.

Focus on the mission. Focus on the mission. Focus on the mission.

CHAPTER TWENTY-THREE

ANOTHER SOLUTION WOULD PRESENT ITSELF

AFTER SAM had started seeing Taylor Stolly, Jenny's relationship with him had all but ended. So she was surprised to find Sam at her door a few weeks later, eagerly explaining how he had made a mistake, how sorry he was, and how he wanted to commit to a fully monogamous relationship with Jenny if she would take him back.

This was the only time Jenny could recall ever seeing Sam appear desperate or not in control in the romantic sphere. It seemed to represent a substantial change in his personality and his way of being. Her training as a counselor informed her that personalities rarely change in a substantial way, but she was able to push back those doubts the same way she had been pushing back the voice of her conscience—farther and farther from the range of her mind until it was barely audible at all.

Sometimes, it felt as though she was living someone else's life.

After their reconciliation, Jenny found herself with erratic emotions. She would harbor anger toward him one moment, then in the next be essentially satisfied with the state of the relationship. She wasn't particularly excited by him, and was far from infatuated, but she was increasingly resigned.

This is going to be as good as it will get. What do I deserve, anyway?

Vacillating somewhere between frustration and contentment, it was less than a week before Jenny started to feel suspicious that Taylor was back in the picture. Sam wanted sex basically every day, and Jenny didn't. Sam had started to push her less and less. Taylor lived a short walk from Sam's place. It started to feel like a math problem with a simple solution—one that she could solve easily even if she didn't want to.

Being with Sam had become important to her, almost without her realizing it had happened. It was as though being without him was no longer optional. This made her thinking collapse in on itself, putting her in a crisis mentality even as she kept her thoughts to herself. Thinking of everything she had gone through with Rio—all of her fears, anxiety, and deep moral compromises (to the point of fearing he had her under his total control)—Jenny realized how much she simply needed not to be alone. She couldn't start over with someone new, someone more sensitive who might see the moat she had built around her emotions and insist on crossing it.

She believed she needed Sam, and she didn't want to imagine a world in which they were no longer together.

This feeling made the days pass in a white nimbus of doubt and fear, alternating with an encroaching numbness.

She had, to an extent, been forced to normalize Rio and what he had done. She knew this had severe consequences for her own psyche.

The murders-suicide had been all over the news. Sam talked about it for a couple of days, but he seemed to believe that the investigators had learned everything they needed to know about Margaret, Rhonda, and Stephen.

Jenny listened to Sam, trying not to react in a visible way.

Rio killed people seemingly without consequences. He had no conscience to bother him—just his obsessive thoughts that he used to fuel his drive. He was sincerely and genuinely invested in his idiosyncratic vision of religion to justify his actions, but the truth was simpler: he got and did what he wanted without any regard for the judgment of normal people.

Jenny had always been a rule follower. But why? Because of the fear of getting caught? She had lived years and years in fear of being captured, like an animal of prey constantly hunted by the stronger and the remorseless.

She was by that point essentially a conspirator in multiple homicides. Nothing she could tell the police or a jury would allow her to walk away from that. She had crossed a line and could never return to the other side.

Maybe her big mistake was caring about the rules at all.

Is Rio corrupting me, or is he exposing my true nature?

Sometimes when she looked at Sam, she allowed herself a gloating feeling. Sam had no idea who he was dealing with. Sam thought he knew how everything worked, how it all added up. But he didn't.

She sat at her desk in her office at the end of a long day seeing clients. The building was quiet. The snow outside her window had mostly melted, with just patches of white where the sun couldn't break through the trees.

She thought about her situation carefully, pulling herself back into her sense of morality, trying to weigh all the factors in the equation. The more she thought about it, the more frustrated she became. Whatever she valued, it didn't line up with how the world worked or how it had treated her. Her anger felt searing, almost reckless.

Am I just naïve?

She was going to have to look out for herself and for what she wanted. She was going to make sure Taylor was kept at arm's length, and she was going to act aggressively, if need be, to keep her away from Sam.

It didn't help that Taylor was so pretty, and younger than Jenny.

Jenny was prepared to defend what she considered her territory. She had conceded enough, across so many dimensions of her life. Here was where she was going to draw the line. The net result of all she was feeling, thinking, and experiencing was making her feel like she needed to embrace risk and no longer run from it.

No more running. Not here.

The test of her resolve came within a few days. Jenny had been looking for signs of suspicious behavior between Sam and Taylor. Taylor lived just a few doors down from Sam, so there was no effective way to create distance between the two. If they wanted to see each other, they needed only to walk about 150 feet and they could be together any time of day or night.

She asked Sam straight-out if he was sleeping with Taylor. He denied it, over and over. She didn't feel comfortable taking his word.

Over the next few weeks, Jenny saw things that led her to believe that Taylor was still in the picture. She found a note from her to Sam in his house. It looked as though it had been outdoors at some point, because it was water-stained. This made Jenny remember Sam telling her that Taylor left notes under the windshield wiper of his car when they had been dating. Sam explained the note away by saying it was left over from that time.

Then why did he save it? Sam insisted that nothing had happened since he and Jenny got back together. But then a few days later, she thought she saw Taylor driving Sam's car when she was going to the grocery store, but she sped by so fast that Jenny couldn't get a good look at the license plate. Maybe there was an innocent explanation, but when Jenny confronted Sam, he continued to deny that anything was going on.

She had never felt this way before; it was as though every threat to her safety and happiness was tied up in this jealousy toward Taylor.

A few days later, Jenny had been rehearsing in her mind what she wanted to say to Sam. She had been building up the courage to finally stand up for herself. Up until then, she kept losing her courage when she really wanted to set things straight. She might be wrong in her suspicions, for one thing. For another, she was terrified of losing Sam and being alone again.

What if Sam simply loved Taylor more and wanted to be with her? What would happen after that? If a client had come to Jenny with this set of thoughts and feelings, Jenny would have recommended that the person take a step back and evaluate what was really going on. But Jenny was in no position to take advice, whether her own or anyone else's. She felt trapped in a corner with events rushing around her, and with no sense of control or even a foundation of morality and rightness.

She was in a terrible place, and it happened so quickly that she failed to see the warning signs within herself. She knew her self-esteem had plummeted, but she couldn't gather the threads of who she used to be in order to feel stable again.

When she thought about it, Taylor was superior to her in every way. She had shining blonde hair, an athletic figure, and was perky and optimistic—Jenny had seen all of these qualities the couple of times she had spotted her on the street when visiting Sam's place. Jenny began to think that any man would prefer Taylor to her.

In the next days, when she was driving to work or sitting in her office between clients, she would have a sort of Socratic interrogation with herself, asking questions and answering them in a slightly different tone of voice.

"Is Taylor prettier than me?"

"Yes."

"Has Taylor committed and abetted multiple terrible felonies?""Probably not."

"If Sam knew the truth about you, what would he do?"

"Leave me and go back to Taylor."

It wasn't unlike the kind of self-referential dialogues Rio indulged in during his counseling sessions with Jenny.

Then, with the afternoon shadows lengthening through the window, the bare tree limbs outside twisting like elbows and fingers, a thought came to her unbidden: maybe Rio's next victim could be Taylor. After all, if Sam was cheating on Jenny with her, she would qualify as evil by Rio's standards.

She felt a terrible wave of nausea and pain in her gut. She was dizzy, as though she was spiraling down.

Who am I?

Jenny pledged to push that awful notion out of her mind and deal with her problems like a normal person. Another solution would present itself. She had no active malice for Taylor, who was just someone trying to be happy in the world, just like Jenny.

But the feelings of jealousy were very hard to shake, and in certain moments they crystallized into rage. Her wish for Taylor to meet with some kind of misfortune took root in her psyche, a compartmentalized desire that she could at once observe and be filled with.

Part of her wanted to talk to Rio about what this was like.

CHAPTER TWENTY-FOUR

A HOLE IN THE MIDDLE OF HER CHEST

BOTH RIO AND JENNY had a lot on their minds when they met for their next counseling appointment. It was a far cry from their very first sessions, which had been marked by long and awkward silences and Rio's vague evasions.

Now Rio had no hesitancy about taking the lead and exploring his thoughts aloud. He was the client, admittedly, and it was his prerogative, but Rio also had no real consideration for other people's feelings or subjective experiences. It was all about his needs, at least until the point at which Jenny would decide to assert herself.

"I'm having doubts about how I handled my symptoms that night," Rio was saying. "I dealt with the obsession over the blood spots by making up an elaborate plan right there in the moment. I'm not sure if this was a good thing to do or not."

Jenny folded her hands in front of her mouth.

News coverage indicated that the three deaths were being considered a murder-suicide, with hints of an affair between Margaret and Stephen. There was speculation that Rhonda had walked in on them, or that she had found out and threatened to divorce Stephen.

Rio had covered his tracks.

"I'm wondering: have I made progress or am I backsliding?" Rio continued.

He had already gone into detail about what he had done that night. She wouldn't listen to details of the crimes, but she allowed him to tell her about his elaborate ruse in order to have an alibi for any of his own blood he spilled in the house.

She didn't want to admit it to him, but she thought the improvised plan was actually ingenious and remarkably creative.

Silence filled the room. Rio looked down at the carpet. He seemed lost in his monumental self-regard. It seemed hugely ironic: here he was, asking her questions that were actually within the realm of the conventionally therapeutic. But Jenny was lost in her own thoughts, her own swell of concerns and worries.

"I need an answer," Rio said, looking up at her. "I stood up to my obsessions like you said. Now I'm not sure what to do."

"Tell me more," Jenny said softly.

"It felt really good at first, defying the OCD," Rio said. "Like nothing I'd ever done before. But now I'm wondering if I stood up to the OCD, or if I defied God."

Jenny paused. "Well, that's the trick, isn't it?"Rio frowned. "What does that mean?"Jenny leaned forward. "Where do your rules come from?" she asked. "Do they come from God? Or are they rationalizations produced by your mind?"

"I don't follow," Rio said with his brow tensed.

"Are your rules and your mission simply things you make up and tell yourself in order to justify your feelings and actions that you would take anyway?"

Rio rubbed the stubble on his chin thoughtfully.

"I've always been this way," he replied. "I was chosen by God."

"Think back. Think hard," Jenny ordered him. "Are you chosen? Or did you have these feelings of hate and violent lust towards women long before you connected them to any divine law? Be honest with yourself."

"I've thought about my compulsions as a mental disorder," Rio said.

This surprised Jenny.

"Be honest with yourself," she said. "Be willing to challenge your beliefs."

"Thinking about it that way enabled me to see a plan of action after I saved Margaret," he added. "I was able to get it under control. But that doesn't make the doubts go away permanently.""People talk about OCD like it's something funny or silly," Jenny said. "It's not. It presents massive challenges for each individual it affects."

Rio nodded, his expression solemn.

"I don't know," he said. "Maybe my urges and compulsions

make it easier for me to believe that I'm a kind of undercover hero, chosen by God, more special than anyone else in the world."

He looked at Jenny with something she had never before seen in his expression: uncertainty and a kind of humbleness. He looked like a child who was expecting some kind of negative reaction from a parent.

"I think it's amazing that you're able to allow that thought to live in your mind," she told him. "It's a clear sign of intelligence and flexibility."

"So let's say it's all really me," he said. "All of it. Just me."

"OK," Jenny said.

She realized that they might be on the verge of a breakthrough. If Rio was able to strip away all of his religious delusions and grandiosity, he might be able to absorb the moral magnitude of what he had done.

"Then I killed all those people and became a great serial killer without any help from God," he said, pride creeping back into his voice. "Without any help from anyone. I made myself special just by declaring it to be true and acting on it. *That's* power."

She hadn't expected this quick shift, but she probably should have. It wasn't as though Rio was going to suddenly develop a human sense of conscience and remorse. Instead, he had shifted even deeper into his narcissism and grandiosity.

It would be deeply fascinating if it wasn't so chilling: he entertained the idea of disconnecting himself from his religious beliefs, but this led to his converting himself into a kind of

God, as opposed to worshipping Him.

Does this make him better or worse than the killer who stepped in here on the very first day? Jenny leaned back in her chair.

"That's not where I was going," she said. "I was hoping we could come to see that the whole idea of killing isn't the best thing to do. I'd like you to start to see the relationship between your desires and the formation of your spiritual worldview, so you can break free from both."

Rio didn't say anything. He had gone inward, staring into the near distance at nothing, his psychological gears clearly turning. His mind was active and energetic. She made a leap herself and thought that he might be envisioning himself as a different kind of killer, unbound by the OCD symptoms and convoluted religious narratives.

Did I just free him to become even worse?

While she tried to put forth a calm manner, she scrambled in her mind for ways to redirect his thought process.

"When you returned to the house with the tow truck, you exposed yourself to law enforcement," she said.

This brought him out of his reverie.

"It was a risk I had to take."

"Maybe yes, maybe no. Who knows?" Jenny kept her tone firm. "But you're on their radar now, one way or the other. Maybe they don't suspect you of anything or the moment, but aren't you tempting fate?"

"Now you sound like the voices," Rio said.

"Maybe the voices are trying to help," Jenny replied.

Or course it ran counter to a constructive course of treatment to recommend giving in to obsessive thoughts. But they had departed from any conventional treatment strategy a long time ago.

"Think about it," Jenny said. "If you commit another murder, the police aren't going to so quickly dismiss any connection they find between you and the crime. They're not going to see a second time as a coincidence, not if they're any good at all. Maybe this is it?" "What do you mean?" "Maybe it's time to stop being a serial killer," Jenny said.

Rio's face froze, and his eyes stared into the distance. Then he seemed to reinhabit his body, and his mouth broke into a wide grin and his eyes gleamed with humor. He nodded at her and wagged his finger, the way you would at a naughty dog.

"Nice try," he said.

There was something so cold and mirthless in his wide grin that Jenny felt a chill run through her entire body.

"You've helped me," he told her. "You really have. You're good at what you do."

"Don't mock me," she said.

"I'm not!" He still had that awful smile on his face. "I mean it! Look, you just made me realize that going back to the house was the right thing to do. Why? Because it was what I decided, and I don't make mistakes."

Part of her was watching this seeming transformation with rapt attention—his body seemed to puff up on the sofa, and he radiated a kind of manic energy. It was like witnessing a chemical chain reaction that she was helpless to stop.

"Now I know I should never underestimate myself," he added. "I should never let my doubts diminish my *power.*"

There was no stopping him.

It was ridiculous to even think that I could.

"All right, you have a good point," she said.

He looked at her. He wasn't even a person. He was a force. He was evil come to life.

"Climb back on the horse and get at it, then," she said.

*What am I doing?*Everything was wrong. Nothing meant anything. Life was nothing but a brutal battle for survival and will.

"You have two more to go, right?" she asked.

He nodded, seeming pleased with her. "Yes," he said. "Two more."

"The mission still exists, then?"*Am I reducing harm or increasing it?*"I know what you're asking me," he said. "You have to understand this: I will still have my slaves in the afterlife. God is real. But my obsessive thoughts are merely of this world. I don't need them to help me find meaning."

It was odd, but in a way, Jenny saw that she had made a positive contribution to her client. Her counseling efforts had led to a breakthrough in Rio's interpretation of the evidence of his experience.

What am I looking for? Validation? Approval?

It wasn't as though she was going to be able to write a book about all of this, explaining how she helped a murderer break through his delusions and find a purity in his perspective on what he did.

Life is nothing but a brutal battle.

"What about you, anyway?" Rio asked. He shifted his focus so quickly, now looking at her like a lab specimen. Not for the first time, she felt that when she talked about her own life, it gave Rio practice at pretending to be a human being. "What's the latest? You still back together with the cop?" She paused. The next moment seemed as though it hung as a sort of miniature eternity.

"I think he's cheating on me," she said.

Rio shifted forward on the sofa. His attention was now very focused.

"You don't say."

"It's someone who Sam had a previous sexual relationship with," Jenny explained. "They live close to each other. I think she's seducing him and leading him to commit infidelity when he's supposed to be faithful to me."

Rio was expressionless.

"She must be pretty," he said.

A sudden lacerating pain ran through both her temples. She pretended to feel nothing.

"Sam certainly thinks so," she said.

Rio leaned back and looked out the window. He seemed to be losing interest. Jenny looked at the clock. Their session was running down to its final minutes.

In the middle of this horrible moment, Jenny had a vision, cartoon-like, of the classic devil and angel perched on both her shoulders. She wondered if this was what it was like for Rio sometimes, the impulses pulling and tearing until there was no center left for guidance.

"It's too bad you're going through that," he finally said, peering up at the gray sky through the glass.

"I'm worried she's going to destroy my life," Jenny said.

"Homewrecker," Rio mused, his gaze still far off in the distance.

He's going to kill anyway.

Some other part of her, deep inside, was screaming in despair.

"What's her name?" Rio asked.

"Taylor," Jenny replied. "Her name is Taylor."

"She's evil to you, isn't she?" Rio asked. He swiveled his gaze back to her, his look expectant.

Jenny nodded.

Rio leaned back and folded his arms.

"Say it," he said.

Jenny stared at him. Her head was pounding.

"Say what?" she asked.

"Say you want me to save her."

The pounding. A hole in the middle of her chest, like she was never going to be able to properly breathe again.

She whispered it.

"What's that?" Rio said. "I must be getting hard of hearing. I thought you said something, but it didn't come through clear enough."

"I think you should save her," Jenny said in a low voice, her eyes burning, her spirit in flames.

"I guess that would help both of us, wouldn't it?" Rio asked. "I get another save, and you get this problem removed from your life. You get the cop all to yourself."

Jenny looked down.

"There's only one problem," Rio said.

Jenny felt tears running down her cheeks.

"What?" she asked.

"It's a logistical question." Rio explained. "You know her. I'm your client. There's a connection there, don't you see? Weren't you just telling me that I've already tempted fate?" Jenny fought to stay in control of herself. She was suddenly afraid that she was going to pass out, tumble out of her chair, and hit her head on the table between them. She steadied herself, still unable to look at him.

"Never mind," she said. "I don't know what I was—"

"Of course, it's not a problem if I do it right," Rio said.

Jenny stayed silent.

"And so what if I come to you for counseling?" he said, seeming to be talking himself into it. "A lot of people do. And hell, if the police come and question you about me, you'll be able to tell them what a good boy I am. Right?" Jenny nodded.

"You said she's pretty," Rio said.

She nodded again.

"Tell me more."

CHAPTER TWENTY-FIVE

PEOPLE PLAYED OUT PATTERNS THEY DIDN'T KNOW THEY HAD

RIO BEGAN PLANNING to make Taylor Stolly his eighth victim.

It was clearly the hand of God that had pointed her out to him, using Jenny as a conduit.

He knew that, normally, Taylor's connection to him through Jenny would be too much of a risk for him to go forward with saving her, but his pushback against his OCD symptoms and his revelations during counseling with Jenny had made his confidence grow to the point that he felt he was entitled to a certain degree of recklessness.

It was also a welcome feature that this killing would tie him even tighter to Jenny, and that he would gain even more leverage and control over her.

But fair was fair. There would be a ninth victim after Taylor, and then Rio would free Jenny once and for all. There would no longer be any risk for her being exposed as the person who shot David Saunders.

Saving Taylor, in some respects, would be easier than planning for a stranger. Jenny had been able to provide a good deal of intelligence on her. He knew where Taylor lived, where she worked, what kind of person she was, and what her daily habits were.

Most importantly, although Jenny wasn't aware of it, she had unwittingly provided him with an ideal alternate suspect in Sam Longford. Longford had a very special significance for Rio. He had investigated other murders Rio had committed. He viewed implicating the policeman as a way to make up for returning to the house where he killed Margaret, Rhonda, and Stephen. It was a way to wipe the slate clean and confuse the police even more than they already were.

Rio started trying to think like Longford as he planned the crime. How would a police officer choose to commit a murder? What would be Longford's motive? How would that motive be expressed in the way things played out? At the same time, Rio was worried that the police might be reluctant to investigate and charge one of their own. It would be necessary to frame Longford as thoroughly as possible. It was of primary importance that Jenny's boyfriend be the chief suspect.

At their next counseling session, Rio detailed a plan that he assumed Jenny would go along with.

"I need you to access Sam Longford's phone," he said.

Jenny looked up, surprised. "Why?" she asked.

"Just for a couple of minutes," Rio explained calmly. "I need you to send a couple of text messages from his phone to yours. I need you to suggest that Longford is really angry with Taylor, to the point of wanting to hurt her."

"What are you—"

"Then I need you to text back, saying that he's made these threats before and that you don't want him to act impulsively. Then you send one more from him, saying something like, 'I wish I could control this rage.'"

Rio waited for a moment, making sure Jenny had absorbed his instructions. He looked at her expression but couldn't read anything there.

"Should I go over it again?" he asked.

"No," Jenny said. He wasn't sure, but she might have been upset. "Are you talking about framing Sam for the murder?"

"Yes," Rio replied.

He was pretty sure she was getting upset. This surprised him.

"I want Sam and I to be together," Jenny said. "I need you to promise that you're not going to do anything to make it look like Sam was involved.""So you're not going to do it?" Rio asked.

He stared at her. It made no sense that she didn't see the beauty of what he was suggesting. It would take care of so much, including her dependence on someone who didn't seem right for her.

"No," she said. "Anyway, it's not possible. He's got his phone with him all the time, and I don't have any way of knowing his passcode."

She might have been lying. Rio watched her.

"All right," he said. "I'll think of something else."

"Leave Sam out of this," she said firmly.

"Leave Sam out of this," Rio repeated.

He had no intention of keeping his word. He would simply have to execute his plan without the assistance of Jenny, who seemed to be having a bout of sentimentality. He needed more information, such as Longford's work schedule, and he was going to have to be creative in the way he obtained it.

"I don't need to make Longford a suspect," Rio told her. "In fact, I already have someone else in mind. I've followed the Taylor woman around enough to see her hanging out with someone I recognize from town. He has a criminal history and a violent temper—he's always getting in bar fights and people know he's volatile."

"OK. Good," Jenny said quietly.

She wasn't aware that this individual didn't exist.

They talked some more, touching on the current state of his OCD symptoms. Rio complimented Jenny for the insights she had provided him with, although she seemed distracted, as though something was the matter. Rio waited until he thought she had let her guard down to ask a question he had been saving up since he first walked in that afternoon.

"What's that?" Rio asked, motioning to a little side table next to the door. On it was a high-quality screwdriver with a distinctive brand marking, the kind of tool that a professional mechanic would buy. It didn't seem like something Jenny would own.

"That screwdriver?" she asked. "It's Sam's. I borrowed it because there's a chair in the waiting room with a loose arm. I need to get it tightened up. It's embarrassing, but I don't own any tools of my own."

"You should have your own tools," he told her.

"I'll keep that in mind," she replied.

"It's a nice one," Rio said, motioning to it. "Is Longford handy?""He definitely cares about his tools," Jenny said, flashing a brief smile. She seemed to genuinely care about the policeman. "Sam's dad was a mechanic, and he gave Sam a bunch of tools a long time ago."

"Looks like Dad had good taste in tools," Rio said.

For the remainder of the session, Rio's primary focus was on how he was going to get that screwdriver. He talked about his house and some politics at work, all the while circling around how to manipulate Jenny. There were only a couple of minutes left in the session when he decided what to do.

"That reminds me," he said. He fished around in his pockets until he found a business card. "Any chance I can get you to make a copy of this for me?"He knew there was a photocopier down the hall, one that was shared by all the offices in the building.

Jenny squinted at the card. "Tax accountant?""Someone at work told me there's things I can do to get creative with my mortgage interest," Rio said, his voice flat and without affect. "Told me to call this guy, but said he wanted me to bring the card back."Jenny looked about to say something, but stopped herself. "OK, sure," she said. "Hang on for just a minute."

He really did have power of control over her.

After she stepped out, Rio pulled out a few tissues from the box on the window ledge and used them to carefully pick up the screwdriver from the table. Not only was it a distinctive tool, it was also part of a set and might even contain a set of Longford's fingerprints. There were all kinds of potential uses for it.

Jenny brought the card and the copy back. Rio thanked her and handed over a roll of pre-folded cash for the session.

"Until next time," he said.

"See you in a week," Jenny replied. They pretty much always said the same words at the end of their sessions now.

Outside, he waited in the truck for a few minutes until he saw the next client go into Jenny's office, a middle-aged man in a puffy coat and long scarf. Then Rio quickly went back inside to the waiting room, where he found the chair with the loose arm and tightened it up. He hoped that Jenny wouldn't think much more about the screwdriver if she didn't notice that the chair had been fixed.

People tended to put things out of their minds that they couldn't explain.

Rio continued to formulate his strategy for saving Taylor. He methodically and conceptually replayed every murder he had committed to date. It was very important that the execution of each crime had a distinct look and feel to it, so that the police would never connect the homicides as the act of a single individual. There was also an element of pride involved, and the need for originality that fed Rio's compulsion to be among the greatest killers of all time.

He wanted to plan out the killing so that all the evidence pointed to Sam Longford. Rio no longer felt as dominated by his obsessions, but he observed a similar attention to detail without letting the voices and urges take over.

It was a fine line—he wanted to know when he was being appropriately detail-oriented without letting the obsessions gain hold over him again. The thoughts were insidious and they were still waiting at every turn. He was continually plagued by distractions. At one point he recalled Jenny telling him that Taylor was pretty, and he got stuck in a loop of fantasizing about assaulting Taylor with Jenny watching. That was too complex, too risky, and would require managing Jenny, but it still kept him from focusing for a couple of days and moving on to more realistic strategies.

He worked to balance creativity, efficiency, and the containment of his obsessions. Finally, a plan started to come together that would adequately address all of the factors involved while also seeming novel compared to the others he had saved. It was after a few times driving through her neighborhood that the strands started to weave themselves together.

Taylor was a jogger. She went for a run exactly three times a week on a schedule. She would even run in the rain when it wasn't coming down too heavy.

That was so important. He couldn't violate the rule about

the rain. God still needed to signal that it was time to cleanse the evil from the Earth.

Taylor's running routes varied, and that made it almost impossible to predict her specific actions on a particular day. There didn't seem to be any pattern to where she ran. Sometimes she would stay in the neighborhood and run in a big circle for about three miles. She had earbuds in every time she ran, which would mean she couldn't hear someone approaching her.

Watching her made it more difficult to control himself.

Other days she would cross over through a wooded area and run through an entirely different neighborhood. She seemed to like variety. She would run on large streets, she would run on side streets—there didn't seem to be a pattern there, either. Every time he followed her at a distance and tried to predict where she would go next, she would make a turn that surprised him. One time she glanced over her shoulder a couple of times as she ran, as though maybe recognizing his truck.

This made him feel more pressure to move up the timetable.

To continue his surveillance and lower his risk of exposure, Rio started parking on the edge of Taylor's neighborhood, pulling his bicycle out of the bed of the pickup truck and cycling around. He wore different hats and jackets each time.

It was this technique that enabled Rio to spot the factor that made it all come together.

A local utility truck was parked in front of one of the homes close to Taylor's single-story cottage. The workers had placed orange construction cones in the street to let passing vehicles know that the truck was parked in an awkward location.

Taylor had come around the corner onto the street, jogging with her hair in a ponytail bobbing under the baseball cap she wore. The construction cones had an unexpected effect on her running path. Instead of moving to the center of the street and simply jogging past the truck, Taylor abruptly turned and made her way down a side street.

People played out patterns they didn't even know they had.

Rio stood there at a distance, wondering if he could position construction cones in such a way to provoke a similar reaction—essentially directing Taylor onto the path he wanted her to follow.

The ideal abduction site was a small path through the woods that connected Taylor's neighborhood with the other one in which she liked to run. The path was about 250 feet long and had several bends in it. Near the halfway point on the path, a person would be out of sight from either side of the woods.

At first, Rio had decided that the path would be the ideal place to actually commit the murder itself, but obsessions encroached in the form of endless questions. Should he kidnap Taylor from her own neighborhood and take her someplace else? Would it be best to simply invade her residence and save her there? How risky was placing cones on the road, and what might a neighbor do if they saw him?

He felt himself giving in again. Sitting in his truck, parked on the side of the highway, he mustered his energy and loudly rejected all the thoughts, yelling out in rage and frustration as cars passed in either direction.

The debate had ended. Taylor would die by the path connecting the two neighborhoods. It was simple—it was a little-trafficked area with places of concealment. There were no cameras there to record what happened. Rio would keep it straightforward. He would lie in wait there and surprise Taylor during her run.

Preparing didn't take much more effort. Rio had access to plenty of orange traffic cones and barrels at work, where they were stacked up in piles behind the garage. He usually carried a few cones in his tow truck when he was on a shift and had to use them pretty often. There were so many lying around that no one would notice the five or six he would need to take. As usual, the most difficult thing to coordinate was the weather. It needed to rain on one of Taylor's scheduled running days—and hopefully not so hard that she might be tempted to skip her exercise.

He had to wait for three long weeks. Finally, the forecast said it would be raining off and on for the next two days, the second of which aligned with Taylor's jogging schedule.

Spring was still weeks away and the temperature was hovering around the freezing point. Rio had some concern that ice might develop, keeping Taylor home, but he kept planning in hope that the second day would be suitable.

He drove out the night before to the neighborhood where Taylor lived and carefully set up the orange cones. He knew that even though the cones were brightly colored, they were actually effectively invisible.

People tended not to closely observe their daily surroundings.

He placed them so they weren't blocking the road but left them in a pattern such that drivers and pedestrians would have to go around them. He knew that Taylor never ran in the middle of the street, so when she encountered them, she would have to turn right or turn left. Turning left would put her into traffic, so Rio was reasonably sure that she would end up going the way he wanted her to—a path that she often opted to follow of her own volition.

Rio needed just one more thing.

Several years before, not long after Rio had just started working as a tow-truck driver, there had been a fatal accident involving several vehicles on Old Baltimore Pike. It took Rio and two other tow-truck drivers to quickly remove totaled cars and a minivan after ambulances took away the injured and killed motorists.

The car Rio was assigned to tow was a Volkswagen Jetta. A mother of two who had been driving it got distracted, wandered out of her lane, and hit a Chevrolet Suburban head-on. Several vehicles behind the suburban weren't able to stop in time, and in total, six vehicles ended up getting involved. The mother had both her children in the car at the time, a young boy and a girl. She and both her children died in the accident. The Volkswagen itself was unrecognizable as having once been a motor vehicle.

Often after these types of accidents, the tow-truck drivers would take anything they wanted from the cars. They might scavenge its various parts, remove any money that might be left in the console, or take away anything else that might be of value. They knew nobody was going to make an issue over a missing pocket knife, a flashlight, or a few dollars in change. Even if a relative of the deceased thought to look for such items, their grief and anguish over losing those killed in the accident would override any desire to insist on investigating. As for the car itself, if it was totaled, no one worried about missing batteries, catalytic converters, fuses, or sound systems.

After Rio towed the Volkswagen back to the yard on a roll-back truck, he looked through the car in search of his reward. Other than a couple of dollars in change under some papers in the glovebox, the only other thing Rio came across was a doll that had belonged to the deceased little girl. It was about eight inches tall, and it had a string in the back that a child could pull in order for it to make a noise.

It wasn't clear what the doll was supposed to say or sound like originally, but in its damaged state from the terrible crash, it could only make a sort of eerie moaning sound. Rio took the doll into the shop, and some of the other workers would pull the string and laugh nervously at the strange and unsettling noise it made. Another consequence of the damage that the doll had sustained was that after its string was pulled back and released, it took several seconds before it made any sound at all. That led to a morbid prank the workers played on each other: one worker would pull the doll's string and slide the doll under another worker's feet when they were looking the other way. The unsuspecting victim would be startled, shocked, and usually mortified by their frightened reaction.

Rio started calling it the "doll grenade," which made his

coworkers laugh. Rio enjoyed their reaction. He didn't often make people laugh.

He also thought the doll made a sound that wasn't completely unlike the noise some people made in his presence just as they were dying.

At first Rio had wondered if the doll was possessed by a demon. But now he knew better. It was just another strange thing in a weird world.

But once having thought about it, Rio couldn't stop thinking about how he wanted to use it when he came upon Taylor on the path. He thought it was a fitting final sound for her to hear in the moments before she paid the price for her evil actions.

CHAPTER TWENTY-SIX

THE RHYTHM OF HIS OBSESSION

RIO FELT POWERFUL, dominant, and in control of everything when the day arrived that he planned to save Taylor. Up until that point, everything had gone more or less as he planned it. The orange traffic cones were in place close to her house. After he went through the usual protocols to make sure no one was following him, he had driven his truck to a commercial lot not far from Taylor's street. The lot contained an abandoned gas station that had been up for sale for more than three years. He parked the truck behind the building and walked into the woods toward her neighborhood.

It had started drizzling just a half hour before.

It was time to save the young woman.

The route in front of him was straightforward. He walked through the shadows of trees undetected until he reached the path. As the time of the killing approached, his anxiety increased and he found himself engaging in counting rituals: steps, his own hand movements, the trees in his path. If he touched a tree with one hand, he'd have to touch the next one with the other, then a third with both hands, to relieve some of the pressure.

He noticed, as he had so many times before, that the obsessions and compulsions were slowing him down significantly. Finally, he stopped walking. A branch cracked under his foot.

Stop, he said to the thoughts, yelling to himself inside.

He took a few steps. Almost beyond his conscious will, he caught himself doing it again. Every time he approached a tree that he needed to go around, he'd touch the opposite side: *left, right, left, right, left*.

The sound of the rain seemed to echo the rhythm of his obsession.

When he reached the path, he was preoccupied because he had passed one more tree on the left than he had on the right. But he was out of trees.

Stop it. Get out of my head.

He stopped talking to himself in his mind. He was alone on the path, with no sign of anyone in either direction, until he saw something: a figure coming toward him, bouncing up and down with the stride of a jogger's figure.

It worked. He lunged back into the trees before she got too close.

He cursed under his breath. He had been so rattled by the obsessive thoughts that he jumped back behind a tree other than the one he had planned to use. This one was about half as wide as the other, but he made the best of the situation by sliding around sideways as she came nearer.

She was jogging faster than usual. Maybe she sensed she needed to get through these woods as quickly as possible. It was a little too remote, too hidden away from the safety of the eyes of others.

Rio slid the doll out of his jacket, pulled the string, and lobbed it up into the air as she reached his position on the path.

It happened so quickly. Taylor paused and looked down at the doll just behind her on the path. She stared at it in shock as she pulled out one earbud.

She stared at the doll on the ground as it let out its unearthly, eerie cry.

Taylor went into a flat-out run.

Her impressive burst of speed was no match for Rio, whose legs were longer and who had the advantage of adrenaline-fueled surprise.

Rio knocked her on the head with a two-pound mallet, sending her tumbling hard into the underbrush to the side of the path. After she fell, it was silent under the trees, save for the gentle sound of the rain trickling through the treetops like the spires of a cathedral.

He had been careful not to hit her too hard. When she came

to semi-consciousness after a couple of moments, she saw Rio standing over her and started to scream. But he produced his Glock 42 pistol and pointed it between her eyes.

When he dragged her into the woods and dominated her, he tried to conjure up images of Jenny watching him with approval. To his surprise, it didn't make the experience more satisfying for him, and he abandoned it before he was finished.

The rain began working to cleanse the Earth. God was in the house.

He felt angry with Jenny for diminishing his experience, but he quickly refocused on the task at hand. He saved her with a single blow from the same mallet: quick and reasonably painless.

"See you soon," he said quietly.

Then he took Sam Longford's screwdriver and drove it deep into Taylor's neck. He considered pulling it back out and dropping it a few hundred yards away so as not to be too obvious, but he didn't trust the police to be smart and thorough enough to find it and pin it to the investigation.

All of a sudden, the sky opened up, rain fell hard and fast, and a wind blew through the branches of the trees. It was happening. He approved. He was cleansing.

Unmitigated power coursed through him. He was not God, but he was of God. He had used his power to make a reality from which others would cower in simpering fear.

He left her there.

Rio was able to resist the obsessions as he made his way through the woods back to his truck. With his power, he was able to make it back in about half the time it had taken before. Once he got in the Tacoma, he watched the road until it was clear before pulling out from behind the abandoned gas station.

He decided to leave the orange cones where they were. They were unmarked, and there was nothing to tie them to Rio or to his job.

He slowly and calmly drove the eight miles back to his house.

No sooner had Rio crossed the ditch behind his house on the carefully laid planks than an older woman walking her dog came across Taylor on the path.

Rio found out about this the next day from a TV news report. He wondered why this woman had been out walking in such heavy rain. He hadn't expected Taylor to be found so quickly, and his mind was quickly clouded with dark thoughts of paranoia.

Had the woman walking her dog seen him?

Did she see him commit the killing or spot him leaving?

Why was she there?

And then it hit him: he had left the doll. He had tossed it into the trees while he was dominating her, though, and maybe it was in a pile of mud and leaves. Maybe the rain had washed away anything that made it distinctive.

You made a mistake.

So many times, he had attracted the attention of his co-workers with those pranks with the doll grenade.

Trying to make people like you. Making them laugh at you like you're some kind of buffoon.

Anger started building inside him, which he tried to placate by fantasizing about killing the woman with the dog. He wrote down her name from the news report.

He fought against committing another off-mission homicide.

The dog must have led the woman to the body. She didn't see anything. If they find the doll, they won't think anything of it and I made sure my DNA isn't on it.

It kept raining.

CHAPTER TWENTY-SEVEN

WHO EXACTLY WAS THE DEVIL?

JENNY PROFOUNDLY DREADED her next session with Rio. She had been numb in the days after learning of Taylor's murder, beyond the landscape of regular human emotions. Whatever Rio was going to tell her when he came in that day, it wasn't going to ground her or allay any of the terrible dread she felt.

He showed up on time and let himself in. She had been looking out at the woods beyond her office window, where the sun struggled to peek through a gray bank of clouds.

For the first part of the session, Rio talked about how he had battled with his obsessions the day of the killing. He talked about the heavy downpour that was a sign of approval and love from God. When he talked about himself running through the woods back to his truck after he had left Taylor, it was with the grandiosity of an Olympic runner describing a gold-medal race. Not the words of a man who had brutally killed a woman before making his escape.

"It was epic," Rio said. "Heroic."She didn't say anything to him.

He looked at her with a deeply cold expression and started going into the details of the homicide. He watched her carefully as he spoke, trying to see if he could read any reaction. She wasn't going to give him any.

"Come on," he said as he stopped mid-story. "What's with you? Aren't you going to say anything? Try to talk me out of doing it again?"

She opened her mouth, but no words came out.

"I'm paying good money for this session," Rio said. "You're supposed to be helping me."

After all that had happened, he sounded almost hurt by her silence.

"You've . . . put me in an impossible situation," Jenny said. "I don't expect you to understand my perspective. But when this all started, I was only thinking one hour at a time. Maybe one minute. Now I can't stop thinking—"

"Quit it," he commanded her. "You're better than this."

Jenny felt her mouth open in shock.

"That woman was evil," he said. "You're too soft, too caught up in your need to feel good, to just admit the facts.""I know you think—""Evil." A coldness passed over Rio's features. "You think she was going to stop doing you wrong? Are you that simple-minded?""I don't—""Let me help you along," Rio said. "I watched her and that boyfriend of yours having sex in his living room. Does that help you understand?"She felt her eyes growing hot. He looked at her with a grim satisfaction, and she was completely unable to tell whether he was telling her the truth or not.

"You mean—""You were right. About all of it." Rio's eyes gleamed. "And they were so loud I could hear them through the window. You want to know what she was saying?"Jenny just shook her head.

"She was saying, 'Oh, Sam. Oh, Sam. Tell me that it's better being inside me than being with that cow Jenny. Tell me how you're going to leave her and come back to me. Keep going, Sam, I'm about to come.'"

Jenny felt a hot anger rise inside her. Everything had spun violently out of her control. Had Sam really done that to her, listened to Taylor talk about her that way while they were making love behind Jenny's back?"Taylor was the devil," Rio said to her firmly. "I need for you to toughen up and look at things the way they really are."

Who exactly was the devil in this situation?

"She was going to take away everything you care about," Rio added.

"The devil," Jenny repeated.

"Do you understand me now?" Rio asked.

"You tell me," Jenny said. "You're the one who killed her."

"You just called her the devil," Rio said.

"I was repeating what you said."

"Don't lie to yourself," Rio told her, as still as a statue.

Jenny felt it again. The hot anger, the jealousy. The fear that what little she had in this world was going to be snatched away.

"She's better off now," Rio said. "I saved her."

"You saved her," Jenny found herself repeating.

Rio just stared and nodded ever so slightly, one of those moments when he seemed to enjoy a grim satisfaction that he had lured Jenny over to his way of looking at the world. Within her anger, Jenny looked up at Rio with her jaw clenched tight.

"You stole the screwdriver," she said.

Rio looked surprised. "You noticed that?" he asked.

"And they found it at the crime scene." Jenny shook her head, trying to think of all the ramifications. "You tried to frame Sam."

Rio held up his hands in a gesture of innocence. "Things come, things go," he said. "Did Longford say anything about the investigators finding it?" "He said they found a screwdriver just like one in his set," Jenny said. "It scared him so much that he went down to his basement to check his tools. He was very relieved when he saw that he still had his full set."

Rio was quiet for almost a full minute. "You replaced it," he said.

It was satisfying, frustrating the meticulous plans of the psychopath in front of her. She felt no real fear—their fortunes were far too intertwined for this small mutual betrayal to cause an irreparable rift.

He sat back on the sofa and pursed his lips, looking at Jenny with no emotion. Finally, he let out a soft whistle.

"You think on your feet," he said.

"I have to," Jenny told him.

"Well, let's keep talking," Rio said. "I got some good news to remind you about. The next one I save is number nine. That's the end of the mission. It needs to be special. She needs to be like none other."

He gave her that look, as though there was some deeply profound hidden meaning behind what he said if only she was clever enough to determine what it was.

Instead of trying to solve his puzzle, Jenny fell back on a summarization technique she had learned in her training. She fell into the act of being his counselor, doing her best to heal him. She intended to solidify the idea in Rio's consciousness that one more killing would be the end of his career.

After all this, she was still trying to reduce overall harm.

"You've made a lot of progress in the time we've worked together," she told him. "Here you are, almost done. You've been brave enough to confront your obsessions, and you've learned about yourself. And now it's almost over. No more mission. Have you thought about what comes next?"

"I haven't really thought about it?" he said.

"But the killing will be over."

"I don't know," he said. "When I set out on this mission, there were some things I believed that I don't really believe anymore. What if my destiny is even greater than I thought? What if I underestimated how magnificent I am?" "You know what the most notorious killers have in common?" Jenny asked him.

"One thing: they all got caught."

Rio's eyes gleamed. "But what if the truly greatest are the ones we've never heard anything about?"She willed herself to take a deep breath, even though it caught in her chest.

"Are there any other goals you have?" she asked him. "There must be something else in life that you can apply your intensity and talent toward.""Lots of things, I guess." He smiled. "I guess I'll have to play it by ear. What, you think I should try to be a movie star?"

He seemed completely serious. She decided to steer the conversation to the ground of the rudimentary empathy skills he had developed.

"We talked before about how you have some psychopathy," she began.

"A little," he repeated. He put up his thumb and forefinger about half an inch apart and let out his humorless laugh.

"It gives you power, but there are downsides as well," she said. "I'm very impressed that you've made the effort to try to learn to see things from the perspectives of other people. It's an ability you can continue to cultivate."

"A hunter should be able to think like his prey," Rio told her.

"It's more than that," she said. "It's like when I read you the story and you weren't able to understand what the author was trying to say about the character. There are deeper levels of life that are available to you."Rio smiled at her. Its meaning was known only to himself.

"So there are things that I've been missing, is what you're telling me," he said.

They looked at one another, both thinking, both calculating. Jenny began to wonder what it was going to really cost her to be free.

CHAPTER TWENTY-EIGHT

JUSTICE
AND REDEMPTION

BACK AT HIS HOUSE, Rio decided to replace the brakes on his pick-up truck. He'd thought he had heard some screeching when he was driving home after he left Taylor in the woods, and this was just the kind of work that tended to calm his mind.

He had to admit it, he was inspired by what Jenny had said about his work developing some form of empathy.

I'm very impressed that you've made the effort to try to learn to see things from the perspectives of other people.

"Wow," he said to himself as he turned and unlocked his tool box. "You impressed her."

He wanted to take it to the next level. After all this time with Jenny, he wanted to really know what she was thinking and feeling.

He didn't really know if Taylor had been sleeping with Longford or not, but she had in the past, and that was enough for him. He told Jenny that Longford was cheating on her because it was what she needed to hear. Longford wasn't right for Jenny, based on what she had told him about their relationship. She could never be happy with someone like that.

Because Rio's understanding of empathy remained superficial at best, he didn't really believe that Jenny's need for Longford was so great that it led her to stand by while Rio eliminated Taylor. Or if the notion entered his mind, he overrode it with a deeply arrogant belief that he knew better than Jenny, who was bound by weakness and illusion.

In fact, he came away from their previous session with the dawning belief that Jenny was attracted to him.

He jacked the pickup truck up in the air, took off the wheels, and arranged all his tools. The work created almost a meditative state for him, and he tried to conjure up Jenny's worldview for examination and evaluation.

Maybe she didn't know how much she wanted Rio. Well, she should. He was unlike anyone she had ever met—powerful and full of purpose. Maybe she had some feelings for Longford that he couldn't understand. Rio thought about things that might make her happy, or make her sad, or make her feel sexually excited.

What does she desire?

The truth was, he knew next to nothing about women. He simply couldn't understand what Jenny might be thinking. He was exhausted and frustrated all of a sudden, as though the mental and emotional effort had drained him.

But he was sure she was part of his life's mission now. There was no way they could ever go back to the way they were before, when they didn't know each other and had only shared that brief encounter at Gazelle Lumber back in 2007.

He needed to try something different.

Rio had been streaming a number of movies over the past few months, in addition to his hardcore pornography habit. He mostly selected films that had strong sexual content, but many of those movies also had romantic storylines.

He had held that aspect of the films in contempt, not believing anything that they depicted could be remotely accurate. He couldn't believe the motives of the characters as they fell in love or got their feelings hurt, assuming that they were as unfeeling and cynical as he was. It had never occurred to him that these stories could be a gateway for him to learn about human nature.

What if those movies weren't all nonsense? What have I been missing out on?

Jenny had told him that there were deeper levels of life available to him. As he worked, he wondered if that had been some kind of code on her part. A hidden message that she wanted him to decipher.

One of the themes he had seen in the movies time and time again was jealousy. One lover would be angry or hurt when their partner was having sex with, or was otherwise romantically engaging with, a third party.

He observed this, but it never made much sense to Rio.

From his point of view, women were simply his property, or a resource to be used and exploited. Their feelings were no more important than those of an animal who was unhappy with its owner.

Rio's extreme narcissism and deep-seated desire to dominate did not leave room for any kind of real understanding that women had feelings. But he was willing to reconsider the notion. Jenny had praised his initial, tentative steps in that direction.

Ultimately, Rio perceived that if he could at least understand something about the feelings of women, and modify his behavior accordingly, he could get more of what he wanted.

His thoughts kept returning to Jenny.

Rio thought about several movies that depicted situations similar to what he thought Jenny was experiencing. They involved a woman who was dating or married to a man, and found out or suspected that the man had another lover. Some of the characters in these movies reacted in an extreme way. Rio discarded those scenarios.

But he detected a pattern: the women who had been cheated on by their boyfriends or husbands became angry at the other woman.

The construct of jealousy as an abstraction wasn't entirely foreign to Rio. He could have described the idea if someone had asked him to. He could understand why a woman in that position might *think* that their competing lover was problematic to their interests, but he couldn't comprehend why the woman *felt* jealous. The "thinking" part made sense to him as a cognitive process, but the "feeling" part did not.

He decided, slipping a brake pad into position, that he was just going to have to believe those emotions were real, even if he couldn't feel them himself.

His cognitive understanding of jealousy boiled down to one thing: sexual competition. In this way, he could understand it as a pragmatic function. If a woman wanted to have sex with a certain man, and that man was having sex with another woman, this created a clear and obvious problem. The woman would then have a number of strategic options, including finding another man, living without the lover, accepting the situation, or somehow eliminating that competition.

As these thoughts passed through his mind with a glimmer of affective understanding, Rio all at once began to appreciate jealousy's true power. As he logically sorted through the options presented by jealousy, there was only one that made complete sense to him: revenge. That was the only way to satisfy the feelings of rage and betrayal that accompanied jealousy. It was, he understood, far more powerful than could be accounted for by the simple dynamics of sexual competition. There were mysteries there for Rio, but he could see that those feelings replaced rational thought and calculation. They took control and necessitated some way of eliminating the third party who had given offense.

It was about more than sex. It was about justice and redemption.

His hands working on the car were essentially independent entities at this point as his mind continued to work. He took the concepts he had just developed and applied them to Jenny's situation.

Jenny had wanted Rio to kill Taylor. It hadn't been his idea.

There was a motive that had been largely hidden to Rio until that moment. Jenny wanted Taylor out of the picture, and she wanted her to suffer. The entire situation clicked into place in Rio's mind, with a clarity of insight that was extremely rare for him.

Does that make Taylor a clean save?

This world of emotional connection, seeing into the heart of someone else, was nothing short of dazzling. He was so amazed by the sensations washing over him that it took a moment for him to process the repercussions for him and Jenny.

When he did, he felt a cold anger that would have profoundly shocked anyone else who might have experienced it in their own mind.

She used me.

Jenny had put Rio in danger in order to satisfy her own needs. He had selected someone with connections that could point back to Rio. She had also frustrated his attempt at framing Longford.

She might not even be attracted to him. Jenny's evil might have clouded her judgment that severely.

What did I expect?

Rio had failed, after all, when he didn't kill Jenny when he had the chance all those years ago. This was his penalty.

Have to set things right.

He had been wondering who his ninth save was going to be.

But it would be difficult, wouldn't it, since Rio had a strong connection to Jenny. She would have to disappear completely, leaving no evidence behind. He was going to have to change his tactics because he had never disposed of a body in that way before.

Jenny had said that when a client has a breakthrough insight, they shouldn't simply stop and be happy with what they had accomplished. Instead, they should push further and try to build on it, and see what else was possible.

Rio racked his mind for a higher-level meaning to what he had been thinking. God was trying to communicate something, if he could only piece it together. It felt, as it often did, as though so much of the world was dark and hidden from him.

One time, Jenny had talked about inductive reasoning, when a person learns from a specific situation and then applies that knowledge to the world in general.

He now knew that Jenny was evil. What did that mean in a larger sense?

Rio believed that Jenny might have once been good, but that she was treacherous. As far back as the first time he had attacked her, he knew that she cavorted with a drug dealer. She was corrupt and dirty.

She had once been good. Probably all of them were at some point. It must have been a natural, universal process.

Therefore, all women must have been evil and none of them could be trusted.

He was almost finished replacing his brakes. He extended

his logic even further, his thoughts unfolding like the wings of a butterfly.

The mission will just be getting started with number nine.

Jenny would be the first kill that Rio made with his eyes wide open. She would be the catalyst for his evolution into a still-higher form of killer. She would not be the Omega, she would be the beginning: the Alpha. She would be Rio's greatest challenge yet, and she would be the wellspring of a new dawn of death and terror.

He had found himself. He had discovered the truth, and thus he was elevated to a higher plane of existence. From this point forward, he would be a superman who indulged his desires with no restrictions whatsoever.

Rio's excitement was indistinguishable from his rage.

He focused on the job at hand. It was time to set his mind to his task. The plan now was to dominate and enslave Jenny with a set of novel tactics, including how he would go in for the kill and what he would do with her afterwards.

All the new skills she had taught him would be crucial to his success.

CHAPTER TWENTY-NINE

IT'S GOING TO BE BEAUTIFUL

A COUPLE OF DAYS before her next scheduled session with Rio, Jenny had a spare hour after a client missed his appointment without calling in to warn her. She found herself out in the waiting room, where she sat in the chair that had once had a loose armrest and had been mysteriously repaired without her knowledge.

The night before, she had been speaking with Sam about what he knew about the Taylor Stolly case—which wasn't much, because he hadn't been assigned to the investigation. The department knew about his prior relationship with Taylor, so he had been kept at arm's length, but a fellow detective who was working the case shared some of the details out of respect for a colleague and because of Sam's loss.

She wasn't able to discern how much Sam might have been grieving for Taylor. She and Sam couldn't read one another.

Sam had told Jenny the day after the murder that he had learned that a screwdriver had been left in Taylor's neck, although Sam didn't have any knowledge about what kind of screwdriver yet—and he didn't seem to have any inkling that it was the same kind that came from the toolset in his basement. By the time he knew, she had replaced it.

Jenny had to go to the bathroom after Sam had told her to try to compose herself. She had suspected, of course, that Rio might have used the screwdriver in committing the crime after she noticed it missing from her office, but hearing about it with such bluntness overwhelmed her with nausea.

When Rio had said he wasn't going to try to frame Sam, she had taken him at his word. At their last counseling session, he had brushed aside her knowledge of his betrayal.

From the time Rio had told her that he knew all about the Big Deal, they had an uneasy alliance that produced a distorted form of mutual reliance. She had actually grown to rely on it, conveniently eluding the fact that she was trusting a psychopath.

She searched herself for regret and remorse. Mostly, she felt a panicky need for self-preservation. She had fooled herself into thinking she could stop running, but now she saw that the entire basis for thinking her alliance with Rio had an expiration date was false and deluded. The only way she would be free of the shooting of David Saunders would be with the death of one of them.

Any jury would surely convict her of conspiracy to commit murder. Somehow, the Big Deal had become the least of her worries.

Even though she had come so far in an attempt to save her own life, she feared Rio and wasn't sure she could stand up to him. But she had to keep reminding herself that her therapeutic approach had essentially freed him from his obsessions and made him more of a monster than ever before.

She had empowered him.

The obsessions used to limit his behavior and govern how many chances he would take. They had reined him in. Now it wasn't clear he saw any limits at all. He was essentially a time bomb of lethal harm.

She thought back to when she had killed David Saunders, when this had all begun. Rio had been the intended target, even if she hadn't even known his name that night in the rain when she had pulled the trigger. Rio should have died that night. He was the man who attacked her, the man who terrorized her, while David was an innocent bystander who came to the scene at the worst possible moment, when Jenny was brutalized and in a panic.

It might be too little and too late, but Jenny was the only one who knew about all the victims Rio had claimed and how dangerous he would continue to be.

In the bathroom that night, trying to stop her hands from shaking, she thought that she would tell Sam and that Sam would kill Rio. But then she realized that Sam wasn't that kind of boyfriend. He would be far more likely to turn her in than commit a homicide to protect her. She was beyond questions of right and wrong in that moment. She just knew that she couldn't trust Sam with her life.

There's no one I can trust.

She fantasized that Rio's psyche might collapse under its own contradiction and fury, and that he might kill himself. But there was no way that was going to happen. Rio was going to play out his psychopathy for as long as he possibly could.

There was only one logical conclusion.

She had no idea how to prepare herself, either physically or mentally, but she knew that even an animal of prey had the instincts to turn and fight its predator when there was no longer any other choice.

It was a cold February day when Rio arrived right on time for his scheduled appointment. It had snowed the night before, and the temperatures had dropped into the twenties before shifting into a freezing rain that coated the trees outside Jenny's office window with glistening ice.

Ordinarily, Jenny would have considered canceling appointments because of the hazardous road conditions, but she was one of the only counselors in the building who kept up a full regular schedule. Each of the clients who arrived that morning talked about the icy roads and the treacherous walkway leading up to the building. Their travails had started to feel like a metaphor for her time slot with Rio.

He was sitting across from her. Silence filled the room. It felt different than usual, more charged and awkward than even their early days of mutual incomprehension.

Suddenly, Rio broke out in a smile that struck Jenny as more like a grimace.

"I've been thinking a lot lately," he said.

He sat stiffly, like a coiled rattlesnake. His attempt at acting casual and pleasant sent a charge of danger through her chest.

"Have you?" she asked.

"You're special," he said. "Really special."

"I appreciate your saying that," Jenny told him.

"How about we take our relationship to the next level?" he asked.

"The next level," she repeated.

She had never been this scared of him before.

"You know," he said. "The romantic level."

Jenny struggled to control her reaction. His smile gained in intensity, reflecting an inner reality that she could only guess at.

"I think we were made for each other," he went on. "We could do great things together. Important stuff."

"What kind of stuff?""Stuff related to mental health and counseling," he said. "We could make a great team. And I've always thought you were pretty."

She forced herself to smile. Outside the window, the ice shone in the afternoon sun.

"You're saying what I've always wanted to hear," she told him. "What took you so long to realize that we were meant to be together?"

"I had to wait until I was sure you were the one," Rio replied without a moment's hesitation. "But now I know."

"It's like God meant it," Jenny shot back. "Don't you agree?"She watched him hesitate. He would never attribute anything to God that he didn't believe was true. She knew his psychology well enough to be sure that was one lie he would never tell.

"I wouldn't say it's what God wants," he said, still smiling. "It's what I want. And I'm great enough that all the world should take notice of my desires. With me, you will also be great. We'll shine."

"Of course you have greatness," she said. "And I've always known it. You're like no one else on this planet. I'm so glad you're finally attracted to me."Rio beamed. He took in flattery like a parched desert floor soaking up rain. She saw him physically puff himself up, his chest rising and his chin jutting in the air as he looked at her lasciviously.

"Why don't you come over to my house tomorrow night?" he asked.

"Why wait?" she asked. "I'll come over tonight."

"Our first time has to be special," he told her. "All good things come to those who wait. Have patience."

"Tomorrow then," she agreed.

"I'll pick you up at the grocery store right down the road," he said as he pointed.

"Good idea. I don't want Sam to know until I can let him down easy. Do you agree?" she asked.

He just smiled.

"Don't tell anyone," he said. "I want our love to be a secret until we're ready to shock the world.""I understand," she said.

"It's going to be beautiful," he said, standing up and peeling off a stack of bills. The chime went off at just that moment to signal the end of the session.

He reached out as they stood next to one another, his fingertips grazing her cheek as he looked into her eyes.

"Beautiful," he repeated.

After he had left, Jenny took a couple of deep breaths in an attempt to compose herself. Then she sat down at her desk with her phone.

The weather app confirmed what she had thought: there was a high probability of rain the next night.

CHAPTER THIRTY
A PLACE WHERE HE COULD THINK

THEY FOLLOWED their plan: Rio would pick up Jenny in the parking lot of the grocery store once she was done seeing appointments for the day. This way, no one at work would see her leaving with a client, which could potentially cost her license to practice. She had told Sam she wasn't feeling well and was going to go home and go to bed, promising to get together with him tomorrow.

She sat in the parking lot, looking up at the cloudy sky. A light drizzle was falling.

They hadn't texted or called to confirm. Rio had said he wanted to keep her out of trouble. Remembering his transparent attempt at manipulation made her anxiety turn into anger.

She'd never been to Rio's house. She didn't know what it was like, how close the neighbors were or if they would be in eyeshot. She didn't know what Rio had in store for her.

Just breathe.

He'd described enough of the house during their counseling sessions that she knew there was a deck out back that over-looked a steep backyard and a few rocking chairs. He only ever used one, of course, because he usually never had guests.

Rio described sitting out there by himself, a place where he could think, undisturbed. Jenny guessed this meant that it was secluded on the deck, with no one able to see him.

That meant no one would be able to see Jenny if they stayed out there together.

There was only about three miles between the grocery store and Rio's house, according to the mapping app on her phone. Quite a distance for walking back to where she had left her car in the parking lot, but she was willing to persevere.

She knew that she didn't want to go inside the house. Once she set foot inside the door, she would be in his world and sub-ject to whatever horrors he might have in store for her. She had little doubt that he had orchestrated and planned out their time together to the minute. She knew how meticulous he was when he was saving a woman.

She wore sneakers so she could be as mobile and agile as possible. Her loaded Glock 42 was in one coat pocket. A spare magazine was in the other. She had taken Rio's advice from months before and chambered a round.

Don't leave any shell casings.

Like watching a movie in her mind, she went through what she wanted to happen. She knew her planning mirrored Rio's like two competing visions of reality.

There were a few minutes to go. Listening to the drops of rain falling harder now on the roof of her car, Jenny carefully wiped down each cartridge in the weapon and all the cartridges in her spare magazine. She had been listening with great care to Rio all this time, after all.

He picked Jenny up right on time—to the minute.

As he was pulling up, Jenny put on her gloves. She got out of her car and climbed into his Tacoma, which was blasting heat.

"It's time," he said, smiling at her.

Her heart pounded in her chest. She gave him a smile and let her hand graze the side of his knee as she buckled her seatbelt.

It was cold out but sweltering inside the truck. Rio had no coat or jacket over his button-down flannel shirt and jeans. If he was carrying a gun on his person, Jenny wasn't able to figure out where he might be concealing it.

They drove into the night.

"It's a little chilly out, but I like the fresh air," Jenny said as Rio made a left turn. "How about we spend some time out on your back deck? I like the idea of being together in the special place where you go to find peace."

Rio grinned good-naturedly.

"I was thinking the same thing might be nice," he told her. "This is going to be one great night."

Jenny was amazed by how isolated Rio's house seemed on its solitary cul-de-sac as they drove through the woods, and how its spotless Victorian exterior made it stand out from every other home in the grid of the housing development.

"Hang on a second," Rio said. "This is my special short-cut."

She sat in the Tacoma's passenger seat and watched him in the headlights as he placed boards over the concrete encasements, got back in, drove them over the drainage ditch, and put the planks back in the bed of his truck. There was something machinelike and robotic in the way he did this, as though there was nothing strange about it.

He has no feelings.

While he was working, Jenny spotted a garage door remote control on the console below the middle of the dashboard. She pocketed it.

Don't want to go into the garage.

When Rio pulled into his driveway, she carefully watched him for signs he was looking for the garage door remote. But he wasn't.

She had her hand in her coat pocket, gripping the pistol hard. Now she let her hand relax.

They walked around the house together.

"I don't care if it's raining," he said as they walked up the steps to the back deck. The ice from earlier in the day had melted. "You OK with visiting out here?" She looked into the house, which was lit up. She saw appliances and a pantry in the spotless kitchen.

"Doesn't bother me at all," she said.

He was behind her and out of her sight for a moment. She took in a quick gasp of air.

Rio had quickly maneuvered to a rocking chair on the other side of a big wooden table. He put his hands on the armrests and smiled.

"Have a seat," he said.

"You're a gracious host," she told him.

"I'd like you to be more than just an ordinary guest," he replied. He seemed completely relaxed and at ease.

It was raining a little harder now.

"I don't want my hair to smell like a wet dog," she laughed as she sat down on the other side of the table. "Do you have a raincoat I can wear?" "Of course I do," Rio said. "I'll be right back." "And maybe a bottle of water while you're inside?" she asked.

She was worried that this would annoy him because he had mentioned that he kept most of his food and drinks in the basement, but he simply smiled as he got up. His curly hair was getting wet in the rain, but he didn't seem to care.

"Anything for you," he said.

He went into the house through a sliding glass door. He had left it unlocked because he didn't need a key to open it.

When he was gone, she looked around the deck to see if there were any areas where an ejected shell casing might fall through the slats. As she was looking under the table, she tilted her head slightly and peered through the rain.

There was something taped under the table on the side that Rio had staked out for himself.

She quickly moved around the table. It was a gun—a Glock 42, the same model she had in her own pocket. It was hanging under the table, secured with a single piece of duct tape.

She thought for a second.

Then she knew what to do.

Jenny pulled out her own pistol, removed the magazine, and racked the slide. The round in the chamber ejected. It started to roll across the table, and she glanced back at the door.

She had seconds at best.

She re-inserted the magazine, carefully pulled on the duct tape under the table, and took Rio's gun and shoved it in her pocket. Then she placed her own gun under the duct tape and pushed it back in place, trying to position the weapon exactly as its twin had been.

Back in the rocking chair, she had time for one deep breath before he returned. He put a bottle of water on the table and handed Jenny an old yellow raincoat.

"Very stylish," she said, trying to smile.

He just looked at her, clearly unsure if she was making a joke or truly liked the drab raincoat.

"You said you wanted a raincoat," he said.

"So I did." She smiled at him. "It's perfect."

Rio went back to his chair on the other side of the table. Jenny slipped the raincoat onto her lap, positioning it like a blanket. He didn't glance under the table or show any sign that anything was out of the ordinary.

"I can see all the work you put into this place," she told him, looking admiringly up at the windows of the upper story.

"It took years," Rio said.

"Did you get your tax situation figured out?"

She didn't know why she had said that. He had stolen Sam's screwdriver that day when she went to copy the business card. He would know she was signaling that she knew exactly what he had done and when.

Don't bait him.

"It doesn't matter too much," Rio told her. "I own this place outright. My main expense is the property tax." The rain fell harder. He sat there in his flannel shirt, showing no sign of inconvenience or discomfort.

"What do you have planned for us tonight?" Jenny said after several moments of silence.

He didn't move or shift in his chair.

"I plan on collecting my ninth slave," he said.

Rain fell down his face. His shirt was soaked. He was as motionless as a statue, with that weird rigidity he evinced when his compulsions were strongest.

"Sounds momentous," she said. "Who do you have in mind?"

Rio's eyes narrowed as he experienced a moment of confusion.

"I don't think you understand," he told her. "You're the ninth. Your evil will be extinguished tonight."

He still didn't move.

"I see," she said. "So that's how I'm going to become a part of your greatness." "I failed all those years ago," he said. "I should have taken you then. Don't think I'm ungrateful for all you've done for me. I'm not. But I did allow you to spread a lot more evil for a really long time."

Her heart was pounding hard.

She made a confused and wounded expression.

"You can't betray me now!" she cried into a wind gust that rose up all of a sudden, pelting them both with rain.

"We'll have plenty of time to talk about it later," he said. "We'll have all of eternity together. And you'll finally know your place."

He reached under the table and raised the pistol at her head. He leaned forward. She was staring into the darkness of a barrel about two feet from her forehead.

"I knew this day would come," Jenny said.

He winced at her. "What do you mean?"

"I've had this coming for a long time," she told him.

He nodded, seeming more convinced of her acceptance of her fate.

"It's good that you understand," he said approvingly.

"Can I make one request?" she asked.

He bit his lower lip. "You're dying tonight, one way or the other," he said. "Your next task will be to prepare our bedroom for my arrival in the afterlife."

"Can you at least get rid of David Saunders's wallet after I'm gone?" she asked. "I don't want to be connected to his death. At least give me that dignity. Don't let my name be associated with his killing."

She was able to slip her hand into the pocket of her coat under the raincoat.

They looked into each other's eyes. The rain fell.

"I burned that a long time ago," he said. "You think I wanted to be caught with it? It's disappeared forever, just like you will be." "Then let's get on with it."

Jenny straightened her neck and held her head up high. Rio gave her a puzzled expression.

"It's not that simple," he said. "We're going to have some fun first. It's time to go inside."

There was a sound of distant thunder. The wind picked up again, blowing his wet hair across his face.

"We're not going inside."

He laughed. "You're not the one to say what's happening next."

"You made two mistakes," she told him.

"You're lecturing me now?" he barked. "You don't seem to understand how this works."

"You didn't maintain control of your weapon, and you got distracted," she told him. "I've learned a lot from you, too. And I won't make the same mistake."

She pulled the pistol from her coat pocket and pointed it at Rio's forehead.

Without hesitation Rio extended his gun toward Jenny's face and pulled the trigger, anticipating the loud report and sharp recoil of his little semi-automatic. But what he heard instead was the delicate click of the firing pin striking nothing but air in an empty chamber. Perhaps half a second passed before his bewilderment gave way to an expression of pure rage. Then something else. The deepest fury one could imagine.

When Jenny pulled the trigger of her gun, the sound it made was anything but delicate. The hollow point caught Rio square in the chest. His gun clattered onto the deck as he lurched backwards over the railing, landing in a lifeless heap on the lawn below.

Jenny calmly placed Rio's gun on the deck before retrieving hers and racking the slide.

"This time I shot the right man."

THE END

ACKNOWLEDGEMENTS

Thank you to Quinton Skinner for his editorial contributions.

ABOUT THE AUTHOR

TODD GRANDE is a professional counselor, counselor educator, and content creator who specializes in personality disorders, addiction, trauma, and psychopathology. He operates a popular YouTube channel in which he covers mental health disorders, personality theory, true crime, relationships, and narcissism. He is a Licensed Professional Counselor of Mental Health and Licensed Chemical Dependency Professional in Delaware and is a National Certified Counselor. He holds a Master's of Science in Community Counseling from Wilmington University and a Ph.D. in Counselor Education and Supervision from Regent University. For many years, Dr. Grande was an associate professor in Wilmington University's Clinical Mental Health Counseling program and provided counseling and consulting services in his community.

CPSIA information can be obtained
at www.ICGtesting.com
Printed in the USA
JSHW032320271021
19898JS00003B/3